Russell West

The Grave
At The Top
Of The Hill

Dear Ruby & Roy
Best wishes
Russell.

The Grave At The Top Of the Hill
ISBN 978-0-9876438-1-0
Copyright © text Russell Westmoreland 2018
Cover Photo: Russell Westmoreland

Second print
First published 2019

rustyswords publishing
Grange, South Australia
Email: rustyswordspublishing@gmail.com

 A catalogue record for this
book is available from the
NATIONAL
LIBRARY   National Library of Australia
OF AUSTRALIA

Dedication

For Wendy and Judy
my co-conspirators

Contents

Whit's fur ye'll no go by ye!

What's meant to happen will happen.

Prologue

The Register, Monday 28 August 1854

STRANDING OF THE MOZAMBIQUE

The following particulars of the stranding and wreck of the Mozambique were brought from the Goolwa by our reporter:-

The Mozambique, from Swan Reach, was driven on shore on the sea-beach outside the Coorong, on Monday the 21st inst. There were 24 passengers on board, besides the crew, consisting of 22 men. No lives were lost, but it is reported that a great amount of suffering had been borne by all on board for several days previous to the wreck, in consequence of the shortage of provisions and the leaky condition of the ship, the pumps being choked.

The first person found to render any assistance to the passengers, was a man named James Law, who resides on the upper Finniss. His statement of the circumstances connected with the rescue is as follows:- 'I had been to Salt Creek in my boat, with flour, sugar and tea, for Mr Bradford, whose station I was at last Monday week. When I had made about 30 miles on my way back, I went on shore, and having pitched my tent for the night and lighted a fire, I heard someone 'cooeying'. This was last Monday night.

I went towards the place and the first person I met was the captain of the vessel, who said they had been wrecked and had nothing to eat. He said there were four females and some children with them, and he would be greatly obliged if I could render them any help. I had only 40 lbs of flour, which I gave him, and told him that I was going to the Elbow (the Goolwa), and would take the females and children with me if he had any men to assist in rowing the boat. I left the next morning in my boat, bringing with me the captain, 4 sailors, 2 children, 4 females, and 5 other passengers. We arrived at the Goolwa on Wednesday morning about 4 o'clock, and sent another of my boats back with provisions for those whom we had left behind.'

On the arrival of Law at the Goolwa with his unfortunate passengers, an express was sent to Adelaide, with all the circumstances, in the expectation that the Government schooner Yatala would be sent round to the assistance of the rest of the passengers and crew. The subjoined further particulars were kindly communicated to our shipping reporter at Port Adelaide, by Mr. J.C. Hawker of H.M.Customs:- 'The ship Mozambique has been totally lost, on the coast outside the Coorong. The Mozambique was loading in the London docks at the same time as the Navarino, and bound for some of the Australian colonies. She stranded, and became a total wreck, at about sixty miles from Port Elliot. It appears that, previous to the final catastrophe, she had been in a leaky state, having eight feet of water in her hold, and was very short of provisions; in fact, they were in a state bordering upon starvation. We learn that provisions were dispatched to the crew and passengers from the Goolwa, and understand that the captain has arrived at Port Elliot.'

∗∗∗∗∗∗∗∗∗∗∗∗∗∗∗∗

Chapter 1
Saturday July 16 2016

The dirt around Alexander Johnston's grave is much harder than the man had imagined. On reflection, he realised that the summer had been the driest on record and autumn had followed the trend. Sweat seeped through his shirt under his armpits and on his back.

Each dull thud made by his spade was accompanied by a rasping grunt. At times he felt he could strike a rhythm to the music pounding out from the party at the reception centre on the other side of Currency Creek. That feeling had passed a little while ago and now each strike of the spade was synchronised to a jolt through his arms and shoulders.

He lifted his head then his shoulders, succumbing to the fatigue until he stretched to his full height. He looked down into the hole and sighed as he calculated that he was probably only half way through digging down to the coffin. He should have brought his pick as well. Annoyed by his foolishness, he questioned his decision to travel light, a choice made because he had wanted to leave his car well away from the cemetery. He knew that this would allow him the best opportunity to slip away quietly if by chance someone did come by.

He realised now how unlikely that was. It was nearly midnight and here he was, in the middle of nowhere, in darkness as black as ink while the moon hid behind the clouds. With a wry smile, he pondered that this cemetery was an unlikely destination for anyone other than himself.

Looking again into the hole, he convinced himself that, if he persisted, he would still complete the task tonight.

He had parked his car a few hundred metres away just off the main road that led to the township of Currency Creek and then to Strathalbyn. The car park served the nature reserve and walking trail. Although it was just across the creek from the reception centre, it was at a lower level than the main road and not visible from it. To make sure the car was hidden, he had squeezed it between the drab grey toilet block and a large, bushy tree.

It had been a simple matter to carry his one tool, the spade, up the hill to the grave site he was now despoiling.

He figured that if all went well, the excavation would take a couple more hours. After that he could extract what he was looking for from the coffin and refill the grave. His reward is small and he will have no trouble carrying it, with the spade, back to his car. He expected to be in bed well before dawn, hopefully a much wealthier man.

He wiped the sweat from his brow. Even though the night was cool, the physical exertion had taken its toll, a surprise to him. He considered himself physically fit and was frustrated by the need to stop frequently.

Rain was forecast for the next couple of days. That meant that any trace of his work would be covered over by nature and the chances were good that no-one would notice in the meantime. He chuckled as he reminded himself.

Let's face it this isn't a cemetery attracting regular visitors.

He realised he had been day dreaming longer than he intended. His clothes were damp with perspiration and, chilled to the bone, he shivered involuntarily. Temporarily revived, he lifted the spade and focused on working to the rhythm of the music still pumping from the party.

The thump-thump bass from the party and the breeze rustling through the tall pine trees surrounded him and took him to another place. Working more freely now, he was so completely absorbed that he did not hear the new sound. A car approached on the narrow dirt road leading to the cemetery from the Mount Compass Road. Too late, he noticed the flicker of light as the car rounded the last corner and pulled up in the car park just outside the gate.

He knew he didn't have time to leave the cemetery unnoticed. Cursing his lack of attention, he looked around for cover. He stealthily crept behind a large pine tree. Leaning his spade against the trunk, he peered around, watching and waiting.

In the dim light, he saw a young man get out of the car. A girl stepped out of the other side. They both wore jeans and sneakers. The young man had a hoodie, with hood pulled forward, while the girl was dressed in a leather jacket and a woollen beanie. They paused at the front of the car and the young man leant her back against the car bonnet. Steam rose with each lusted breath they took. Their bodies melded as one and they kissed long and deep. As their bodies parted, the young man took the girl's hand and they ran the few metres from the car into the cemetery, closing the gate behind them.

They laughed as they walked along the path leading through the centre of the cemetery, stopping at a wooden bench under a large lime tree. They were only twenty metres away from Alexander Johnston's grave in row two, but the dense foliage of the tree shaded the moonlight and the couple were embraced by comforting darkness when they sat.

The young man drew the girl in and wrapped his arms around her. Pulling in closer, she rested her head against his chest. The gravedigger listened to them but couldn't discern what they were saying.

The girl tilted her head, looked up at the young man and stretched up to put her lips to his. After they kiss, she looked into his eyes and murmured 'I need to tell you something.'

He held her eyes. 'I love you too.'

'What? That's not what I was going to say. What made you think I was going to say that?'

'Well don't you?'

'Of course, I do, stupid.' They both laughed, eyes locked in teen ardor. When they stopped she lowered her head and looked at her feet.

She continued, 'I have something really important to tell you.'

The gravedigger was impatient with this sudden diversion. He couldn't stop fidgeting, frustrated and annoyed he was unable to continue with his work, or to move undetected from his hiding place. He wanted to see if he had an escape route and stepped carefully around the tree trunk. An unseen root was the landing point for his first step and he stumbled forward, brushing against his spade. Despite his frantic attempts to catch it, the spade clattered on a concrete gravestone.

The noise startled the couple and as he whipped his head around, the young man caught a movement out the corner of his eye.

He jumped up and called out, 'Who's there?'

The gravedigger lay prostrate on the bed of pine needles and leaves, trying to stay silent. He heard his heart pound in his chest like the sound of a hundred drummers. He cursed under his breath, hoping he could stay quiet long enough to outlast the couple's curiosity.

Damn, this should have been so simple.

The young man stepped closer.

'Come out, I know someone's there.'

Silence.

'Come back, babe, no-one's here.'

'Nah, there is. I saw someone.' He trod slowly but deliberately in the blackness toward the gravedigger.

'Come on, pervert. Show your face.'

The gravedigger lay still. He hoped beyond hope that the couple would just go. This wasn't meant to happen; he had intended to slip away if someone came. He should have been more alert. He wondered if he could still make a run for it, get away while he could. That would certainly draw attention to the disturbed grave. He wanted the young man to back off; if he didn't, he would almost certainly find the disturbed grave.

The gravedigger decided to wait. He felt his heart pounding, every breath he took sounded like the snort of an angry bull.

The young man didn't back off. He was cautiously moving forward, determined to find the root of the noise.

The gravedigger was cornered. Fearful, he sprang to his feet and rushed the few metres between them. His sudden movement startled the young man and he pushed him in the chest before he had time to react. The young man fell to the ground bewildered.

The girl's scream pierced the gentleness of the breeze in the trees. The gravedigger turned toward her and in the split second he looked at her, she gasped, his face clear in the light of the moon. She knew him.

'What are you doing?' she shrieked.

The gravedigger turned and walked away. He needed time to think.

The young man rose from the ground and strode with purpose after the gravedigger. Furious and embarrassed at losing the first round, he was intent on teaching his assailant a lesson. Muttering obscene threats under his breath he didn't count on anything other than belting the living daylights out of his attacker. That turned out to be his weakness. Out of view, the gravedigger had returned to the tree where he had hidden and picked up his spade. The young man pulled up as he saw the gravedigger rushing at him spade raised above his head like a medieval warrior. He retreated, acutely aware how ill prepared he was to defend himself.

Expecting the gravedigger to strike at his head or on the side of his body, he lifted his arms high and crossed them across his head. Instead the gravedigger thrust the spade forward and low, smashing it into the young man's groin. He fell to the ground writhing, summoning barely enough breath to call to the girl.

'Run, get out of here, now!'

Terrified, she ran toward the gate, hoping to reach the safety of the car. The gravedigger sensed her first move and dashed across, blocking her escape. He stood, legs parted, holding the spade across his body. She spun and ran in the opposite direction, away from the car. The young man was back on his feet and ran to join her, stumbling as the clamping pain clawed at his gut with every step.

They trampled between graves in the cemetery downhill toward Currency Creek, further into darkness. They knew, and they knew their attacker knew, that he now could not let them escape. They could sense him chasing them. They forged their way forward, blind and terrified.

They ran down the slope toward the bottom corner of the cemetery. They knew the place well - it's been a long time haunt of young people living Tom Sawyer-like adventures. As they ran, they tripped on exposed tree roots, but somehow managed to keep their feet. Nearing the bottom, the young man turned back and reckoned they had been out-running the gravedigger.

'Keep going,' he urged her. At the end of the cemetery was a stile across the fence to the bush outside. He helped her over and then pulled himself across, still smarting from the pain in his groin. They stood on a sloping pathway leading down to the creek – the same path the gravedigger used to come up to the cemetery. They stumbled on the steps descending the hill, catching on the thorns of prickle bushes growing from the side of the path. Close to the bottom, the pathway steps ran out and instead the ground became rough and uneven.

They held hands as they attempted to pick up speed but the young man made a poor footing and slipped on the scree, dragging her with him. They slid to the bottom of the path where it intersected a hiking trail. To the right they would reach the car park and the main road. The left led away, to the waterfall. They stalled, considering their options.

'Which way?' she gasped. He motioned toward the waterfall.

'He's going to think we'll go to the road. This way.'

They turned left, away from the road. The rocks on the path jutted out irregularly and the going was rough, even in sneakers. The path was narrow and they had to run single file. The young man led the way. After around two hundred metres, he stopped. They were next to a narrow track, almost hidden, sloping up the hill to an old copper mine shaft. Again, they paused. They couldn't detect any sounds other than the running water of the creek and very faintly the revellers at the wedding reception some five hundred metres away from them.

'In here,' he said, 'Hopefully he doesn't know about this place and we can out wait him.'

He led her into the mine entrance, about twenty metres long. Mid-way along the entry passage they had to almost bend double to clamber through. It was pitch black even with the half-moon light outside. They reached the end of the passage and turned right. This part of the tunnel was about five metres long and higher. They could stand comfortably and at the end there was a secondary shaft rising vertically to the surface three metres above their heads. Looking up, they saw the sky above, pillowed clouds moving slowly across in front of the stars. At the top of the shaft was a grate intended to protect unwary hikers from falling in. There was only one way out, the way they came. The young man signalled her to stay very quiet. 'I'm going to call for help,' she whispered, as she pulled her mobile phone from her jeans.

The phone dimly illuminated the space.

'I'm not getting a signal.'

'Damn. Let's just wait.'

It was twenty two minutes later when she pulled her phone out to check the time. 11:35.

'Surely we'll be safe now. He must have gone the other way.'

'Just a bit more,' the young man said.

Shortly after, he parted his lips to suggest it was time to move. He paused as he caught a new sound.

'Did you hear that? Sounds like footsteps.'

They sensed as much as heard the man's presence as he tentatively stepped inside the mine. The young man raised his index finger to his lips.

The gravedigger had discarded his spade during his scramble down the hill and then followed the path back to the main road. He was convinced they had not gone that way and retraced his steps. As he walked, he realised how he had let the sudden interruption get out of control. He knew he should have backed off when the couple discovered him, made some excuse no matter how feeble. Now, he had made it escalate. *Damn his temper*. Nearing the mine, he wondered if this could be their refuge. He wanted the chance to talk with them. *If he could just talk to them, perhaps he could diffuse the situation*. He stepped hesitantly into the blackness of the mine.

Hearing the footfalls closer, the young man understood there was only one way for the couple to escape. In the glow of the faint moonlight coming down the vertical shaft, he watched for any sign of movement, waiting for the moment the man turned into the passage where they were hidden. He sprang forward, bent low as he reached full speed and buried his shoulder into the gravedigger's mid drift, forcing the breath from his lungs.

'Go, run now,' the young man yelled. The girl squeezed through the small gap between the men. She crouched low in the entry passage, gasping as she reached the entrance to the mine. She looked back into the mine but saw nothing in the blackness. She felt sick at the scuffling, grunting sounds of combat as the two wrestled in the narrow space.

Her mind filled with terror, dread and panic. Tears streamed down her face as she stood shivering in the cool night air. Nothing in her life experience prepared her for this moment.

She was so alone even knowing that Kyle was so close, fighting to protect her, to save himself.

Fearing for him, she wondered if she should go back and help ... somehow ... how? At that moment she wasn't sure if it was fear or logic that told her that she should run for help. Glancing back only briefly, she turned right, back along the path the way they came.

The young man and the gravedigger were locked in a fierce tussle pushing and hitting each other but in the narrow confines of the tunnel each found it hard to gain an ascendancy over the other. After less than a minute that seemed like an hour, the young man was able to push the gravedigger with some force, knocking him off balance so that he fell to the ground. Stepping over him, he gasped as he made his way to the mine opening. The gravedigger rose to his knees, his hand pushing against a fist sized rock on the ground. He picked it up and ran after the young man. He reached him as he was about to clamber, crouched, through the lowest section of the tunnel.

The gravedigger stretched forward. His fingers clutched the young man's belt, pulling him backwards sharply, until he fell onto his back. The man dropped to his knees. Looking into the terrified eyes of the boy beneath him, he raised his right hand above his head and with as much force as he could summon, smashed the rock into the bewildered face, hitting him again and again until he lay bloodied and motionless.

The gravedigger lifted himself from the ground and felt with shock the stickiness of his bloodied hands.

What happened to diffusing the situation?

He pounded his palm against his forehead as he struggled for rationality, realising he had now committed an abominable crime, one he would never have imagined himself capable of.

His moment of guilt and self-retribution was soon supplanted by an instinct to survive, regardless of the consequences. He had to make a choice. Stop the girl from getting to help, or make sure the young man was better concealed. He pulled the body to the back of the mine and rushed outside to chase the girl. He wondered how far away she was.

The girl ran, stumbling across the inhospitable rocks and brushing through the long grass and bamboo growing on the side of the creek. She held her hand over her mouth, partly in anguish, partly the result of shock invading her body.

How did this happen? Why? Why is he doing this to them?

She dragged one foot after the other. Shock and fear drained her of energy. She found it increasingly difficult to focus her eyes on the path ahead. A large stone poked from the path, obscured by a small overgrowing bush, and her foot clipped it as she passed. Already unbalanced, it was enough to send her hurtling forward and she crashed onto the loose stones that edged the path.

She lifted herself to her feet. Her palms were shredded, tiny stones embedded under her skin. Strangely, after the initial stinging, she didn't feel pain in her hands. It was her left knee that caused her more distress. She felt down to the hole in her jeans and brought up her hand, her fingers sticky with blood.

The girl tried to resume running. Her knee impeded her and she barely hobbled along the path. She couldn't have felt more miserable, despondent and helpless.

Her mind raced, her body hurt. She felt so alone. She desperately wanted to know that Kyle was safe and pleaded there was somewhere she could hide until he came for her.

In a fleeting moment of clarity, she decided her best choice was to run to the car. It allowed her the best chance to escape … her only way to help Kyle. She could call someone, the police, if she could get to the safety of the car. She searched for the path leading back up to the cemetery.

The path was less obvious from this direction and she missed it. Running a few more metres, she could pick out the faint sound of the reception only two hundred metres ahead. She realised she may be closer to help than she had thought.

Exhausted, she paused for breath under the large square concrete pylons supporting the railway bridge crossing Currency Creek.

She gulped for air, hunched over, her hands resting on her knees, the left still oozing blood. She couldn't stay here.

Oh, Kyle, please come. She desperately wanted this nightmare to finish.

The gravedigger was also exhausted and slowed to a walk as he approached the railway bridge just a few metres ahead. He had exerted himself physically for over an hour now. He feared she was already safely away from him.

His mind was now catching up with his actions. The horror of what he had done to the young man repulsed him. He was sure the girl recognised him in the cemetery and that realisation dispatched him into a corridor of panic. As he walked, he realised he had reacted on first impulse and he could have dealt with the couple differently. He could have made some excuse, walked away. But now, now he was a killer... a murderer.

He could have quit then, let the girl go and just got the hell away. Maybe headed interstate or up bush. *Coober Pedy, isn't that where people went when they didn't want to be found?*

At that moment, he glimpsed a slight movement in the moonlight. *Oh, god, it's her.* He had known her most of her life. If he walked away now, she would surely report what happened. Now or never, he pondered. The gravedigger's fight or flight instinct was making choices as he stood. He could run, get away while he could, leave this place forever and become someone else. Or, he could finish what he started, repulsive as it was. In a split second, he made his decision.

He could sense her breathing as he moved forward as silently as he could, holding his breath. Too late she noticed him and screamed for help. The sound of her pleas could not reach the revellers at the party over the sound of Tina Turner beating out 'Nutbush City Limits.'

The gravedigger grabbed her by the shoulders and met her eyes. They stared at the fear in each other's faces, the moment frozen in time. She struggled against his grip, screaming. He pushed her backwards into the water. As she fell back, she clawed at him but all she could grab was his woollen sweater, enough to pull him toward her.

'Bitch' he muttered under his breath as he stumbled into the water after her. It was more than a metre deep and he lunged in an effort to reach her before she got up again. Before she was on her knees, he was behind her. He wrapped his hands around her slender neck and easily pushed her down. In a rage, he held her head under the water until she moved no more.

No bubbles rose to the surface and he knew it was done.

Chapter 2
Saturday July 16 2016

The gravedigger realised he dare not leave her where she was. He must move her, and eventually the young man's body too, somewhere away from the cemetery. Pulling the girl from the water, he lifted her slight body over his shoulder.

He carried her two hundred metres and paused in the darkness before he entered the open space of the car park. His car was well hidden next to the toilet block. Satisfied no-one was nearby, he crossed quickly and threw her indelicately into the back of the big 4x4 utility vehicle and covered her with hessian bags.

He contemplated going back for the young man, but realised his body would be much heavier and needed to be carried much further. For the time being, he resolved, disposing of the girl must be his focus.

It was almost midnight when he inserted his key to start his car engine. Pausing, he wound down his window. The sound of cars accelerating away nearby signalled the party was now breaking up and people were leaving. He decided he couldn't afford to put his headlights on while there was other traffic around - exiting the car park now would draw unwanted attention at this time of night. He watched, waiting until the sound of the last car speeding away faded and the lights dimmed on the other side of the creek. For ten minutes he waited, gripped by anxiety. He had no idea where he should go or what he should do. He compelled himself to think - he decided he would take the girl as far away as he could. The young man was hidden for now. He reasoned that he could make her drowning appear accidental to deflect attention away from Currency Creek.

The gravedigger engaged the car's gear and eased out of the carpark. He drove eight kilometres to Goolwa. The town's streets were quiet and empty - even the pubs were darkened. Deciding to take Barrage Road following the banks of the Murray River, he passed the yacht club and the aquatic club. Minutes later, he reached the barrages that separate the river from the sea, restricting access of salt water into the freshwater system.

Turning off Barrage Road onto the side road leading to the Beacon 19 boat ramp, he saw nothing but darkness in the houses of the barrage supervisors. He drove two and a half kilometres further, his mind playing over the night's events. There were no street lights here. The narrow road was flanked by the shadowy sand hills on the right and the lanky long reeds growing in the river on the left. Within the narrow tunnel of his present, he struggled to organise his thoughts.

How did it go so wrong? He expected to be home by now, soaking in the enjoyment of his discovery, content in the knowledge he may never need to work again. Instead, he was dealing with an unfolding nightmare. He cursed his impetuosity – he wished he had allowed the couple to be on their way. *Was the prize worth this cost?*

The last two hours were like cotton wool in his brain – an amorphous collection of threads that he couldn't untangle.

He snapped his brain into clearer focus. *What's done is done.* He couldn't change what happened, but he mustn't allow his guilt to bring him down. He must save himself.

The car park at the boat ramp was empty, just as he would have expected. He pulled to the side, cautious not to put the wheels on the soft sandy verge. *Can't be too careful.*

As he lifted the body from the back of the 4x4, he no longer thought of her as the vibrant young girl he chased and killed – now she was just a thing, a threat to his freedom. Her body was colder now. Once he recovered from the initial shock of her coldness, it allowed him to delineate her past living presence from the object he now handled. Placing her on the ground, he was taken aback when he noticed the state of her body. Her arms and legs were covered with abrasions and bruises, bringing him back to the horror of what he had done. With that realisation, he was seized by panic – the control he had forced on himself was replaced by fear, fear that he was unable to escape the guilt and ultimately the penalty for his wrongdoings.

He felt the cold sweat on his brow and stepped away from his car. His gullet closed and his mouth was so dry he worried he would retch. Doubling over, he breathed deeply until he regained physical control. Still he was unable to control his mind and it told him he must do better – to find a different solution.

Desperate, he reflected on his choice to make the girl's death look like an accident. The realisation struck him like lightning.

Her discovery must point to a violent assault. That will account for the wounds on her body. Maybe they will blame the young man, at least if they don't find his body. Yes, it will be better this way.

The gravedigger looked out onto the river at Rabbit Island, one hundred and fifty metres away, where the pelicans and ibises were resting for the night. Satisfied with his isolation, he removed the girl's clothes to her underwear. He was guilt-ridden and ashamed, but if his scenario was going to appear realistic he must take off her underwear too. Trying not to look, he stripped her bra and panties. After he collected the rest of her clothes, he returned to the car to throw the pile into the tray. He would dispose of them later.

His hand discerned the outline of the mobile phone in the back pocket of her jeans. The gravedigger, now killer, removed it and walked down the ramp. Hurling the phone as far as possible into the dark water, he heard, rather than saw, the splash before it sank to the muddy floor.

He lifted the girl and carried her to the water's edge about fifty metres west of the ramp, taking care not to step into soft mud where he might leave tell-tale footprints.

Although she was light, he struggled to heave her out into the reeds that poke through the cold black water. He wanted to hide her out from the shore among the tall grasses. Instead she lay at the edge, only a couple of metres from the shore. He couldn't risk going out any further to adjust her position. She was not hidden very well, but he reasoned it wouldn't matter; it would keep the police away from the cemetery long enough.

The gravedigger must make one more stop. He drove back along Barrage Road and then cut away from the river, toward Goolwa Beach.

****

Five minutes later, he arrived at the car park at the beach, deserted but lit by a chrome moon. To his left was the café popular with beachgoers, now closed for the winter. On the right was the tower used by lifesavers to scan the white capped waves and the golden beach during summer. Early in the morning after sunrise, there would be more than a score of people who would brave the winter chill to walk along the shore. Many of the walkers would bring dogs and allow them to run unleashed on the sand. He needed to find a place where the dogs would be unlikely to go.

He gathered the girl's clothes and the hessian bags covering her and walked down to the beach. The wind was stronger down here, a southerly straight off the South Pole. His sweater was wet and he was bitterly cold.

The sand moved under his feet as he trudged along the shoreline, heading west, toward Victor Harbor. The moon shone an even light - on any other night he would appreciate its beautiful silver reflection on the expanse of sea to his left. Absorbed by his task, he didn't notice.

The only sound he perceived was the wind and the surf breaking on the sand, rhythmic in its primitive night dance.

He walked a few hundred metres along the shore before deciding he was far enough. Weariness and cold gnawed at his body and he feared he would collapse exhausted if he didn't hurry.

Turning right, he stepped over the low wire fence, inadequately protecting the delicate seaside vegetation against people and their dogs. He slogged up the steep sand hill covered with bushes and grasses that fought the wind and salt every day and night just to survive.

There was no path within a hundred metres of where he now stood, two thirds up the leeward side of the sand hill. This was remote enough; surely an unsuspecting beachgoer would not come up here.

The sand was soft and easy to dig into, so he excavated with his hands. He paused as he was reminded of the blood that had covered them after his brutal assault on the young man. Because his hands had been in the water, they were clean but he dreaded that he had blood on his sweater and pants.

He made a hole to knee depth and placed the girl's clothes and hessian bags at the bottom. Working the fine sand to make the surface as consistent as possible compared to the surrounding area, he re-filled the hole. He looked at his work, satisfied. The overnight wind would finish the job, leaving no trace he was here.

Although still wet and cold, he was no longer dismayed by hypothermia overpowering him. His physical exertion was enough to warm his body. Turning, he climbed across the top of the sand hill, down the windward side and up the next. There he dug another hole. He took off his pants, shoes and sweater and buried them. Once finished, he stumbled near naked down the sand hill to the beach.

Exhausted, he tramped back to his car. After checking the car park was still deserted, he climbed into the 4x4 and started the ignition. He resisted turning on the headlights until he was back on the road. The drive home was uneventful and he didn't see another vehicle. He couldn't believe his luck so far, but he was also vain enough to put this down to the care he was taking to prevent being connected to the crimes.

He was frustrated his plans to rob the grave were thwarted. In a whirlwind of emotions, he initially felt immense guilt, sorrow and disgust at his actions. Yet these feelings were soon followed by a sense bordering pride at his ability to survive. Finally he experienced only relief and tiredness.

Arriving home, he unlocked the door and collapsed on the sofa. Tonight he would be alone – that was part of the plan. He chose this night so he wouldn't need to explain why he was out so late doing God knows what.

He could have stayed on the sofa all night had he not succumbed to the cold, still dressed only in his underpants. He shook himself awake and forced himself into the bathroom and looked in the mirror. He had his hands to his face and imagined that the blood had stained them crimson red. His eyes were puffed and his hair dishevelled from the wind. Once the steam from the shower was eking into the room, clouding the mirror, he stumbled into the cubicle and allowed the water to soak every pore of his skin. He scrubbed his nails and hands to make sure there was no stain left on them. He tried to wash the guilt away but it stuck to him like a feather to sticky fingers.

Why did the boy rush him? It would have been alright if the stupid kids hadn't forced him to act without allowing him time to think things through. What were they doing there anyway? If they hadn't shown up, everything would have gone to plan.

He fell into a disrupted sleep, waking often in a cold sweat with the awareness of what he had done. For now his life must go back to normal until this debacle blew over. If he got the chance, he would return to the grave, but he had to stay patient. The grave had been in place for one hundred and fifty years already. It still protected the reward he sought. With good fortune, he would get back before anyone investigated the desecration of Alexander Johnston's grave and what was buried in it.

Chapter 3
Tuesday 4th July 1854

'Well, there 'tis Ruby, that's the last of it.'

Alexander Johnston set the bowl down on the kitchen table.

'So there's nothing left in the tent?'

'Aye and I'm nae sorry to be finished with it. I'll start pulling it down tomorrow so we can sell it. There are always new people coming into town. I'm sure one of them would be glad for a tent in good condition.'

While many new settlers lived in shelters constructed only from wooden posts and ladies' linen, Alexander and Rubina Johnston had enjoyed the luxury of the canvas tent he had purchased in the goldfields. Alexander felt a restored faith in his ability to provide for his family now he had finished their fine new house. It was one of the first permanent constructions in the Goolwa.

Later to be known simply as Goolwa, the locality derived its name from the aboriginal word for elbow, a description of its position on the lower reaches of the River Murray

The town lay a few kilometres from the mouth of the river. Many ship captains and, indeed, the government of the day, predicted that one day the Goolwa would be a thriving town. All types of goods unloaded from a southern sea port would be transferred at the wharf for their journey by paddle steamers to the multitude of towns setting up along the river's fifteen hundred mile length.

This dream brought Alexander to the Goolwa. Rubina had always followed where her husband took her, sometimes with apprehension but on this occasion she embraced the relocation. However, the path to the Goolwa had been laboured.

Alexander was a mariner, first and foremost. Born in 1817 at Cockenzie, Scotland, a small town on the Firth of Forth, he took to a life on ships for no reason other than that the men in his family had always been sailors.

In 1841, he married Rubina Seton and soon after they bore a wee bairn, Donald. They were keen for their son to have greater opportunities than they believed Scotland could offer, so Alexander seized the chance to crew on the Admiral, a ship bound for Melbourne, Australia. They hastily booked passage for Rubina and Donald and they would arrive only three weeks after Alexander.

The family settled in Melbourne in July 1851. However, Alexander soon learnt that opportunities for a sailor in Melbourne were limited. Then a chance meeting at an alehouse changed his fortunes forever.

An Irishman, Paddy Murphy impressed Alexander with his enthusiasm.

'If you're a brave man, Alexander, a fortune is waiting for you.' He was referring to the goldfields springing up all over the young colony of Victoria. 'But,' he said, 'it's only those that get in early that get the prime digs.'

Alexander looked at him, intrigued by the man with a ruddy face, twinkling eyes and passion embedded in his voice.

'If you're of a mind to go and if you have few pounds to invest, you can be my partner. 'Tis as wealthy men we can return to Melbourne, my friend.' Paddy didn't disclose to Alexander that he had no financial contribution to offer the partnership.

However, the opportunity excited Alexander, especially if he could team with a man like Paddy, who knew the ropes. Over the coming weeks he spent more time with the Irishman, waiting for news of the next rush.

Finally in September The Argus in Melbourne published details of a new strike at Mount Alexander and for Alexander Johnston, this was the opening he was looking for, one he could never have hoped to find in Scotland. The fact the location shared his name he took as the most positive omen he could have wished for.

At Paddy's urging, he invested nearly all his remaining savings into a horse and cart, some elementary digging tools and provisions to get them started. He found boarding for Rubina and Donald in Melbourne and on the 15th of September, Alexander and Paddy made their way to Mount Alexander, eighty miles north-west of Melbourne.

Like most of the men who came in search of gold, the pair possessed no mining experience, but they were toughened, hard-working men with a determination to make good in their new homeland.

They lived in a canvas tent in the small community of Chewton, making their way every day to the tiny eight foot by eight foot plot allocated to them. There they worked alongside like-minded, hard-working, sometimes hard-drinking, hard-fighting men.

Alexander was able to steer clear of trouble. A small, wiry man, he was strong and could work as hard as any man, but he also knew his limitations in a bar brawl. Paddy was not quite so inclined and his drinking and short temper got him into trouble daily.

After six months, the two were dispirited. When their money ran short, Alexander sold the horse and cart to pay for more provisions for himself and Paddy. He sent the balance to Melbourne to pay for continued board for Rubina and Donald.

The occasional shout of glee from a neighbouring dig when a strike was made added to their despair. By April, Alexander and Paddy were falling apart. Paddy started to earn a bad name amongst the small community, looking for loose women to sleep with and belligerent men to fight against.

It was a huge relief, then, on a sunny but cold afternoon in May when Alexander's spade hit a rock with an unfamiliar thud. He lifted a single nugget out of the hole. Feeling it tenderly with his calloused hands, he guessed it weighed over three pounds. As he washed it, he kept his excitement subdued until Paddy returned an hour later.

For a change, Paddy was sober, but held an unopened whiskey bottle, tucked carefully under his right arm.

'Paddy, I have news. I've struck gold.'

When he saw the size of the nugget, Paddy was dumbfounded. He had seen many of the other diggers on his way back after spending the afternoon tucked in the arms and legs of Molly Maguire. He couldn't believe that the news hadn't spread like wildfire across the site.

'I've not said a word to anyone, Paddy. This is a big one and we cannae risk being robbed.'

Paddy whooped and wrapped Alexander in his big arms.

'I don't care. Tonight we celebrate, my friend.'

It took every ounce of energy Alexander possessed to convince Paddy not to drink hard that night. Early the next morning, after a sleepless night guarding their find, the two men took their nugget to the post office in the new township of Castlemaine for assaying.

To their unbridled delight, the nugget weighed in a few ounces less than four pounds. The valuer deemed it to be eighty percent pure gold and offered the men £205 for the fifty-one ounces, an offer they readily accepted.

The magnitude of their wealth temporarily subdued Paddy's outgoing, ebullient nature and he listened carefully as Alexander laid out a plan to protect it.

'Paddy, the worst thing we can do now is squander the money recklessly. We have to make sure we dinnae leave here as broke as we came.'

'But just a little now surely can do no harm. Faith, we've worked bloody hard and risked everything. What is it all for if we can't enjoy ourselves a little? I've a mind to spend a few days in the alehouse and the nights in Molly's bed.'

'That's nae what I'm here for, Paddy. I want a better life for my family and I'll nae have all my efforts wasted with nought to show.'

Eventually, Alexander convinced Paddy to exercise a small degree of caution. As a compromise to Paddy's inclinations, they deposited £25 each in their own names and the balance in a joint fund until they decided on the future of their venture.

Paddy found it difficult to contemplate plans for the future. He spent his days drinking and fighting on the goldfields or lavishing Molly Maguire with extravagances she'd never before experienced. On the other hand, Alexander became increasingly desperate to leave the squalor in which they lived - to reunite his family in their own home and to fulfil his dream to master his own ship based out of the growing Melbourne port.

Sudden wealth exacerbated the breakdown of the pair's relationship and they argued daily about the direction they should take. Eventually, one night at the end of May, Alexander confronted Paddy in their tent.

'Paddy, my friend, I have decided to return to Melbourne. I need to be with my family. I'll be gone at the end of the week.'

'Bloody hell, man! We've just had our only big break and now you want to give it all away. Who knows how much more gold is buried out there?' Paddy exploded, waving his arm in the general direction of the dig.

'I'll sign my rights in the site over to you. You can keep all you find. I need to look after Ruby and Donald and, if I'm honest with you, Paddy, you've nae been pulling your weight lately.'

Paddy vented his anger and frustration by throwing anything loose against the walls of the tent. To avoid a physical exchange, Alexander left through the open flap into the cool, clear night, past the throng of miners gathered to investigate the ruckus. He did not stop until he reached the outskirts of Chewton. When he returned to the tent an hour later, the crowd had dispersed and the tent was empty.

Paddy grew increasingly sullen and spent less time at the dig and more in the bars and Molly's brothel. By the end of the week, Alexander rarely saw him.

Late on the day before he planned to leave, Alexander was packing his tools when a digger from a nearby site approached him.

'Alexander, a moment.'

'Fergus, good afternoon. Looks like a bonnie evening. Have you had luck today?'

'No, I wanted to talk to you about Paddy Murphy.'

Alexander groaned, fearing the worst, without knowing what the worst could be. He suspected Paddy was locked up in a cell, drunken and battered.

'What's he done?'

'Are you not leaving tomorrow?'

Alexander was perplexed. 'I've made no secret of that, Fergus, but what's that to do with Paddy?'

'Now that he's gone, I wondered if I could take over your site.'

'What do you mean "gone"?'

It was Fergus' turn to look perplexed. 'He's left Chewton, Alexander, drunk as any man I have seen - with that bloody Molly Maguire. Taking her to Sydney, he said. She says they are getting married. Faith, she'll fleece that man like a merino sheep, fool that he is.'

Shocked, but privately thankful, Alexander told the man he would sign the papers over, allowing him to dig the site. He quickly gathered his tools and made his way back to town. There he found the tent stripped of all evidence of Paddy Murphy.

The following morning, Alexander made his way to Castlemaine to make arrangements to transfer his share of the joint account he held with Paddy into his own name. He walked through the Post Office doors shortly after ten in the morning.

He left at eleven, despondent in the knowledge Paddy had cleared all the funds from the account the previous day, transferring £25 into Alexander's account and the balance of over £120 into his own. Alexander cursed his naivety for trusting the drunken, belligerent Irishman and not protecting his money better.

He calculated he now retained only £45 after the money he sent to Melbourne for Rubina and Donald, still a reasonable sum but surely not enough to fulfil his dreams.

The rest of the afternoon, Alexander sat in his tent dwelling on his misfortune and bad judgement. He resolved to leave the goldfields the next morning and to dedicate himself to making sure in future he provided for his family the way a responsible man should.

That night, he made arrangements to travel by wagon back to Melbourne. He allowed himself the luxury of a single ale and returned to his tent for a night of unsettled sleep.

At dawn the next morning, he pulled down and packed the canvas tent. He didn't cast a backward glance as he departed on the wagon, silently cursing the man he thought his trusted partner.

Early in 1853, Alexander was back in Melbourne when he received a letter from his cousin, George Bain Johnston, also called Geordie by his family and friends. George was twelve years younger than Alexander but, even as a young man, had earned a reputation as a fine sailor and a man connected with people of influence.

Also from Cockenzie, George worked for Captain Hew Cadell and joined the crew of The Lioness, a three masted schooner which Cadell sailed from Scotland to Port Melbourne. Like Alexander, he then rushed to the goldfields, arriving not long after Alexander had left. While there he heard of his cousin's lucky strike and his sudden departure. This didn't shock George. He knew his cousin would be keen to consolidate his success for his family's benefit.

George experienced less success than Alexander on the diggings, but on the other hand lost less as well. When Hew Cadell's son, Francis, offered him the chance to join a new shipping venture at the Goolwa, George left immediately for South Australia. The letter George wrote to his cousin encouraged Alexander to meet him there.

In May, almost a year to the day since Alexander struck gold, the cousins met at a tea house in Melbourne.

'Alexander, you must come. The opportunities on the river are boundless. You heard of the exploration by Charles Sturt?'

'Aye, and others since. What makes you believe the opportunities are on the river and nae by sea? Geordie, you and I are both men of the sea, nae the river.' Alexander knew he was being cautious even though he trusted George implicitly.

'I'd have been the first to agree, but you have seen how the inland is opening up. There are few roads and fewer that are suited for cartage. The land is unfriendly, but the river! The river provides passage to the inland.'

'Are you certain 'tis navigable?'

The question was the one that George could not answer with certainty. 'Well, Alexander, I'll be honest. It's nae been proven but plenty believe 'twill by the end of the year. Cousin, I'm telling you it will provide excellent prospects for mariners like us.'

'I'll discuss it with Ruby, George and let you know before you leave tomorrow.'

'I can ask nae more than that, Alexander.' He slapped his cousin on the back.

Alexander hurried home to share the discussion with his wife, undecided whether he was prepared to take the risk. Two minutes into the conversation, Alexander knew the move to the convict free colony of South Australia was already decided.

'Geordie and Elizabeth!' Ruby squealed. She was fond of George's wife and they shared the same religious convictions. 'Oh, Alexander, it sounds grand. We must go.' She knew she was having more to say in this decision than a wife should, but her glee was unconstrained.

For his part, Alexander still felt remorseful about his disaster on the goldfield. He was inclined to acquiesce to Rubina's clear choice, but could not avoid misgivings.

'Rube, we must exercise care. We cannae be sure the river trade will grow the way Geordie promotes.'

'Well, Alexander, if it does nae, are we any worse off?'

They travelled to the Goolwa in January 1854.

Once settled, Alexander found work as a sailor easy to come by. George introduced him to Francis Cadell and while Alexander lacked George's personal charm, he and Francis hit it off well. A proud man extremely embarrassed by his poor business acumen, Alexander had confided his loss of fortune only to Rubina. She comforted and assured him it was probably God's will they should not be afforded wealth. She was grateful they retained enough money to establish a home in the free colony, perhaps enough left for Alexander to join in a small business enterprise.

Alexander remained somewhat bitter, but felt thankful his wife was a kind, understanding woman who would support him without question. He wanted to make sure he returned her kindness and love; above all he desperately wanted her to believe in him.

In March, he identified an opportunity to buy a small block of land and he purchased lot 25 in Newacott Place for £22/10/- . On the lot he erected the canvas tent he used in the goldfields. This was to be the family home while he built a more substantial dwelling.

Alexander and Rubina had £20 left in their savings, enough to engage the town builder, carpenter and undertaker, Alfred Bates, to help Alexander erect the house. They designed a simple cottage, comprising four rooms. A bedroom faced the front on the left with a generous sitting room on the right featuring a fine fireplace and chimney. The kitchen behind also had a fireplace for their cooking and shared the chimney with the living room. Next to the kitchen on the left at the rear was Donald's room.

They built the walls using local limestone and mortar, and the floors and ceilings from solid pine wood. Under the kitchen floor was a large underground water tank, which in short time would be filled with rainwater from the roof guttering. The house was built in the Scottish custom without a verandah to shield the hot Australian sun but it was a firm construction and one of the first in the Goolwa.

As they stood in their new kitchen, Alexander and Rubina glowed in their contentment.

Chapter 4
Sunday, July 17 2016

It's just gone 7.00 when I wake. Yesterday was a better day. Better than most since I arrived in Goolwa, eighteen months ago. I'm trying to leave behind the shadows of my past life that still take me to dark places too often.

Just when I felt my life at Loxton was settled, it was brought down. I enjoyed a good career as a Physical Education teacher at Loxton High School, not a high paying job and not a lot of prospects for advancement, but I loved my lifestyle, in a small community where I made a difference in kids' lives.

My fulfilment flourished when I introduced the kayak program to the school and it looked possible that a couple of my students would earn scholarships into an elite course in Adelaide.

After I read newspaper reports about the growth in drug trafficking and crime in rural towns, I figured my program would help in some way to keep kids occupied with something worthwhile. Yeah, I felt good.

One of the kids that signed up was Emma Satchin, a pretty 15 year old, who exuded confidence to burn. She led a team of catty young girls in year 10 and to me it seemed she set an example for the other girls. She knew how to bend the rules, or break them if she had to. In her closed group, she set her own rules. I was surprised when she joined the kayak program. She wasn't particularly gifted but she had a determination to stand out from the crowd.

For a while I thought that the kayak program gave Emma some direction, just like two or three of the boys that were slightly older than her. They'd made a choice to train four nights a week and once on the weekend. For these kids this was a better choice than to loiter in the town's main street or to ride their dirt bikes around on one of their father's properties. It was a big commitment for kids in their teens. As I said, it made me feel good.

What I didn't see and now curse every day was that Emma's real motivation was Jake, one of the boys on the squad. He was big, strong and talented, almost certain to pick up a scholarship. After training, the two of them would walk from the river toward the town hand in hand, burbling teenage conversation. It seemed harmless enough.

One Friday in November I was summoned to Principal John Manton's office. That was the day my world started to crumble. To my surprise, Emma's parents sat opposite John, but even more off-putting was the presence of one of the town's coppers, who I didn't know.

I recall the conversation only too well.

'Take a seat,' John had said without any pleasantries or introductions. Numbly, I did exactly as he said, wondering what the hell was coming next. I did figure it wasn't going to be good.

'This is Greg Satchin, Emma's father, and her mother, Pat.'

I knew that Greg was once a farmer. After some hard times, he had given up working the land and now owned one of the tyre retailers in the town's main street. The family lived in a modest house on the street behind.

I had heard that Greg possessed the typical forthrightness of a farmer and tried to exercise strict discipline with his children. It seemed to me that this strictness may have inflamed the rebellion Emma showed. I had no doubt she was a handful for both her parents.

While I was sizing up the Satchins, John continued to talk, introducing the policeman. I was so pre-occupied I missed his name and had to shake myself to re-focus on what John said.

'We are here because Emma's parents are very concerned about some things they have discovered recently. I am concerned because they may involve you.'

I was bewildered, becoming visibly frustrated.

'Go on. What are these "things"?'

John was looking a bit flustered.

'I'm sorry. I'll get to the point. Mrs Satchin found a pack of condoms in Emma's bag earlier this week - the bag she uses for kayak training. She's also been getting home much later from training than she should.'

'And this affects me how?' I retorted.

'Emma said she's had sex with you.' There it was. Greg had become impatient with John's considered delivery and had decided to get straight to the point. I sat agape.

Apparently he had pressed Emma, wanting to know why she had the condoms and who she was intending to sleep with. I suspect out of exasperation she retaliated by saying she was already sexually active. She was heading down a one way street by now but didn't want to bring Jake into the discussion. When her father confronted her, she offered up the next person she thought of – me.

My protests to the accusations were to no avail. I don't know whether John believed me or not. In the end it didn't matter. The copper told me that it was now a police investigation and that I faced a jail term if it turned out Emma's story could be proven. Then John Manton said the issue had also gone to the highest levels of the education department and even the State Minister for Education was calling for blood. I walked out of the meeting suspended from teaching, only two weeks before the school year finished. It was unlikely I would be back at school for the rest of the year. To make matters worse, the kayak program was also suspended.

As it happened, I was cleared of all accusations, but it took four weeks and during that time I couldn't set foot in the town without the glares of the townspeople and, on two occasions, verbal attacks. Word spread fast and I was considered as good as guilty. My confidence was shattered – the town I had grown to love and the joy I got from teaching and the kayak program were becoming distant memories. I frequently slipped into deeply depressive states. There were days I wouldn't leave my small rented house on the outskirts of town.

Such was my despair that I didn't wait for the town to accept me again. John Manton told me he couldn't risk the controversy of starting up the kayak program again, but that I could resume teaching in the first term of the new school year.

I decided to leave Loxton, to leave teaching and to discard my old identity with its tarnished image. I packed up two of my favoured K1 kayaks, a few paddles and my clothes and headed south.

Reflecting now on my misfortunes, I am feeling myself slip into my old pattern of bitterness and anxiety. I drag myself out of bed. I need to force myself to re-focus on better days like yesterday. I decide to prepare a breakfast of bacon and eggs in the hope of lifting my spirits.

Walking past the mirror, I realise that the image reflecting back at me, while not perfect, is still good. My hair is thick and black, with a strong curl that cuts across the top of my forehead.

It is starting to show some salt and pepper signs on the sides, but my bright green eyes are the focus of most people when they look at me, so the aging of my hair is not as obvious as it might be.

Since arriving in Goolwa I have paddled with a new intensity and as a result my body is nicely toned especially for a forty-one year old. I have a new career mowing lawns and maintaining gardens for many of Goolwa's holiday homes. I spend most of my time outdoors and together with the hours out on the water over a lot of years, I am tanned to an even golden colour. Even in winter I am blessed with a healthy appearance. Yep, things could be worse.

For a moment I'm surprised by my vanity, a contradiction to the man tormented by the injustices of my past. I soon remember why. For the last few months I have fallen out of my ritual of shaving daily, something to which I adhered strongly for over twenty years. I now sport a fashionable three day growth most of the time, encouraged by Sally who says she prefers a man who isn't pristine, as she calls it.

As I heat the frypan and throw in the bacon rashers, I reflect on last night. Sally came over after her shift at the library and we shared a couple of glasses of McLaren Vale Shiraz with a bowl of chilli prawn pasta she'd cooked up effortlessly. She has been good for me since I arrived in Goolwa.

Sally is in her early thirties, confident and comfortable in herself. She's a natural red head with a burning orange tinge to it, perfecting her wide blue eyes. To complete her stereotypical Irish heritage, her skin is pale with pretty freckles that dot her upper cheeks on each side of her nose. Because, she says, she tends to burn easily, she's never been an outdoors sort of person. Physical fitness doesn't interest her much. Nonetheless, she has a petite figure and looks her perfect self in nothing dressier than tight fitting jeans and a white shirt.

We met at a cricket match on the town oval, where she was watching her brother Riley bat for the A's. We were both ordering beers at the bar and she took the initiative, introducing herself as Sally O'Brien and I responded as Carl Johnson.

'So, Mr Johnson, I haven't seen you around here before. Have you a holiday home in our lovely little town or maybe you've heard what a great place it is to live?' The formality of my name and the playfulness in her tone completely smashed through my defences. We chatted comfortably for the rest of the afternoon.

Over the past few months we have spent increasing amounts of time together - walking, going to the movies in Victor Harbor, or out for a meal, sometimes just talking. Our relationship has blossomed into one that is filled with happiness, tenderness and hope.

We have a wonderfully romantic and physical connection. She loves the sense of touch and can lift my mood by simply resting her hand on mine or stroking my back. For all of that, our relationship is not one full of steamy sexual passion and for me that is just fine right now. The things I appreciate most about Sally are the things I need – trust, warmth, care and humour.

Her easy conversation is comforting after what I left behind and even though I still dread those occasional dark episodes, the sun always shines a little brighter when I am with Sally.

She left early last night. After our pasta we made some small talk on the back deck. Then she headed off to meet girlfriends for a night out listening to blues and jazz in nearby Port Elliot. Anticipating a big night she slept at a friend's house. It suited me because I had a task I wanted to get stuck into as well.

I can't wait to see her again tonight.

Chapter 5
Sunday, July 17 2016

During the night a south westerly breeze sprang up, teasing the river into small waves tipped with white caps.

On Rabbit Island, pelicans huddled together to lessen the chill of the wind, uncaring about what was happening on the water. Two boats moored out from the boat ramp rose and fell with the swells and made minor adjustments to their position swinging around to face their bows into the wind. The girl's body was moving too and within a couple of hours the wind had coaxed her away from the tender hold of the reeds. Once free, she floated out from the shore. Naked, unencumbered by wet clothes, she drifted on a morbid journey east toward the river's mouth. She would arrive at the river's mouth in just a few hours.

The wide concrete driveway of the boat ramp allowed two or three boats to comfortably launch simultaneously. On the western side, two wooden walkways ran along the side of the ramp. The one closest to the ramp was fitted with sturdy poles at the end to allow boats to be tied off for passenger and goods loading. Rocks littered the riverbed under the walkways, some poking curiously through the water surface. The girl's journey was complete by dawn as she came to a rest under the walkway closest to the ramp, held gently by the sturdy poles and the curious rocks so she did not drift any further. By the time the sun rose over Rabbit Island and the pelicans prepared themselves for the day ahead, the wind had dropped to a mere zephyr and the water was so flat that the only disturbance to its sheen were the insects playing on its surface.

The girl's body was at rest.

******

It's much later in the morning than Jock and Trev intended when they arrived to launch their small craft. They were not experienced fishermen but that hadn't diminished their enthusiasm. The older of the two, Jock, had just bought his first boat and spent most of the previous week preparing his rods and reels, not to mention ensuring that the boat's motor and safety equipment was all in order.

Despite his detailed planning through the week, their launch was delayed by a flat tyre, not ten minutes after they left the farm just out of Strathalbyn. After changing the tyre, they had a clear run to Goolwa. There they stopped at the service station to fill the boat with fuel and to pick up ice for the esky and bait for the fish.

The sky was clear, the wind low. The water was still and pelicans on the bank of Rabbit Island were reflected on the mirrored water. It promised to be a perfect day if the fish were on the bite. They had been discussing with relish the prospect of catching their fill of Coorong Mullet or Mulloway and the accolades they would receive from their wives for the freshly caught fish grilled on the barbecue.

The passenger, Trev, was the other man's son in law. He stepped out of the car. He didn't really like the old man. *He could be a grumpy old turd.* Trev only agreed to come out fishing at the encouragement of his wife. He was surprised to find that he now looked forward to the day. He smiled as he thought how happy Jock was with his new toy. The drive down was easy and the two conversed freely and for once Jock hadn't harangued him about selling a few head of cattle now that prices were on the rise.

He walked down to the edge of the ramp and waited for Jock to reverse the trailer toward him. He looked up at the sky. It looked like the weather forecast was going to be spot on, cool with a light breeze.

He guided Jock as he reversed the boat toward him. The trailer approached and he walked backward down the ramp.

'Jock, to the left, mate', Trev called as he signaled with an outstretched arm.

Jock made the correction, continuing until the trailer was in the water to the top of its wheels. He put the car in park, engaged the handbrake and cut the engine. Getting out of the car, he felt a bit of stiffness from sitting in the car and the effect of age on his knees. He joined his son in law behind the car and together they disengaged the boat and floated it off the trailer.

'Just hold it there while I park the car, Trev. I'll give you a hand to pull it over so we can tie it up over there,' he said pointing to the poles at the end of the walkway.

Trev knew he could do it by himself, but he figured that this was the old man's special day. *No harm in doing things his way.*

After he parked the car, Jock walked back and grabbed a rope fastened to the stern of the boat. He started along the walkway, Trev following with his rope attached to the bow. Once the boat was positioned along the walkway, they tied the ropes to the poles.

'Can't believe there's no-one else down here today. It's too good to be true.'

'Too right. Why don't you go grab the esky and the other stuff that's got to go on the boat? I'll hop in and get her ready. Oh, don't forget the smaller esky, I brought a couple of beers along.'

'No worries, give me your keys and I'll lock the car.' The young man grinned, humoured by Jock's reference to a couple of beers. *The old guy isn't prone to extravagance.*

Jock climbed into the boat. He fiddled around moving the safety vests and fishing rods to the places he wanted them. By the time he was finished, Trev was standing on the walkway next to the boat with the larger esky, the one with the bait.

Turning to take the esky from his son in law, Jock saw something floating in the water.

'What the hell is that? Oh, shit!'

'What is it?'

'Get down here, look. For God's sake, it's a fucking body!'

Trev jumped into the boat and bent down to look under the walkway. He stumbled backward as he saw the body; naked, bruised and battered.

There would be no fishing today.

Chapter 6
Sunday, July 17 2016

After breakfast, I throw on some clothes and head to the back shed. It looks like a beautiful day. If the wind doesn't spring up, I may fit in a paddle this afternoon. If it does, then I might switch to a surf at Goolwa Beach. Either way, afterwards I'll meet up with Sally for a walk on the beach.

The repairs I made last night to the steering mechanism on the kayak and patching the hole with fibreglass look to have held. *Good – the boat is now ready for use again.*

Amy Richards is the one concession I've made to my old life since I came to Goolwa. I was paddling on the river at North Goolwa, off Liverpool Road about a year ago, when I pulled into the shore for a rest and re-hydration. Amy was sitting on a seat and wandered over to check out my boat. She had done some paddling during a high school aquatics program and had really enjoyed it. The boats she had used were built for stability so she was fascinated how different mine looked.

'It's so narrow,' she said, 'how does someone your size even fit into it?' She came across as a bright and articulate sixteen-year-old; I reminded myself of the risks engaging with teenage girls, so I stayed aloof. She may have thought I was rude.

Over the course of the next few weeks, I often saw Amy as I paddled on a Saturday afternoon. We would exchange hellos and she would occasionally watch as I trained. Sometimes when I paddled close to shore for a break, she would wander over for a brief chat.

One Saturday, Amy asked if she could try paddling a racing kayak. I was surprised by the enthusiasm she showed. I was even more surprised that I was tempted by the opportunity to coach again. I guess my confidence and trust in human nature was restored the more time I spent with Sally.

Not long after, Saturday afternoons became a regular two-person training session. She was a fast learner and quickly adapted to the instability of the K1 even on days when the water was choppy due to wind or the wash from rivercraft.

Although Amy was not beautiful, she had that prettiness girls develop as they grow to womanhood. She seemed to be experimenting with hair colours, clothes and piercings, a contrast to her relatively shy nature. Her brown eyes rarely made direct contact and her speech was always soft and restrained. She lacks the self-assurance of Emma … *my god, why is she my reference point?*

Our first sessions were quiet affairs. I helped her improve her stroke and challenged her with sprints. We talked about kayak technique but whenever the discussion turned to personal matters, I deftly diverted it.

Over time, I relaxed a little and Amy started to open up about her life. I heard about her father and mother. Sometimes she spoke about them fondly, but more often the cracks in their relationship were obvious.

'Mum's alright, I guess,' she had once said, 'but she doesn't stand up for me when Dad goes on one of his rants. He just doesn't get me, not like golden boy, Brock.' She was referring to her brother, a couple of years older than her.

'What do you mean?' I had asked.

'Brock is good at sports. That's all that's important to Dad – footy and cricket. As long as Brock is good at them, he can do what he wants. The truth is Brock's a dick. He's always having a go at me, just because I'm not interested in the things he is.'

'So, what do your parents think about you paddling?' I was keen to make sure I wasn't setting myself up for another parental conflict.

'Oh, they think it's great. Dad says it's not a real sport but at least it's getting me out of my bedroom. He wants me to be more normal. He thinks I'm a freak … so does Brock.'

'Because of your hair and piercings?'

'That and other stuff. Mainly I tried to look different just to annoy them. It doesn't bother me so much now 'coz I know what I want to do.'

'Oh yeah, what's that?' I was starting to get interested in where Amy was headed.

'I'm going back to school, night school. I want to get into Uni. Anything would be better than staying a checkout chick.'

'What are you planning to study?'

'I want to be a teacher,' she said. *Of all things.*

Months later I am still reserved, always coaching from my boat rather than too close. If she notices or finds it strange, she never says anything and, well, I feel like my life is getting back on track.

Amy is quite petite and only about one hundred and sixty centimetres tall, so she doesn't have the long arms and legs to become an elite kayaker. But then, I'm not coaching her to make her one and I no longer have any interest in pursuing that objective. However, she is picking up the principles well, using her legs and stomach muscles to give her the drive through her stroke. She has trimmed off a bit of the puppy fat she sported when I first met her and she is now a little broader across the shoulders from the work she has done.

Yesterday was a challenging training session for the most unexpected reason. For a change, we headed off from the ramp near the scout hall at Goolwa North and then paddled further north toward Currency Creek and the River Finniss. Keeping left of Goose Island and the Billy Goat Islands, we entered the waterway of Currency Creek, its mouth wide and enveloping. The afternoon breeze whipped up a wave as the creek entered the river, but it didn't seem to worry Amy. Undaunted, she was keen for the new challenge.

She was uncharacteristically chatty yesterday and opened up a bit more about her deepening relationship with Kyle, who I don't recall ever meeting.

'He's so nice, Carl. He really cares about me. I think I love him.'

'That's a big call, Amy. Have you had a serious relationship before?'

'No,' she said defensively, 'but that doesn't matter. I know how I feel about him and it's good. Well, it's good for me anyway. Mum and Dad aren't so keen.'

'Maybe they are just being cautious. You are their only daughter and they wouldn't want you to get hurt.'

'Yeah, right.' Her tone was caustic.

I sensed she had more to tell me but our discussion soon dissolved into more mundane matters like whether the wind was going to spring up on us when we headed back.

We paddled in a further two kilometres and we could see ahead that the creek suddenly narrowed to about fifty metres. The water was much calmer here so we sprinted the last five hundred metres to the narrowing.

We paddled on slowly. After we passed through the neck, the creek opened out again. In further, a huge flock of black swans were startled by our sudden appearance and took to flight. There must have been a couple of hundred birds and as they laboured their way into the air, the beating of their large wings on the water created a drumming noise like I'd never heard before. Amy and I sat in wonderment as we watched the black cloud of birds fly on another few hundred metres before settling back on the water.

For no apparent reason, Amy picked up on our earlier conversation, but in a very different tone. She was serious, almost troubled.

As I reflect on the conversation this morning, I wonder how well I dealt with it.

Amy had started tentatively. 'Carl, can I tell you something, you know, just between you and me?'

'Sure,' I had responded, without a clue where she was going.

'I'm pregnant,' she blurted. Regaining composure, she looked across to me. 'I found out a couple of weeks ago. I'm nine weeks now.'

Although I was shocked by her admission, I tried to keep my voice as calm and detached as I could – the last thing I wanted was to get embroiled in the problems of a second teenage girl.

'So, the father is….'

'Kyle, of course.'

' Right. Does he know?'

'Not yet, but I will tell him soon. I'm keeping the baby.'

'Will he be there for you?' I asked tentatively.

'I think so. We love each other.' After a pause, Amy continued. 'But it's not Kyle I'm worried about. It's Mum and Dad.'

'You haven't told them yet? Amy, you're very young with your whole life ahead of you. They need to know.'

'You think I don't know that. I'm not stupid.' Tears were now rolling down her face.

We were just sitting in the middle of the creek. I shuffled in the boat feeling increasingly uncomfortable.

'They will be so disappointed and Dad will go ballistic.'

'You don't know, Amy. They may be more supportive than you think.'

'No, you don't know, Carl. Dad hates him. He will be so angry with me and I'm scared what he will do to Kyle. He thinks Kyle's a no hoper; says because he got into trouble when he was a kid, he won't ever change.'

'Do you believe that?' I asked, trying to change the tone a little.

'No. He's the warmest, most gentle person I have ever met. Dad would never take my feelings into account though. He treats me like a little kid. I'm almost an adult.'

'Amy, you're right. You're nearly an adult, but you're not one yet. Listen, I will always be here for you to talk to.' I could hardly believe the words were coming out of my mouth! 'The thing is, you have to talk to your parents and Kyle.'

Amy looked at me through reddened eyes and muttered, 'I know.'

On our trip back to the ramp, we didn't return to the subject of her pregnancy. Honestly, I didn't feel comfortable in bringing it up again. Nonetheless, as uncomfortable as it was, I felt closer to Amy, as a friend and a mentor. I realised I was capable of trusting again and being trusted again.

Amy decided to hole the kayak as she came into shore. In fairness, she probably didn't "decide"' to hole it, but she did go into the bank at the wrong place too fast, hitting a rock right on the front of the keel, tipping the boat and somehow fouling the rudder mechanism. She immediately burst into uncontrolled tears. While I felt some annoyance at her recklessness, I soon realised that what she needed was a little bit of empathy.

Once we got out of the kayaks, I wanted to walk around to her and hold her in close. Instead, I gently placed one arm around her shoulders while she wept. Still, I couldn't help but wonder if I was starting to cross that line I feared so much, a feeling that became intense as she pulled in close and leaned her head against my chest.

'It will be ok, Amy. Just tell your parents and Kyle and let it unfold from there. Once you have shared it you can start planning next steps. You don't have to do it on your own.'

'I know. What about your boat?'

'Oh, don't worry about that,' I said. 'It's just a boat and I can fix it. You'll be alright?'

'Yes. Thanks for listening, Carl.'

She unwrapped from my embrace and walked slowly toward her house, a forlorn, troubled young lady.

Today I look at my repairs satisfied they are good. *I hope Amy has been able to talk with her parents and Kyle and they give her the support she needs.*

Chapter 7
Sunday, July 17 2016

Riley O'Brien was one of three police officers stationed at Goolwa. He was the senior, supported by Constable Rachel Cross, posted to the town two years ago, and Probationary Constable Phil Reid, who joined the team only six months earlier. Riley was born and bred Goolwa, leaving only while he undertook his training at the Largs Bay Police Academy in Adelaide.

Unlike most of his colleagues, he was delighted to receive a rural posting once he graduated and even more pleased to return to his home town. The cops he knew would be uncomfortable working among people they knew, including friends, family and the kids they grew up with. Riley regarded it a privilege. *After all, didn't he join the force to serve the community, his community?* What's more it meant he had the opportunity to live near his family - his parents and his sister Sally, who now shared a rented house with him at Goolwa Beach.

Early Sunday morning he was eating toast at his kitchen table, lost in his own thoughts. At 38 years, he almost had his life in order. His musing was broken by Sally bursting through the back door.

'Hi, Sal. Have a good night?'

'Great. We saw some really funky bands and it's always great to catch up with the girls, or should I say, your fan club.'

Riley already knew where this conversation was going. On previous occasions he'd attempted, unsuccessfully, to deflect her. Now, he just found it easier to let her have her say.

'Oh, yeah. What's up now?'

'You know what's up, Riley. My friends can't understand why you're not already taken. They all say you are the most eligible bachelor in town.'

It was a title commonly expressed around Goolwa but Riley was mostly oblivious to it. He had had his share of relationships in Goolwa and neighbouring towns. For all that, he hadn't yet found someone to spend his life with.

Sally continued, warming to her teasing. 'Anna calls you George Clooney in uniform.' She gave him a cheeky grin.

'Does she now? Are you finished?' He was keen to wrap up the conversation.

'Well, actually, no I'm not.'

'Ok, actually I am,' he said. 'I've got to get to the footy club and then to work.'

He knew that his job and community interests got in the way of him meeting the right person but he had no intention of giving them up. Once a very serviceable player for the Goolwa Magpies he no longer played AFL football, a sacrifice to advance his career. However, he remained involved with the club and served on the club management committee.

'See, there you are, Riley. Always so involved, it's no wonder you don't have time for a serious relationship. What are you going to the club for today?' She was curious why he would be going into the club so early before work.

'It was my turn to be property steward yesterday, so I've got to drop all the gear from the game back to the club.'

Sally held her thumb and finger to her nose. The last time Riley performed the task, she had shared a ride home in his car. In the back seat were the used guernseys from the game, reeking of the sour and sharp smells of male sweat and liniment.

'Yuk. Never, ever ask me to wash those filthy clothes. I don't know what those boys do when they play footy, but they are rank. Who's got that lucky job?'

'Cheryl Higgins. Peter's wife. She's volunteered to wash them all year.'

'Poor thing. What was she thinking taking that thankless task on?'

'Volunteers are what makes the club tick, Sally, and I guess if you are married to a club legend, you are going to get roped in.'

Peter Higgins played as a ruckman with the club until a knee injury in a grand final forced him into retirement. Coincidentally the club's winning percentage dropped for a few years. Truthfully, Riley and others in the club couldn't deny that his retirement had hurt the club's competitiveness. He had also earnt a long suspension in the same match following a spontaneous and unwarranted physical confrontation with an umpire. This fact had long been forgotten by the club faithful and he was still esteemed as a legend.

Riley capped his head and paused at the back door.

'Ok, I've gotta go. I should finish around 5.00. Are you home tonight?'

'Yep, I'm catching up with Carl for a walk on the beach later but I should be home for dinner. Have a good day, Riley.'

Riley entered through the oval gate shortly after nine and drove along an asphalt roadway that rimmed the playing arena. Although the ground was deserted today, he could visualise cars parked perpendicular to the boundary. He could almost hear the cacophony of blasting horns each time a goal was scored, providing encouragement to the players. He wistfully recalled the feeling on the ground.

He drove to the far side of the oval where the double storey clubrooms were located. Peter Higgins' Toyota Hilux was parked outside.

Riley gathered the bag of smelly clothes and as he walked through the front door of the club, he was greeted by Peter from behind the bar. He was a large man standing nearly two metres tall and as broad as an axe handle across the shoulders. Regardless of his legend status, he struck an imposing figure.

Like Riley, Peter was raised in Goolwa. His family could trace its origins in the area to the 1840's when Thomas Walter Higgins had built Higginsbrook. In its time, it was an impressive tract of land stretching from Currency Creek to Port Elliot, running 1,400 head of cattle. A jovial man, Peter often joked that it must have been the other side of the family that inherited the wealth because he certainly hadn't.

'Morning, Pete. You're here early.'

'Yeah, there was a twenty-first birthday party here last night so I have a bit of tidying up to do in this bar area. I tell you, mate, if people treated their homes how they treat this place, I wouldn't want an invitation to dinner. Bloody pigs, they are.'

'Jeez, you're a bit grouchy this morning. You usually take all this in your stride.'

'Just over it, I guess. The shitty tasks always fall back to the committee members, have you noticed? You've got the guernseys there? I won't be hanging around too long. Better take them home so Cheryl can clean them up.'

'They didn't get too dirty yesterday,' Riley said. 'Not many of our blokes went in anywhere near hard enough. I reckon it's our worst effort so far this year.'

Before Peter could comment, Riley's mobile phone rang. As he answered, Peter clutched the bag and took it out to his car.

He was about to walk back into the club, when Riley burst through from inside.

'Sorry, Pete, gotta go. Looks like we've had a drowning in the river.'

******

The traffic was light and cleared the way for Riley as he engaged the patrol car's flashing lights. He called to ensure an ambulance had been dispatched, but he suspected from the description the witnesses gave emergency services it was probably too late for the girl. From the time he received the call, it took him nine minutes to drive from the football oval to the boat ramp.

Arriving at the site, Riley approached the fishermen who stood, pale and shaken, smoking alongside their car. They pointed him to the body and he stepped warily onto the boat where he saw the motionless form on the foredeck.

'Who took her out of the water?' Riley called to the fishermen.

'We wanted to be sure she wasn't still alive,' the older man said.

Riley leant over the body. What he saw shocked him. Although he had been in the force for years, the sight of a dead person never sat well with him. But it's not the image of the battered and bloated body that most unsettled him.

His eyes widened as he realised with absolute certainty the identity of the girl. She was Amy Richards, the daughter of Michael Richards. Riley was acquainted with Michael through the Goolwa Football Club where they were both committee members. Holding back rising nausea, he looked up as the ambulance arrived, red and blue lights flashing.

The two green suited paramedics joined Riley on the deck of the boat. The taller man knelt to examine the body while the other stood next to Riley.

'Beautiful day, isn't it? Perfect for a spot of fishing, but I guess not for these blokes now,' he said, pointing back to Jock and Trev.

He looked down at his partner who returned the look with a shake of his head.

'Not for this lass, either,' the kneeling man said. 'There's nothing we can do for her now. I'll tell you what, though, if you want my opinion, there is no way this is just a skinny-dip gone wrong."

'What do you mean?' asked Riley.

'Have a look at the bruising on her,' he replied, pointing to the back of her neck. 'Also, I'd think all these scrapes on her knees are pre-death. I'm no pathologist, but I reckon this girl met with foul play.'

'Ok, thanks, guys. I guess you boys won't be hanging around then.'

'As I said, mate, nothing we can do for her. I'm afraid she's all yours now.'

Riley made the necessary call to the Major Crime Investigation Branch in Adelaide. A few minutes later he received a return call.

'Sergeant O'Brien?'

'Yes'

'Detective Inspector Paul Smith here. I hear you have a body down there and you think there are suspicious circumstances around the death.'

'That's right, sir.' Riley talked Smith through the discovery and condition of the body, then paused waiting for a response.

'Yes, well, I agree it needs further investigation. I'll need to pull a forensics team together. We should be able to get the chopper down, so let's say around two hours, midday. In the meantime, can you make sure that the site is secured? I don't want anyone inadvertently fucking up our crime scene.'

Riley read between the lines. Smith was implying that country cops didn't know how to manage evidence protection.

'No problem, sir. We will get it locked up tight.'

He hung up, immediately securing the site with black and yellow tape. Then he blocked the road with his car leaving the lights flashing. As soon as he finished, Constable Rachel Cross arrived, parking her patrol car alongside Riley's.

As she exited the vehicle, he called to her.

'Rachel, can you stay there and watch the barricade? Make sure no-one comes through unless they are authorised. I'm just going to be taking statements from these guys,' he said, pointing to the fishermen.

Smith arrived early in the afternoon, the chopper depositing him and the three member forensic team at the entry to the car park. After unloading their gear, the chopper quickly ascended. Having disturbed the tranquillity for a few minutes, it headed north, sound gradually fading.

While Paul Smith punched a number into his phone as soon as the noise of the helicopter subsided, the forensic team members introduced themselves to Riley and Rachel and started unpacking their cases. Finishing his call, Smith strode to Riley and Rachel.

'Morning, I'm Detective Inspector Paul Smith. As you know, I'm heading up the investigation.' He turned to Rachel. 'So, love, any chance you can organise a coffee? White with two, thanks.'

I'm guessing you're Sergeant O'Brien? Where's our body?'

'Yes, sir, just down here,' Riley said, noting Rachel slamming the door in disgust as she got into the patrol car. He would need to talk to her later. His immediate assessment of Smith was that he might well be a chauvinistic, arrogant prick. He was happy not to be in the clutch of one of the large city units - they were all too often cemented in the misogynistic and hierarchical culture of decades past.

He led Smith to the small marquee erected to offer some privacy and dignity to Amy's lifeless body. Smith glanced in, paying scant attention to her and stepped out. He spent the next ten minutes reviewing the fishermen's statements with Riley while the investigators commenced their examination of the scene. A female forensic officer and one of her male colleagues collected pieces of foreign material in the surrounding area -

cigarette butts, coffee cups and other items that might provide clues, either now or later, to what happened to Amy. The third member of the forensic team photographed and measured the dozen or so tyre tracks on the verges of the car park. He did the same with any footprints he found.

Smith pulled Riley aside.

'I need a word in private, O'Brien.'

'Yes, sir.' They walked along the road away from the car park.

The DI stopped and turned to Riley. 'The thing is, Sergeant, as you may know our major crime division is snowed under at the moment. Frankly, we don't have the resources to handle this one on our own. I understand you have been doing some training in major crime investigation so I have spoken with your chief and he's okay with me seconding you to assist. It is actually pretty useful having someone with local knowledge on the team.'

'Thank you, sir. What do you want me to do?' Riley privately felt excited and a little anxious about what had just been proposed.

'Let's understand two things, O'Brien. Firstly, you are still going to have to pull your weight with the station down here, that's part of the deal. Secondly, what I say goes, alright…. no heroics, no Lone Ranger antics. If you can't work under my direction, I don't want you. Understood?'

'Clear as a bell, sir. '

It was mid-afternoon by the time Amy's body was taken by the coroner and Smith released Riley to talk to her parents.

Looking directly into Riley's eyes, he instructed him 'I want to know every move our girl made in the twelve hours before she was last seen.

'And, O'Brien,' he called over his shoulder as he turned to walk away, 'I noticed some grey nomads camped in Winnebagos on the road back there. On your way out, check if any of them saw or heard anything.'

Smith ambled toward the small group of reporters waiting on the other side of the delineated zone. The question in his mind as he approached was how much he should tell them. *Was it just a drowning at this stage or should he confirm that they were investigating a likely crime?*

As he walked, the answer became obvious. *The reporters would have figured Major Crime detectives wouldn't be there if it was just a case of accidental drowning.*

Chapter 8
Monday 14th August 1854

Although he was not a hard drinking man, Alexander frequented the newly built Goolwa Hotel most afternoons. He liked to catch up on local news, in particular any new ventures in the town that could be advantageous to him.

He always sat at the same table in the corner, with an acquaintance, Joseph Tripp. Joe was a fisherman who worked along the Coorong, the long narrow lagoon that ran parallel to the coast line flanked by high sandy dunes for nearly one hundred miles.

'I tell you, Alexander I travel from Finniss and Strathalbyn in the north through to Salt Creek in the east. There int a person in this town that knows more than me about what's going on hereabouts.'

Alexander had to admit this made him a very valuable source of information. However, in many ways, Joe reminded Alexander of Paddy Murphy, so he was always wary about how much he shared with him.

'Aye, that's true, Joseph. I wonder if that will continue to be true with all that's planned for this town.'

Joe Tripp was a big man with rough, calloused hands and a ruddy face ravaged by the sun. He was rarely seen without a pipe in his mouth and, when in town, without a glass of rum in his hand.

After taking a swig of rum, Joe retorted. 'Plans, bloody plans. If you want to see where things are really progressing you need to go east. There int no future here.'

The two men sat at their usual table without speaking for several minutes. The silence was broken when they were approached by Alexander's cousin, George Bain Johnston.

Since moving to the Goolwa, George had become actively involved with Francis Cadell in the push to promote trade along the length of the River Murray. George's success as a mariner had seen him become a captain of a vessel in Cadell's employ and he was now in the process of forming his own venture.

He had already secured Charles Murphy as a partner, but knowing his cousin to be a reliable sailor, if not a proven business man, he was keen to offer him the opportunity to join as a third partner.

'Good evening, Tripp. Alexander, may I have a word.'

George generally avoided entering into conversation with Tripp, a man he did not respect. In his view, the man was coarse and abrupt, although he did concede that he couldn't point to any specific wrongdoing on his part. Tripp sat firmly planted with his drink and cast him a scornful look. George turned his back to the fisherman and addressed Alexander quietly.

"Ruby and Donald are well, Alexander?'

George was, unlike Alexander, a man of solid build, barrel chested and at least six inches taller. His face was round and generous and like most men of the era sported a full beard that was neatly trimmed. In other respects he resembled Alexander, with soft green eyes and dark hair parted on the left with a dominant wave as it spread across the top of his head. As always, George wore a white shirt with upturned collar, a pressed dark jacket and bow tie.

'They are well. Thank you for asking, George. And Elizabeth, she is well, I trust.'

George's wife, Elizabeth, and Alexander's wife, Rubina, had developed a close relationship and the pair was instrumental in establishing a Wesleyan Church in the Goolwa.

'She is in a state of excitement, Alexander. The parish will have a full time minister from September.'

Alexander knew that George had more on his mind and waited for him to continue.

'So, Alexander, have you thought any further about investing in Johnston and Murphy? This is a prime chance to get in early on the river trade and even after building your house, you must have some funds to spare.'

Alexander had not corrected George's notion that he still had most of his gold digging fortune and he was now embarrassed that the matter of his personal wealth had come up in front of Joe. He felt backed into a corner and that sooner or later the truth would eventually be revealed, damaging his credibility in the town.

Alexander was keen to tag along on the coattails of his successful cousin, but he knew that at present he would be unable to procure the funding that George expected.

'Well, George, I've had it under consideration, I have. I have nae yet made up my mind if 'tis the right thing to do just now.'

In fact, he suspected it was exactly the right thing just now and the best opportunity for him to realise his dreams. If only he was able to lay his hands on another hundred pounds or two.

'Alexander, the offer cannae stay open for ever. Please, think about what it could mean for your family's future. Is that nae what you came here for?'

'Aye, 'tis George. I'll let ye know.'

George left the pair, perplexed by Alexander's apparent reluctance. As he walked away, he questioned if he truly thought bringing Alexander into the partnership was a good idea. At the same time he also knew that to do otherwise would lead to difficult conversations with Elizabeth.

Joe turned to Alexander. 'You're not really considering this folly are you, Alexander? Ask me there's more than one in this town, your cousin included, that have high opinions of theirselves. Mark my words, they will wish they'd stayed in the goldfields.'

As Alexander took a swig of his ale and pondered, Joe continued, inclining his head toward the eight men in deep conversation at a table on the other side of the saloon.

'Look at them fools. They're wasting their time with some fantastic notion they can organise a regatta for all the boats from here to Victor Harbor. A celebration, they says, for the first anniversary of the launching of a cargo ship built hereabouts. Bloody fools. I int partaking with my boat and most of the other fishermen think the same. As for the whalers, them selfish bastards wouldn't give a tinker's cuss for some tin pot regatta if there's a whale anywhere in these waters.'

'I dinnae ken, Joseph' replied Alexander, 'I can see fortuitous happenings here. Look around. This inn was nae here a year ago and Mr Goode is opening his store next door very soon. We are going to have a police station here next year and talk is there will be another two hotels in the town soon. '

'Bah, what's the good of hotels and shops if the town don't grow and as for the police station, we all knows that's because of the problems with the blacks in town. I know the blackfellas well, Alexander, and the thing is them's good people, but not with liquor in their belly. We just got to keep them out of town is all.'

Alexander, however, remained unconvinced.

'You're missing the point, Joe. Now we have the railway from Port Elliot, we can transport cargo by sea, bring it here on the railway and then boat it along the river. Look at our wharf now, equal to any in the colonies I'd wager. And, look, Cadell and Randell proved how far you can take a boat along the river, all the way into New South Wales and I hear it might be that you can go even further north, along the Murrumbidgee.'

'Railway, ha? Governor Henry bloody Young is another fool emptying the colony's treasury with that folly. This colony's gone broke once and it's on its way again. Every clever person is making their fortunes in the Victorian goldfields, not this shit hole.'

Alexander was not to be deterred. 'Joe, this is the time for the Goolwa. Where do you think the flour and meat for the goldfields is going to come from? They'll open up the land around here and we can ship along the river for much less than it will cost by bullock. You're right, though, a lot of people are leaving here thinking they will make their money from gold. That means there will be less competition here when the river trade takes off.'

'Well, you can have it, friend. Anyone thinks this place has a future is loose in the head. If I could raise the money I'd be heading to them goldfields or home to Wiltshire.'

'Aye, well, I'm going home. I need to think about George's proposal and discuss it with Rubina.'

'You're a bloody fool, Alexander.'

Chapter 9
Sunday, July 17 2016

A short time after leaving Smith, Riley was back in his car. The campers hadn't seen or heard anything. One couple retired to bed around 9.00 and the other couple before 10.30. One said the last car they heard going toward the ramp was shortly after dark, at 5.30, but they were unable to provide any further useful information.

He called into the barrage supervisors' cottages a couple of hundred metres farther on but they also were unable to recall any cars in the area after dark.

As Riley drove through town to the other side of Goolwa, he thought about how he would tell Amy's parents. He didn't know her father very well, even though they did play football together when Michael was at the end of his playing days and Riley was at the start of his. He also knew him through the football club committee, on which they both served. It was customary for the committee to meet informally for dinner on the Friday night before every home game, but for some reason, Riley and Michael had shared only brief conversations. He couldn't explain why, but he found it difficult to warm to Michael – maybe, he reasoned, they were just different people.

He swung the police car onto Liverpool Road toward Goolwa North and turned his mind to other people close to him that would be impacted by the news. His friend Carl Johnson had been coaching Amy. Riley knew from his sister Sally that this 'project' had changed Carl, turning him from someone who was often withdrawn and morose into a person who now seemed to have found purpose.

Riley suddenly banged his hand on the car steering wheel as he realised that he should have told Paul Smith about Carl's relationship with Amy, Sally and, of course, himself. Consumed by the stress of the situation and the many ways it could play out, Riley arrived at Amy's parents' house without any memory of the drive there.

He sat in the car for a few minutes composing his thoughts. For now he had to take one step at a time, follow the process just as he was trained and deal with each new piece of information as it unfolded. And, he should tell Smith about Carl at his first opportunity.

Riley looked at the house, a neat transportable of the type common in this holiday town even amongst the permanent residents. The lawn was freshly mowed and the garden neatly maintained, crowded with succulents that grew well in the sandy soil. A large shady gum tree stood majestic at one corner of the house. On the gravel driveway was Michael's four wheel drive twin cab Nissan and at the end of the drive was a path that forked to the left. The pathway terminated at a set of four steps rising up to the covered porch where the front door waited for Riley.

Standing at the doorway, he again struggled to remember how he got there. He reminded himself to focus. He raised his hand to knock on the door but hesitated as he heard raised voices inside, muffled but clearly emotional. Moments later, he knocked and waited as the voices inside fell silent.

The door opened to reveal a woman who looked to be in her early forties, smooth skinned and fair haired. Riley saw her face was slightly flushed, perhaps a result of the conversation just terminated mid-sentence.

She looked quizzically at Riley and he was momentarily taken aback by the strong resemblance to the girl whose body he had just left.

'Hello, officer, can I help you?'

'Hello Mrs Richards, I'm Sergeant O'Brien. Is Michael at home?' he asked.

Her expression remained confused, but she called to her husband, who arrived at the door moments later. Michael was a tall man reaching over one hundred and ninety centimetres and it was clear that Amy's diminutive build was inherited from her mother. His face had a ruddy complexion and his hairline receded substantially. Riley recalled that he had sardonically said that his hair loss was the result of running his own building supplies wholesale company and raising a teenage daughter.

Standing behind his wife, Michael greeted him. 'Oh, hello, Riley, I didn't expect to see you here. Is something wrong at the club?'

Karen Richards expected the conversation to move to matters concerning the football club and turned to walk to the kitchen.

'Sorry, Mrs Richards, this concerns you as well. Do you mind if I come in?'

The next two minutes were amongst the worst of Riley's career. In his job, he had, on occasions, broken bad news to families, but mostly as a result of a car accident. A death was a death, of course, but the viciousness seemingly associated with this one seemed to make it so much more horrendous.

Once Riley broke the tragic news, Karen Richards' eyes widened in disbelief until realisation hit and she burst into tears. She buried her head deep into Michael's shoulder while he sat in stunned silence. Riley offered them a glass of water. They didn't respond, so he went into the kitchen, poured two glasses and set them on a coffee table in front of them.

At this stage, he had only told them that Amy was dead. He now had to expand on the way they believed that she died and, as sensitively as he could, extract necessary information that may help their enquiry.

'Karen and Michael, I need to tell you more about Amy's death that you will find very painful. Please let me know if you want me to repeat anything or to explain further and I will as much as I can.

'The thing is, we believe that Amy was murdered.' He saw the anguish in Karen's face but felt he must go on to avoid subjecting them to a tortuous, slow release of bad news.

'There is every likelihood she was sexually assaulted either before or after she was killed. We can't be positive about how she died but I can say that drowning looks to have been the most likely cause.'

'How do you know she may have been sexually assaulted... raped, that's what you mean isn't it? You must have a reason for thinking that,' Michael challenged, his voice laced with icy aggression. Karen sobbed louder and looked up at Riley with pleading eyes, not wanting to hear the answer she feared was coming.

'Amy was naked when she was found. There is no sign of her clothes, but we have a team searching the whole area.'

'Oh, my poor baby,' Karen whispered.

Riley shuffled uncomfortably as he drew a deep breath and faced them. 'Would you mind if I asked you some questions that might help us in our investigation?'

'I want to catch this bastard more than you do,' Michael muttered with venom. 'What do you need to know?'

'OK, I'll keep the questions to the minimum that I can for now. I know you are going to need some time to deal with this. Can you tell me the last time you saw Amy?'

Karen drew strength from being able to participate in the conversation rather than just listen with no control over what was being said.

'We saw her at around 11.30 yesterday morning, just before we left home. We went to my sister's birthday party in Adelaide. Michael didn't really want to go, football on Saturday, you know, but he decided at the last minute he would come with me.'

'And do you know what Amy was going to be doing later in the day?' Riley questioned.

Michael responded, 'She was going for a paddle with that Carl bloke. I know she wouldn't have missed it for the world. Really taken to it she has, I mean had. It's done her good, too. She's not as rebellious as she used to be.'

'After that,' Michael continued, 'she was going to go out with her boyfriend, Kyle… Kyle Hooper.'

Riley knew Kyle. He had seen him around town. The kid had got into a bit of minor trouble as a teenager but as far as he knew had grown into a reasonable and mature young adult.

'Did she see him, do you know? What were they going to be doing?'

'I suppose they caught up.' Karen was a little more composed, even as tears welled in her desperate eyes. 'Amy said they were going to Victor Harbor for a bit and then come back and watch Netflix. It doesn't look like they did… there's not an empty glass or potato chip packet to be seen.'

'So you don't think she's been home? Did that concern you?' asked Riley.

'That's actually what we were arguing about when you arrived, Riley, 'said Michael. 'We didn't get home until late and didn't look in on Amy's room until this morning. We thought maybe she had stayed over at Kyle's instead of coming back here. And I have to tell you I'm not that keen on Kyle. You know he's been in trouble before, don't you? You don't think that Kyle….' He left the sentence unfinished.

Riley frowned. 'We can't be sure of anything right now. We just have to gather the facts and put them together until we know what's happened.

'Your son, Brock? Was he at home last night?'

Michael answered, 'No, he was at some footy show. He probably stayed over at one of his mates. That's not unusual though. He's twenty and sowing his seeds. We don't keep much of a leash on him.'

'I assume that Amy has a mobile phone and you've tried that?'

'Yes, of course, maybe a dozen times. It keeps going straight to her voicemail.'

'Can you give me the number, please? We'd like to find it if we can.'

Riley wrote the number on his notepad as Michael called it out, before looking up at the despondent parents.

'There's one more thing I need to ask you and it's going to be difficult. We need to have one of you do a formal identification. Amy's been taken to Adelaide. The pathologist will need to conduct a post mortem to identify cause and time of death and so on. I can arrange for you to be taken as soon as you are ready – is that all right?'

Karen and Michael looked at each other, before Michael replied. 'We will both go.'

'I want to see my little girl,' Karen added in a quivering voice, tears now streaming down her face.

'Ok I'll call you soon to arrange a time for the pickup. I'm so sorry to be bringing you such sad news. I can also arrange some counselling if you feel you'd like it. Just let me know.'

As he walked to the door, Karen suddenly grasped his forearm. 'Wait, Riley. You haven't mentioned Amy's car. It's not here. Do you know where it is? Was it with her?'

Riley's jaw dropped for a moment as he realised his oversight. He should have asked that question already and he was reminded how much he was still to learn about investigative procedures. He had assumed that Kyle would be driving whenever they went out. He recalled his old tutor warning "assume makes an ass out of you and me". Still he'd fallen for it.

'No, we haven't located her car. Can you give me some details?'

Michael answered, 'It's an old Mazda 323, 1996 I think, orange, rego number VWA 612. If it wasn't with Amy, where is it?'

Riley turned to leave. 'If Amy was murdered we will be doing everything we can to find who is responsible. That'll include finding her car.'

By the time Riley was back in his car it was dark, winter chill starting to settle in. The street lights illuminated the drizzling rain that now fell, shards of light creating the illusion of one of those firecrackers that gives off a golden shower.

Before he started his car, he rang Paul Smith and updated him on his discussion with the Richards. He told Smith about Amy's plans to paddle with Carl Johnson and then to go out with Kyle Hooper. Finally, he explained Michael's disdain for Kyle and the apparent disappearance of Amy's car and mobile phone.

'Ok, Riley, get out an alert on the car as quickly as you can and see if we can triangulate the location of Amy's phone. The forensics team is just finishing their work down at the ramp and I expect a briefing from them in the next hour or so. Preliminary view is that they don't have much to work on from the site though.

'I expect the draft results from the post mortem later tonight. Lucky for our investigation, those guys are super busy and they've been given overtime authority, so I got them to prioritise this one.

'Right now, I'm going to pay a visit on Kyle Hooper. Let's see what he has to say … assuming he hasn't flown the coop.'

'Anything else you need from me, sir?'

'Well, unless Kyle is our killer and I wrap this up tonight,' Smith continued, 'I want to interview this Carl fellow tomorrow morning, then we will talk to the manager at the supermarket where Amy worked. I know it's late now but after you get the alert out on the car, I need you to make sure you have a full name and address for Carl.'

Riley decided it was the time to declare. 'Well, sir, I need to talk to you about him. His name is Carl Johnson and in fact he's a friend of mine, not particularly close, but he's been seeing my sister, Sally, for a while now.'

Smith drew a breath before he responded. 'Well I guess I don't need to remind you to stay objective on this. He's not a suspect .... yet. If that changes we may need to re-visit your involvement in this investigation, O'Brien. Anyway, it should make the introduction brief, tomorrow.'

Smith's change of tone, referring to him as O'Brien instead of Riley, wasn't lost on him as he started the car and headed back to the station.

****

Chapter 10
Sunday, July 17 2016

Paul Smith was driven by PC Phil Reid to the small home in Goolwa North. In the glow of the streetlight, he could see that the front yard was unkempt. The lawn had been mowed but it was clear that the weeds in the garden beds had not been attended to in some time. He pulled a torch from his pocket and shone it across the house. Paint was peeling from the timber. The carport attached to the side of the house was empty and there was no sign that a car had been under the roof for a while. The carport was cluttered with old furniture, a lawnmower and a couple of bicycles.

He saw no sign of Amy's car.

The pair walked to the front door and Smith noted that the paint here was peeling too and the curtains inside were badly worn.   There was light coming from inside the house, so it appeared at least that someone was home. He knocked sharply and waited for an answer.

A few moments later, a woman in her forties opened the door. Smith quickly appraised her. Vicky Hooper had dull brown hair with grey streaks, tied back into a neat ponytail. The track suit she wore and the slippers on her feet were clean but had seen better days.   He saw tired lines around her eyes. Nonetheless, she would have been clearly attractive as a younger woman. *Maybe she just no longer has desire or money to put appearance as her top priority.*

'Mrs Hooper?'

'Yes, can I help you?' she asked from behind a screen door. If it was intended to provide security it would offer only minimal protection against a serious intruder.

'I'm looking for Kyle. Is he at home?'

'Who are you and what do you want with Kyle?'

'I'm sorry,' Smith replied, showing his identification, 'I am Detective Inspector Paul Smith and this is Police Constable Reid. I'm hoping Kyle can help us with an investigation we are conducting.'

'He's not here. I don't know where he is', she said. Smith could not help but see the sense of dread that wiped across her face. 'What investigation?' As she said the words, she recalled the news reports she had seen on TV only ten minutes earlier about a girl drowning in the river nearby and the suggestion of foul play. 'What's happened?'

'Is Mr Hooper at home?'

'There is no Mr Hooper. He shot through and left Kyle & me alone eight years ago. Please tell me what you want Kyle for. I'm so worried about him. He hasn't been home since yesterday afternoon.'

Smith looked at her and felt her anxiety.

'Perhaps we could come in and have a chat.'

As they walked through to the living area, Smith observed that most of the walls were faded and the carpets well worn. The kitchen adjoining the living area was freshly painted, neat and clean. The television was on in the corner of the room. Vicky Hooper picked up a remote control and turned it off. She offered Smith and Reid seats on a sofa.

Smith began, 'We are investigating the death of a girl in the River Murray.'

'Yes, I saw it on the news, awful.'

'We believe that the girl is Amy Richards. We are waiting on formal identification but we are very confident it is her.'

Vicky's eyes and mouth opened wide and she raised her hands to cover her mouth. 'Kyle's been seeing Amy!'

'Yes, I know. That's why I am here. Now, you said you don't know where Kyle is. Is it unusual for him to be out of touch for over twenty four hours?'

She looked up with sad eyes. 'Maybe three or four years ago, when he was quite rebellious, but not now. He's a good boy.

'You have to understand that when his dad left, he was just a kid, ten years old. He adored his dad and really missed having a father figure in his daily life. He fell in with some rough kids, but he came good. He does what he can around here, painted my kitchen last week, but he's got his own life too. I have to respect that. What's he got to do with Amy drowning?'

'Maybe nothing,' Smith replied, 'but we have to build a full picture about Amy's last movements, particularly because she seems to have drowned in suspicious circumstances. I can't give you more details than that, but I do need to know what Kyle was doing last evening.'

'He was seeing Amy. He said something about them going out for a while and then going to Amy's to watch Netflix. I assumed he spent the night there, but I did get a bit worried when I didn't hear from him this morning. He's not answering his mobile phone either.'

'Do you know where he might have gone if he wasn't with Amy?'

'No, I don't. He doesn't drive so it can't be too far. Oh, god, I hope he's ok. Please find him, Mr Smith.'

'We will be doing our best, Mrs Hooper. Can you please let me have his mobile phone number?'

She sounded it out and Reid wrote the number onto his notepad.

'We will be in touch with you as soon as we have anything,' he said as he rose, 'but in the meantime, please call me as soon as possible if Kyle gets in touch. It's important for us to talk to him.'

As they walked from the front door, Vicky Hooper wondered whether Kyle was alright but also was he connected in any way to Amy's death. The worry lines on her forehead formed deep creases as she closed the door.

Smith opened the car door, looked back to the house and wondered whether Kyle was alright and was he involved in any way with Amy's death. *Where are you, Kyle?*

*****

The gravedigger sat in front of his television, waiting for the 8.30 news update to come on. He had seen the report earlier in the evening, showing police at the boat ramp. An inspector was talking to reporters, telling them what they knew, which was not much. Investigators in yellow suits came in and out of a marquee in the background. He was sure that the girl's body would be in there.

The image had suddenly brought back the horror of the night before. He had broken into a cold sweat, the nausea building in his gullet until he had rushed to the toilet and thrown up.

He was more composed now. When the news update switched to the report of the death in Goolwa, he craned toward the television, anxious to absorb every piece of data.

As it finished, he sank back into his chair. His rational mind told him everything was alright. There was nothing to suggest to the police that there was a connection between the girl's death and the dug up grave at Currency Creek. What's more, there was no reason why he should be connected.

He had time to plan his next step carefully.

*****

Smith was asleep, although not soundly, when his mobile phone rang. He woke, confused momentarily as he adjusted to the realisation that he was in a motel room. He had decided to base himself in Goolwa for the week. This case was most likely going to be his sole focus, unless they had all totally misread the circumstances around the girl's death.

He glanced at the digital alarm clock which showed 12:45 in brilliant blue.

'Smith here. That better be you, Doc'

'Glad to hear someone wants to talk to me at this ungodly hour.'

Ray Dennis was a highly experienced pathologist and Paul Smith was more than satisfied when he was assigned to this case. He knew the turnaround would be quick and the results would be accurate and concise.

'Who said I *want* to talk to you? What have you got?'

'Ok,' Dennis responded, switching to report mode, 'let me confirm the things you already suspect. Firstly, the girl was drowned. Secondly, the abrasions and contusions on her arms and legs are consistent with a struggle or some rough handling. Looks like she might have fallen to the ground with the dirt and other materials embedded in her skin.

'Next, there are a couple of things you might be expecting. She has marks that look like the grip of someone's hands around the back of the neck. I'd suggest that's consistent with someone forcing her under the water. Also, we have some fibres under two of her fingernails, so your attacker – you would guess I'm calling it in as murder – is gonna have some clothes we can potentially match. We'll run some tests to see what we can find. In reality, that might not help much until you have a suspect and some clothes to match it to.'

'Time of death, Doc?'

'Well, hard to say. She's been in the water for a while. If I were to give you an estimate, I'd be putting it within eight to twelve hours before the body was found. Probably one or two hours either side of midnight.'

'OK, thanks, Doc, anything else?'

'Well, Paul, I haven't told you the things I'm pretty sure you're not expecting.'

Paul wondered why these guys all liked to string out their own little mystery story. 'It's late, mate, just give it to me so I can get some sleep'

'Ok. First, she has no signs of recent sexual activity.'

'What?' Smith bolted upright in the bed. 'So we are not talking a sex attack.'

'That's right, Paul. And the next big surprise, our girl was nine weeks pregnant.'

'Fuck me.' Smith blinked his eyes a few times to convince himself he had heard correctly. 'Ok, thanks, Doc. I've got some serious thinking to do.'

'No problems. Look we are still running a couple of other tests. I'll feed them through to you as soon as I can if there are any new developments. Otherwise I'll have the report to you by tomorrow night.'

'Cheers …. And thanks, Doc.'

Smith started running through the possibilities.

If sex wasn't the motive, what was? The baby? Something else entirely?

Who was the father – Kyle Hooper, someone else? Carl Johnson?

Why was she naked? Was it an attempt to disguise the real reason she was killed? What was she doing early Sunday morning? Where the hell is Kyle Hooper?

He realised he wouldn't sleep any more tonight so he got out of bed, put the kettle on, went to the toilet, made a coffee and sat at the table with pen and paper until dawn.

Chapter 11
Wednesday 23 August 1854

'Mister Varcoe, I really don't know how I can thank you enough for your kindness. I'm sure we would be much the worse if you hadn't shown us such hospitality.'

The woman speaking was Catharine Delaney, one of the passengers on the ill-fated Mozambique. The barque had washed up on the beach outside the Coorong a couple of days earlier, after listing badly for almost a week.

She was talking to John Varcoe, the owner and publican of the Goolwa Hotel. He had provided rooms, clothing and food for the stranded passengers on their arrival at the Goolwa. He was keen for his hotel to be known as an honest and welcoming establishment throughout the young colony.

Also talking in the group in the front room of the hotel were the Mozambique's captain, William Corcoran, John Varcoe's wife, Mary and several others of the passengers and crew from the ill-fated ship.

The captain, William Corcoran spoke next.

'Yes, Mister Varcoe, we are all much indebted to you. Thank you also for arranging the salvage of goods from the ship. I fear she has made her last journey, so I don't expect there will be too much of her we can save. I am thinking that you might be able to use some of the ship's items here, in your hotel. It would be a gesture of our gratitude for your kindness. I shall of course need to procure approval from the ship's insurer.'

'What did you have in mind, Captain?'

'I'm sure you could use the tables and chairs, they survived the wreck in good shape.'

'Indeed they did, Captain, they are stored in my stables out back, together with the figurehead from the ship.'

'Ah, yes,' Captain Corcoran said, 'I think she would look fine above your hotel, Mister Varcoe. It will act as a permanent reminder to all who sail in these waters that the Goolwa Hotel is a friend to seafaring folk.'

'Well, I would be most honoured, Captain, and for the table and chairs as well. Of course, I am sure you will all wish to continue your journey as soon as arrangements can be made, but until then, Mary and I would like to extend our welcome to you.

'Now, Missus Delaney, have you news of your belongings?'

'Thank you, Mister Varcoe. I received two of my trunks but I regret one is still missing. Unfortunately, it is the one that contains all my jewellery. Do you think it will be found?'

Aged in her early forties, Catharine Delaney presented as a confident, upright woman whose bearing made an impression as soon as she walked into a room.

Alexander Johnston and Joe Tripp certainly noticed her enter. They had, of course, heard about the wreck of the Mozambique and the rescue of the crew and passengers. It was said that all the cargo had been recovered, although perishables and foodstuffs were ruined.

They listened intently as Catharine Delaney spoke. Town gossip was that she was the wife of a wealthy Irish pastoralist, Padraic Delaney, and that she travelled to the colonies in search of land.

Alexander reflected on the conversation he had with one of the ship's crew who consumed too much rum on the night of their rescue.

'Ach,' he had told Alexander and Joe, 'that Padraic Delaney, he dotes on that woman. Hear tell he does nought but shower her with gifts, anything she wants – jewellery, perfumes and the finest clothing I have ever seen on a woman.

'She wears different jewellery every day. She has so much that the captain was paid by Delaney to put a twenty four hour guard on her cabin for the whole of the journey from Southampton. Apparently the man did not blanch at the fee. Her trunk must have treasures worthy of a princess.'

Alexander and Joe, always eager for gossip, plied the man with more rum as he continued to unravel his knowledge of the intriguing Irish woman.

'My friends, you have been generous in sharing the rum of this fine establishment. So, I am going to share a secret with you', he had continued as he waved a drunken finger in front of his mouth.

'One of the pieces she wore bears the name "Albert's Folly".' Unable to hold back, Joe had interjected, 'I am thinking this tale int no more than some idiot's folly.'

'No listen, man,' the sailor objected, 'apparently a few months before Prince Albert wed Queen Victoria, he commissioned one of London's finest jewellers, George Fotheringham, to design and manufacture an emerald necklace fit for his bride, the Queen. The jeweller created the masterpiece, just as Albert wanted and passed it to him personally. Fotheringham, lucky sod, banked the grand sum of £4,000.

'Anyways, despite Albert's best intentions, the necklace never graced Victoria's neck. The word is, a few weeks before their wedding, the Queen announces to Albert that she don't like emeralds no more. Can you imagine?

'So then, Albert, poor bastard, goes back to the jeweller and commissions him to make a replacement in quick time.'

Alexander and Joe were enthralled.

'So what happened to the necklace, this Albert's Folly?' Alexander asked.

'Well, then, George Fotheringham is disappointed and says to Albert "what do I do with this piece of shite?" And then Albert says to him he can sell it for a fine price but he demands that it has to be done as discretely as possible so that the Queen never learns of his serious error. So, it takes Fotheringham two years but then he sells it to a very happy Padraic Delaney at a considerable discount to its original price. Everyone's happy except poor bloody Albert.'

Alexander refocussed his attention to the present. Like every other person in the room, he strained to hear John Varcoe's response to Catharine Delaney's question as to whether her trunk might be found.

'I'm sorry to say, ma'am, but we brought every item that we could find, on the ship and on the shore. It's likely the tide washed your trunk to sea. There's no probability it will be found. I can assure you that the Captain and I made sure that the salvage was closely supervised. If the trunk was there we would have found it.'

Catharine was upset, of course, although it was not the financial loss that troubled her.

'Oh, dear, Padraic will be so annoyed. Of course, it's all insured through Lloyds of London, so we will recover the value. It's just that Padraic chose some of my jewellery himself and it means so much to him. I think I must rest before I send word to him.'

She departed as she entered, with every eye in the room upon her.

Alexander grabbed Joe on the forearm.

'Come over here where we can talk privately.'

Tripp followed him to a table on the far side of the room.

'A great opportunity may await us here, Joseph,' whispered Alexander.

The big fisherman stared at him, bumfuzzled.

Alexander continued, 'If they haven't found the trunk in the ship or on the shore, it's either been washed out of the ship to the bottom of the sea, or it's been taken away and down the coast some ways. And I'll wager the latter.'

'But surely someone looked along the coast for it,' Joe argued.

'Well, this is the point. The captain and his crew dinnae ken these waters. John Varcoe is a clever man, but he's no sailor. If that trunk floated out of that ship, I have a fair idea where it's going to land ashore.'

'So, tell them, man. There might be a reward in this.'

Alexander looked at Tripp carefully, before continuing. He considered the risk of the proposal he was about to put to him. Deep in his conscience, he weighed up the morality. He knew that once spoken, his proposal couldn't be taken back.

'I'm nae thinking of a reward, Joe. I'd like to think myself an honest man, but I've lost out badly by being honest and trusting. Back in Scotland, I saw what these landowners did to hardworking folk on their lands. Back in the famine, those people ate well every day and bought their fine clothes and jewels while decent, ordinary people either starved to death or migrated to America or Canada or here.

'Nay, I'm thinking, if we find that jewellery, we keep it. She said she's insured, so she's nae losing, nae matter how much her type deserve it. And for us, 'twill change our lives. Forget your gold rush, Joe, this will be an easier treasure to dig up.'

Joe's eyes were transfixed on Alexander. 'So, how?'

'Here's my plan. You will take me along the Coorong in your boat tomorrow night. As far as anyone knows, I am fishing with you. I'll tell you where to beach your boat. We cross the sand hills to the sea and mayhap I find the trunk. Albert's Folly is the piece we need to find.'

'You're mad, man. Even if you do find it, how could you sell it? The whole colony will know about it and every scrupulous trader will recognise it by sight.'

'All right, Joe. Firstly, I won't be looking to sell it in South Australia. I'm going to Swan Hill on Cadell's boat in a few days. From there I'll make my way to Melbourne. From my experience there are nae too many scrupulous traders in that town.

'I may nae get four thousand pounds for it, but even if I only get two thousand, that's three hundred for you and seventeen hundred for me.'

'Wait. You're only giving me three hundred, that's only …'

'Fifteen percent, Joe, that's what I'll pay you for the use of your boat. That's fair, I'll be the one finding the trunk and selling the goods.'

Joe protested, 'I want no less than a third, Alexander.'

'One quarter, or I'll find another boat.'

Finally, they reached an agreement and the conspirators made arrangements to leave the Goolwa at sunset the following night, so that they could quietly slip away under the cover of darkness.

Chapter 12
Monday July 18 2016

It was 6.40 when Paul Smith opened the door of the police station. After his sleep deprived night, he was grateful that he was able to get a take away coffee from the café next door to the motel.

Phil Reid was on the desk and looked up. 'Morning, Sir.'

'Morning, PC Reid. I want a briefing session with O'Brien and Cross. They can update you after. Is there a room we can use?'

'Through there, sir. It's all decked out with what you will need.'

Smith walked into the room where he saw Riley and Rachel in conversation. As soon as he entered, their discussion stopped. Smith had no way of knowing, but Riley had spent the previous twenty minutes reassuring Rachel that, notwithstanding Smith's treatment of her the day before, she was a valued member of the team and a good cop, highly respected by other local cops and the community.

Moments later, the lead member of the forensics team, Shelley Harrison walked through the door.

'Ok, folks, let's just put together what we have on this case so far.'
Smith walked over to the whiteboard. He looked at the team, waving a marker to make sure he had the attention of them all. Satisfied, he turned to the board and wrote in the centre:
'AMY RICHARDS
DROWNED
SUSPECTED MURDER
NO SEXUAL ASSAULT
BEACON 19 RAMP'

The team drew a collective breath. If he had any doubt, Smith now knew he had their attention.

'Excuse me, sir, no sexual assault?' Rachel asked, hand raised like a school kid.

'That's right, Cross. I got confirmation from the pathologist last night.'

'But, sir, she was naked. Why? Maybe she did drown skinny dipping.'

'That's a fair enough deduction, Cross, but the pathologist is convinced that the marks on her body suggest she was held under the water.'

He continued briefing the team on the results of the post mortem, assured that he had their full engagement.

'I got a call from Ray Dennis this morning with the toxicology results. It seems there were no drugs or alcohol in her system. That could indicate two things. Firstly it reduces the possibility she drowned skinny dipping. More importantly, we can downplay the likelihood that this was a drug deal gone wrong, unless of course Kyle is a user or dealer.'

'One other very important piece of information – our girl was nine weeks pregnant. At this stage, we don't know who else was aware, including her parents and boyfriend.'

Every mind in the room considered the possibilities as Smith called Shelley Harrison to the front.

'Ok,' she started, 'I don't think I can compete with those revelations. Yesterday the team collected a good deal of material at the boat ramp. At this stage, I can't tell you that it's any more than rubbish.

'We've also photographed all the tyre tracks in the area and cross-checked them against retail tyre brands and the cars they match. The list is too long to help at this stage.

'Sir, if I can just add one observation. In my mind, the boat ramp is probably not where Amy was drowned. I think it is likely that the body drifted toward the mouth before becoming lodged under the walkway.'

'So, your team is also investigating other sites upstream from the ramp?'

'They will be onto it today, sir.'

'Good. Riley, how about sharing what came out of your interviews yesterday?'

Riley read from his notes, sharing with the team his interviews with the fishermen, the Winnebago campers, the barrage supervisors and finally, Michael and Karen Richards.

'One thing we know for sure is that Amy's car is missing. There's been no reported sighting of it since the alert was put out last night.

'Amy's mobile phone is still missing as well. It appears to be turned off and efforts to triangulate its location haven't been successful.'

Smith took the front again and gave an account of his visit to Vicky Hooper, including the apparent disappearance of Kyle Hooper, who was supposed to have been with Amy the previous night.

'Rachel, Kyle's phone appears to be off or out of range too, but can you see if you can get that one located as well as Amy's. Who knows, we might get lucky. Ok, anyone else got any other information to share? If not we'll move on.'

After an appropriate pause, Smith strode to the whiteboard and wrote a new heading - 'EVIDENCE'.

The group fired suggestions at him, which he listed on the board. He stepped back and reviewed the list:

Weapon - no

Amy's Clothes – where?

Amy's Car – where?

Amy's Phone – not responsive, where?

Fibres under fingernails - what are they?

Amy pregnancy - who knew? Who is father (Kyle Hooper?)?

Material under skin – struggle

Bruises around neck - forced

Naked, but no sexual activity – why?

'Right,' Smith announced, 'More questions than answers there, people. Ok, let's look at what motives might exist, from what we already know'

Again the group brainstormed, but was only able to come up with a short list

They all sat staring at the list on the board:

MOTIVES

Sexual assault –no!

Pregnancy – why?

Car theft

Drugs?

Random

Other – what?

Why was she naked?

'Well, doesn't this highlight how much we don't know?'

'Sir,' Riley chimed in, 'isn't murder a bit drastic if you just want to steal an old car?'

'Agree, Riley, but let's leave it on the list for now. Let's move on. What about opportunity? Who do we think had the chance to kill her, whatever the reason?'

He wrote '*OPPORTUNITY*' as a new heading.

'Kyle Hooper must be there, mustn't he? He is supposedly who she was with last,' Riley said.

'We don't know for sure that she met up with him, so I'm putting Carl Johnson up as well. We believe he spent time with her earlier in the day and is the last person we know for certain that saw her alive.' Smith looked directly at Riley, waiting for an objection. There was none.

When Riley spoke, he offered, 'I think Michael Richards needs to go up. I know he was theoretically in Adelaide, but we only have his wife's word for that. Who knows, perhaps he got angry because his daughter was pregnant to someone he didn't like.'

'Ok, good. It's a long shot but I agree we need to pursue it. Two more things about him though. Firstly, we don't yet know if he was aware his daughter was pregnant. Secondly, we only have the parents say so that Amy didn't go home. What if she did and that's when she told them she was pregnant? Dad gets angry and does her in. Is there a record of violent behaviour, Riley or Rachel?'

Rachel shook her head and looked at Riley for confirmation.

'Not to my knowledge, sir,' he answered. 'But, let's say that's how it went, why would he take her all the way past the barrages to drown her? It doesn't seem likely.'

'Some good points there. I think we need to verify his story so let's leave him on the list for now. Ok, we are starting to talk about suspects, it seems, so unless you can think of anyone else that had the opportunity, let's list out who we think is most likely to be of interest, at this stage.

A new heading was written on the board and after a few minutes a short list was on the board:

POSSIBLE SUSPECTS

Kyle Hooper (pregnancy, drugs?)

Michael Richards (pregnancy, abuse?)

Carl Johnson

Random/Drug dealer

'What about the brother, Brock?' Shelley suggested.

'Why do you offer him up, Shelley?'

'Well, only because he's obviously close to his sister, I mean as a relative, plus we don't really know where he was or what he was doing. Do we know how he got on with her or Kyle?'

'Another long shot, I think. Anyway let's add him to the list. Something might come out to clear him or involve him down the track,' Smith reasoned.

'At this stage,' he continued, 'I think Kyle Hooper is our primary focus. He needs to be. We suspect he was the last person that saw Amy and now he has disappeared. So here's what I think we need to do next.'

He lifted the marker to the board:

NEXT STEPS

Find Kyle Hooper!

Find the car (RO'B)

Find the phones (RC)

Identify material under Amy's skin (SH)

Interview Carl Johnson (PS/RO'B)

Interview Michael Richards (check if home all night) (PS)

Further Leads –Supermarket ref Amy work history etc (PS/RO'B)

Ears open any witnesses in town – any unusual activities (All)

Follow up PM - DNA (foetus for paternity) (PS)

'Ok, any questions? If not, let's get to it. Above all, remember your ABC – assume nothing, believe nothing, check everything.

'Now, Riley, let's get to Carl Johnson's place before he goes too far. Rachel, I'll want you to come with me later today when I talk with Michael Richards, so make sure you're around mid-afternoon.'

Rachel looked quizzically at Riley, searching for some sort of explanation, but he had his face down to his notes and didn't look at her.

Chapter 13
Monday July 18 2016

I am up a bit later than usual this morning. Fortunately, I don't have a lot of urgent work to do, so I am affording myself the luxury of a morning training session on the river. The temperature is mild and like yesterday the breeze is light, so I am expecting the water to be calm.

It's 7.30 as I load my kayak and paddle onto the roof racks. *This is just what I need to dust off some cobwebs.*

The surf was clean yesterday and I enjoyed a good hour in the cool water. Invigorated, I raced home for a quick shower, returning to the beach right on 4.00, the time Sally and I agreed to meet.

As I pulled into the car park, she stood, waving, looking beautiful in blue jeans, a white windcheater and sneakers. She had walked to the beach from her house only five minutes away. We kissed as I got out the car and I held her in a welcome hug.

We headed along the beach toward Middleton and Victor Harbor. Quite often we took a coffee on the walk, but the beachside café closes for winter so yesterday we just held hands as we strolled. The breeze had dropped off and the winter sun warmed our faces.

The sea was grey-green as it always is at this time of year, but even in its dullness it had an appeal, different to the brilliant blue of summer. The white surf as the waves tumbled seemed to mirror the fluffy white clouds in the blue sky above.

One of the things we love about walking on the beach in winter is the absence of people around us. The expanse of sand, the roar of the sea and the migrating birds passing through above turns it into our own special place.

After we walked for nearly an hour, we turned back toward the car park. We talked about all sorts of nothing – whose gardens I would be tending this week, which book Sally was reading, how her family was going and on and on.

She has never probed my family history. She knows my parents have died and that I have no siblings, but she realises it is not something I want to talk about, so she leaves the topic alone. Another of my closed spaces.

It was almost dark when we noticed the sunset was not one respecting the passing of a bright sunny day. In the last few minutes, grey clouds had come in from the south west and now covered the horizon. Within a few minutes we were caught in drizzling rain.

We stepped up our pace a bit, but it was clear that there was no shelter between us and the car park. Even though we ran, we were drenched by the time we climbed in the car. The rain maintained a steady drizzle that kept up until we arrived back at my house.

After we got inside, I fetched an oversized dressing gown for Sally, while I put on a track pants and a tee shirt. By the time I put our clothes into the dryer, Sally had the kettle on.

We sat side by side on the sofa, drinking our coffee, laughing about our misadventure. I don't know who made the first move, but it seemed no time at all before we ambled hand in hand to the bedroom.

We stood facing each other, looking into each other's eyes as I undid the tie around the robe and she allowed it to slip off her shoulders to the floor.

Our night passed through phases of tenderly holding and kissing each other, lovemaking and sleeping. I woke this morning with her pale back and shoulders facing me, her red hair gently falling across the pillow and my arm, which lay across hers, holding her. I felt like never before, very much falling in love with this woman who saved me from self-obliteration.

My contented reflection on the past twenty four hours is broken by a car pulling up near me. To my surprise, it is a police car and as Riley gets out of the car, I expect he has come looking for Sally. He is probably just checking on her because she forgot to let him know she wasn't going home last night. I admire the bond they share and how they seem to always look out for each other.

A second man gets out the car and by his manner and his dress, I am pretty confident he's not one of the local constabulary. He has the look of a city cop who has seen the best and worst of people, but he always expects and acts like the next will be one of the worst.

'Hi, Riley, are you looking for Sally? She's inside.'

Riley shakes his head and looks serious, 'Hi Carl. No, I'm not here for Sally. This is official business I'm afraid.'

The second man walks between Riley and me, annoying me for a moment. He flashes police identification at me.

'Mr Johnson, my name is Paul Smith. I am a Detective Inspector with the Major Crimes Investigation Branch. Can we have a word?'

'Of course,' I say but don't invite them in.

'We are investigating the death of a person known to you - Amy Richards.'

'Amy?' I stare at him until I realise my mouth is still open.

'That's right, sir. She was found deceased yesterday morning and we believe that the circumstances are suspicious.'

I can only stutter out words. 'But, but I saw her on Saturday. How... when did this happen?'

'According to our estimates, it was sometime late on Saturday or early on Sunday. Tell me about your relationship with Amy.'

'Well, she just started kayaking and I was, I guess, training her a bit. Nothing competitive, just an interest. How did she die?'

'She drowned. When did you see her last, Mr Johnson?'

'Saturday afternoon. I don't know, I didn't wear my watch but I guess she left me about 3.30. She was going home and then I think she was going out with her boyfriend.'

'Yes, Kyle Hooper. What do you know about him?'

'Not a lot I'm afraid. She seemed keen on him, though.'

'Why do you say that?'

I look across at Riley, before answering. 'She told me yesterday that she was pregnant. She also said that she knew that Kyle would be there for her.'

'She told you? Do you think that her parents or Hooper knew about the pregnancy?' Smith asks.

'Certainly not at the time I saw her. She agonised over telling her parents. She worried that her dad would get angry. Apparently he's not keen on Kyle.'

'Why do you think she told you this, Mr Johnson?'

'I think she was pretty worked up about telling them and I suppose we were just out on the water chatting about things when she came out with it. Maybe she wanted some advice.'

'Did you give it to her?'

'Well, I just said that I'd be there if she wanted someone to talk to but I said the first thing she needed to do was tell the people that should know first.'

Riley speaks for the first time since our introductions. 'Do you know where Kyle Hooper might be, Carl?'

My eyes turn away from Smith and I realise that I have been staring at him the whole time of our conversation.

'No idea, I'm afraid. You said there were suspicious circumstances. Why?'

'There are indications she was held under the water.'

'Oh my god,' I mutter, 'How are her parents?'

'As you would expect,' Riley responds, 'they are pretty cut up. They are in Adelaide doing identification now.'

Another thought crosses my mind. 'Why did you ask me if I knew where Kyle was? Haven't you spoken with him yet?'

'No, we haven't been able to locate him or Amy's car. Tell me, did you speak to Amy by phone after you saw her on Saturday.'

'No, we were going to go for a paddle this afternoon. Usually, she would ring if she couldn't go, but I haven't heard from her.'

'One last thing,' Smith asks, 'Can you tell me what you were doing on Saturday night?'

'I stayed here, alone. Sally, my girlfriend, er ... Riley's sister, went out and I fixed Amy's kayak. She ran it aground and put a hole in it on Saturday.'

'We may need to talk again, Mr Johnson, but if you think of anything, anything at all that may help us, please don't hesitate to call me.' Smith passes me a card and turns to walk.

'Riley, what ...' I call.

'Sorry, Carl, we have to keep moving.'

Riley closes the door of the car and drives away. I stand looking after them, stunned and confused. I see no sense strapping the kayak on the roof racks and I walk inside, trying to make sense of it all.

Sally is standing in the kitchen in my dressing gown.

'Did I hear Riley's voice?'

I just nod.

'I heard another voice as well,' she says, but simultaneously sees the expression on my face. 'My god, you look drained, what's happened.'

'Amy's been killed.'

I relay my discussion with Riley and Paul Smith to her and sink onto a chair at the table.

'I'll get us a coffee.' Sally offers.

Chapter 14
Friday 25 August 1854

Alexander told Rubina that he was going away for a couple of days with Joe Tripp, ostensibly to do some fishing in the Coorong. He avoided telling her about the search for the necklace mainly because he was certain it would get a reaction he dreaded. He knew Rubina would try to talk him out of it. While she made it clear to Alexander that she did not like Joseph Tripp, she would not interfere with her husband's business. She was raised in a family where the man dictated every decision in the house, from what time meals would be eaten to what activities could be undertaken on the Sabbath. A wife's role, she understood, was to make sure that her husband's decisions were implemented without question by her and every other member of the house.

Notwithstanding that, Rubina knew that Alexander respected and sought her opinion on any matters that would affect the wellbeing of the family, and for that she loved him deeply. While she had no hesitation in discussing matters freely with Alexander, her upbringing always provided a boundary beyond which she would not venture.

Alexander's real concern in discussing this issue with Rubina was that he knew she would find his opportunism distasteful, from both a religious and a moral perspective. Rubina read the bible daily and took pride that she lived her life according to the ten commandments, as well as all the other teachings in the good book. While Rubina would not have preached to Alexander about his lack of virtue, he felt pangs of guilt as though she had.

'So, do you have all that you need, Alexander?'

She was, of course, accustomed to Alexander being away from home. As a mariner, he probably spent more of their married life at sea than at home with his family. That had not, however, diminished their love and their utter faithfulness to each other.

'I do, my lovely. I expect that I will be back in three days, with a bag full of fish. Just make sure that Donald keeps up with chopping the wood for the fireplace. I've taught him how to do it properly and it will help build the laddie up.'

He pecked her on the cheek as he walked to the door. He lifted his swag to his shoulder and walked out the front door of the house onto Newacott Place.

It was only a short walk down to the river and by the time he could see the water shimmering in the late afternoon sun, he also saw Joe Tripp's small fishing boat moored below. Joe was busy arranging the sails and waved to Alexander as he saw him making his way down the hill on the narrow pathway.

It was shortly after five in the evening when the small boat cast off. The sun was setting on what had been an unusually warm day and the water settled down to a mirrored glass surface. They could see pelicans gliding slowly and deliberately near the riverbank, occasionally dipping their substantial beaks into the water, before lifting their heads to watch the boat pass by.

Occasionally, a tern would dive from high above to seize one of the small fish venturing too close to the water's surface and paying the ultimate price. *The never-ending food cycle!* The fish feed on the insects flirting on the water surface; the birds feed on the fish looking for the insects. Who ate the birds, Alexander wondered?

It was dark by the time Joe had taken the boat out of view of the town and the light wind allowed them to cut a steady swathe through the water. By nine o'clock, they were several miles from the Goolwa and Joe steered the boat into shore, a place concealed by reeds and occupied only by the animals of the river. They had made a quiet exit from the town. Although Alexander did not withhold the fact that he was going away, neither man wanted to draw attention to where they were going and, more particularly, why they were going. The fewer questions asked the better.

They made camp on the riverbank and cooked a simple dinner of beans and damper. Joe, as was his custom, downed half a bottle of rum while Alexander brewed a billy of tea. They settled for the night under a starry, cloud free night.

The pair woke early the next morning and made porridge for breakfast before packing camp and reboarding Joe's boat. It seemed like nothing had changed from the day before: pelicans were drifting along the river and the terns were swooping on the fish chasing the insects on the surface of the water. Alexander loved the river life, its calmness compared to the sea, with which he was so much more familiar. Despite this calmness, he also paradoxically appreciated the vibrancy of the never ending activity on and near the river.

The breeze stayed light all day and the slow flow of the river meant that their progress toward the Murray's mouth was sure and steady. Alexander passed the time in wonderment of the river. He contemplated the fact that the water they were now cutting through originated in the snow covered mountains on the eastern ranges over a thousand miles away. In his mind, he questioned how long a drop of water melted from the snow actually took to reach the mouth of the river, a journey where it would be transformed from crystal clarity to a murky brown and finally part of the saline mass of the Southern Ocean.

Alexander's pondering was interrupted in mid-afternoon when Joe announced that they were nearing the river mouth. Joe had been quiet all day and Alexander took this to be characteristic of the life of a lone fisherman, lost in his own thoughts, comfortable in his own company.

While Joe had done it several times, Alexander had never crossed the mouth into the Coorong and had not quite understood why it was as treacherous as people had said it could be. Surely not as dangerous as a wild sea. However, he reserved judgement, knowing that a number of experienced sailors had already lost their lives attempting the crossing.

The mouth itself was wide but shallow. The surf beyond the mouth was strong and the river flow was subdued in comparison. Because the sandbar at the mouth continually moved, each crossing was different to the one before. Today, the strength of the incoming tide washed over the sandbar pushing aside the fresh water with contempt as the sea sought to take occupancy in the river and the Coorong on the other side.

The water bubbled and bounced as though it was boiling in a cauldron.

'Hold on, Alexander, this is going to be a rough one,' Joe called from the tiller at the rear of the boat. Alexander had been sitting in the middle of the boat but now moved to the bow so that he could grip both sides and keep out of the way of the boom, should it unexpectedly swing around.

It took Joe almost an hour and most of the strength he possessed before the little boat reached the quieter waters of the Coorong. Although Alexander was an experienced sailor and had sailed many of the wildest seas on Earth, his face was ashen as he looked back at Joe. For his part, the fisherman looked exhausted but poised.

'All right, let's get going.'

The water in the Coorong, while calmer than the whirlpool they had just come through, carried a slight swell from the wind that swept down the length of the waterway. This was what Alexander felt much more comfortable with and feeling the fresh breeze in his face restored his composure in just a few minutes.

'So, where do you think this wreck is then, Alexander?'

'From what they've said, I think we should set camp about a mile further on. We can cross the sand hills there across to the beach and we should be able to see the Mozambique from there.'

By five, they had beached the boat, Joe dragging the anchor up the sandy shore, while Alexander unloaded the provisions.

'Alexander, do we set camp and make for the wreck tomorrow?'

'I think we should go tonight.'

In the remaining light they headed up and over the sand hills between the Coorong and the beach. It was not far but the sand was soft and fine and the hill was high, so it was hard going.

Alexander was fitter and lighter than Joe and was able to make better progress than the big fisherman. When he reached the top of the sand hill he could see along the coast for several miles, although the failing light would take that from them in a few minutes. Alexander looked to the right, back toward the river mouth... nothing. Turning his head to the left, he saw what he was looking for. Only a few hundred yards from where they stood was the Mozambique, gradually being torn apart by the endless buffeting of the powerful surf, lifting and dropping the barque like a piece of balsa.

'There she be,' said Alexander, pointing to the ship while Joe made the last few steps to the top of the hill.

'Thank God,' Joe doubled over, gasping for breath. 'You go on. I'll catch up in a bit.'

The sun had set and the dark enveloping him when Alexander got to the site of the abandoned wreck. Aided by the light of his oil lamp, he could see that nearly all the cargo had already been recovered, other than a few crates containing spilled flour, sugar, tea and other spoiled foodstuffs. However, he remained convinced that Catharine's trunk with its treasures must be on the beach somewhere and walked along the sand, following the direction he knew the tide must have flowed.

He walked to the east, into the biting wind that had grown in intensity and dropped in temperature. Alexander was intent on looking at what was on the sand at water's edge. He failed to see the dark form that shadowed him from behind. He suddenly felt the presence and, thinking it was Joe Tripp, he turned to wait for him to catch up.

Instead, he saw the figure stop abruptly and raise his right arm. He was no more than ten yards from him. The man held a spear in his right hand, shaking it vigorously and making as if to throw. Alexander gently placed his lantern on the ground. He raised his hands, his open palms facing the man to show that he was unarmed and meant him no harm.

The men stood facing each other for what Alexander felt was several minutes but was in reality less than fifteen seconds. The other man yelled something at him which he did not understand. While he had seen aboriginal men before along

Page | 112

various parts of the river and closer to the Goolwa, he had never had occasion to attempt to speak with them, let alone learn their language.

He opened his mouth to say something, anything, to diffuse the standoff, when he heard more of the unintelligible language from behind the man. This time he recognised that it was Joe Tripp's voice.

After a short discussion in the aboriginal tongue, the man dropped his arm, Alexander relieved that the threat of a spear through his chest had passed, for the time being at least.

Joe explained to him that the man was Lenny Kerpany – a member of the Lugundi tribe, one of the eighteen tribes of the Ngarrindjeri nation. His tribe lived on the eastern side of the Murray Mouth. The Lugundi were successful hunters along the reaches of the Coorong and were well fed with the plentiful fish they caught from its waters.

Lenny was a solid man dressed in furs. His hair was wild from the winds that carried along the Coorong and his face pock marked from the smallpox epidemic that swept among his people when he was a child. He was lucky to have survived. Many of the boys and girls his age had died from the disease and the numbers in the Lugundi tribe had almost halved since the white man had come.

Over many years Lenny had seen Lugundi women seized and taken away by the whalers and sealers from the southern coast and Kangaroo Island. His initial reaction on seeing Alexander with his lantern was that the white man was one of these and this was why he had shaken his spear at him angrily.

Joe had learned the Ngarrindjeri language on his many fishing expeditions. He jabbered at him in the man's tongue before turning back to Alexander.

'He thought you was a whaler or sealer.'

Alexander looked at him dumbly.

'Them scum have been stealing their women for years. Anyway, I convinced him you were just a poxy little Scotsman with no balls.' Joe burst into raucous laughter before speaking again with Lenny.

After several exchanges, Joe again spoke in English.

'Lenny says more of the cargo was washed ashore further to the east, but before you get your hopes up, his people have taken anything that was attractive. Says his women are now dressed with many pieces of jewellery. So, I suppose that's that, Alexander. No fortune for us.'

Joe invited Lenny to join them for supper and the two returned back along the shore toward the wreck of the Mozambique

Disheartened, Alexander meandered in the direction that Lenny had pointed, where the aboriginals had discovered the jewellery.

He had only walked a short distance along the beach when he came across a trunk bearing the name Catharine Delaney. The lid of the trunk lay open and as he peered in Alexander could see that it seemed empty apart from a few sodden undergarments.

He moved these aside and lifted a leather pouch that poked from the sandy sediment at the base of the trunk. He held it close to his lantern and his eyes widened with astonishment and delight when he read the imprint *Geo. Fotheringham & Son, London, 1840.* He opened the draw string. Inside the pouch was an emerald necklace. He was sure it was Albert's Folly, spoken of by Catharine Delaney.

Alexander walked back to the campsite, carefully concealing the pouch inside his jacket. Joe had lit a fire and baked a fish. They talked as they ate, Joe interpreting between Alexander and Lenny. After shaking hands with the two white men, the aboriginal left them, illuminated by the light of a bright moon until his silhouette sank behind the sand hills.

Once Lenny had left and Alexander was sure that he was no longer in earshot, he withdrew the pouch from his jacket and showed it to Joe.

'Are you sure that's it? It don't look too special to me.'

'It has to be, Joe. These are emeralds alright. We are going to be rich, friend.'

At that, Joe ran to the boat and returned with his half-full bottle of rum. He took a deep swig and handed the bottle to Alexander. Although he did not drink rum often, Alexander made an exception and took a draw from the bottle.

The two danced and whooped around the fire before settling down to contemplate how they would use their yet to be converted fortune.

Eventually, Joe fell into a drunken slumber, while Alexander reminded himself over and over that he could not allow himself to again be robbed of a fortune, an even bigger one this time. He slept with one eye open until a cold dawn broke over the shimmering waters of the Coorong.

Chapter 15
Monday July 18 2016

The two policemen left Carl Johnson's house and Riley drove toward the supermarket in the shopping centre on the edge of town.

'So, what did you make of your friend Carl's reaction?' Smith queried, critically appraising Riley.

'Well, sir, he looked shocked and upset. More than I have ever seen him before. I can't believe he could be involved in Amy's death.'

'Well, I appreciate your assessment based on your friendship with him, but in the end the evidence will tell us whether he is or not. I'm actually more interested now in Amy's relationship with her boyfriend and her father.

'I understand you know the father as well, but it's going to be hard for you to press him on his relationship with his daughter. So, just so you know, that's why I will take Rachel with me to have a little chat with him this afternoon. While we are doing that, I want you to do background checking on Kyle Hooper and Carl Johnson and for Christ's sake let's see if we can find Kyle and that goddam car.'

Riley pulled the car into the shopping centre car park. It had barely stopped before Smith stepped out and stretched.

'Right, let's see if we get any more little surprises from this lot.'

As the policemen got out of the car, Riley was called by a man accompanied by a woman pushing a shopping trolley. A small child sat in the trolley eagerly licking at an ice cream in a cone. The man was Peter Higgins, who Riley had left at the football club earlier the previous day.

'Riley, I just heard. The drowned girl yesterday was Amy Richards.'

Paul Smith put himself between Higgins and Riley.

'Excuse me, sir, I'm Detective Inspector Paul Smith. Do you mind if I ask how you found out it was Amy that drowned. We haven't released her name.'

'Oh, right. Well I'm on the football committee with her father, Michael, same as Riley is. I happened to phone him this morning and he told me. Tragic accident. '

Riley interrupted, 'Well, Peter, I think at this stage, we need to just support Michael and Karen as best we can. They are obviously pretty shaken up.'

'Do you mind me asking, is it usual for a drowning to require a Detective Inspector to come down to our little town all the way from Adelaide? It's got the whole town buzzing.'

'Mr, err...'

'Higgins, Peter Higgins. And this is Cheryl, my wife, and granddaughter, Lily.'

'Yes, well, Mr Higgins, the town needs to stop speculating and let us get on with our work. What we are doing is not unusual for this situation and as soon as we can clear it up, I will leave your little town in peace.'

Smith walked away.

'Shit, he's a bit of a dick isn't he, Riley?'

'I wouldn't know. I guess it's a bit frustrating dealing with gossip when you are trying to run an investigation. Anyway, how are you, Cheryl?'

She spoke for the first time. 'Oh, I'm good thanks, Riley. I have to admit that I'm a bit tired at the moment. I've been looking after the grandkids a bit lately and they can be a bit wearing. Lucky the other two are at school but when you get all three together, I'm buggered at the end of the day. Pete usually finds something better to do, club business or something, once he's had enough,' she laughed.

'I shouldn't complain though. I'd rather be in our shoes than in poor Karen and Michael's.'

Riley made his farewells and hastened to catch up to Paul Smith as he walked into the supermarket. Smith strolled to the nearest checkout and showed his identification to the operator.

'I'd like to talk to your manager, please, love.'

The girl at the checkout was only about sixteen, and frowned, clearly concerned.

'Is this about Amy?'

'What do you know about Amy?' Smith asked.

'Didn't she drown?' the girl looked agape at him. 'Was she murdered?'

'Why do you think it was Amy? We haven't released any names.'

'Everyone knows. Mr Collins told us all at a staff meeting this morning.'

'How about you just get Mr Collins for us.'

The girl looked at Riley, then rushed toward the back of the store. An elderly lady waiting in the queue stood open-mouthed at the conversation she had just overheard. In Riley's mind was the sure knowledge that the whole town would be talking about Amy Richard's murder by drowning before the afternoon was over.

A man in his early fifties walked from the back of the store with the checkout operator following a few steps behind. He was a short, stout, balding man, dressed in black trousers and a white shirt with a collar too small for his bull like neck. His tie was loosened and the top button of his shirt undone. He appeared flustered, a man who was always stressed and today was no better than the rest

He introduced himself as Kym Collins and asked the policemen to follow him to his office.

The office was austere and messy. Each wall was covered in sales charts, memos from head office and award certificates recognising the store's customer service. On the desk were piles of paperwork, with one corner reserved for a photograph of his wife and two pre-teen daughters. Collins' chair was old and dated with holes in the arms where years of wear had taken their toll. Beside his own chair, the office had two visitors' chairs, although one was occupied by cartons of potato chips.

Collins apologised as he lifted the cartons and placed them on top of others covering the floor. Smith and O'Brien sat on the chairs and waited for Collins to sit.

'I'm sorry, Detective Inspector, it's a bit hectic today. I've had three people call in sick and of course there's the tragedy with Amy Richards.'

'Yes, I'd like to ask you about that. How did you find out about Amy?'

'I rang her father this morning because she hadn't come in or let me know she'd be late. I'd seen about the drowning on the news last night, of course, but I was staggered when he told me it was Amy. Is it right she was murdered?'

'That's one possibility we are investigating. Tell me about Amy.'

'Well,' Collins started, 'She is a good worker, one of my best. She's reliable, always on time and she is prepared to work.'

Smith asked, 'How long has she worked here?'

'She came straight after she left school, a couple of years ago. I think she lost her way a bit at school and left as soon as she could. She only works as a casual here, about fifteen hours a week. I'd have given her more if I could but I don't have the budget. Anyway, she didn't seem interested in more hours.'

'Why do you think that was?'

'Of late, she'd been talking about going back to school, night time, I imagine. She wanted to get into Uni to become a teacher. I don't know, I think in some ways she felt like she had been sort of disadvantaged and that made her leave school sooner than she should have. Now she feels she's got some direction.'

'What do you mean "disadvantaged"?'

'Not sure. I can't really explain it. I don't think she got a lot of encouragement from her father. He seemed to have a big influence on her but maybe not in a way she was entirely happy with.'

Smith looked across to Riley to make sure he had noted the comment.

'What about her boyfriend? What can you tell us about him?'

'Kyle? Not much. He'd meet her after work sometimes. They seemed to get on alright. He was pretty protective of her too. I wonder if maybe he was even partly the reason why she seemed to get a bit more direction; he's still at school and wants to go on to Uni next year.'

Smith considered for a moment before asking, 'When you say that Kyle was protective, did you mean in relation to her relationship with her father?'

'No, no, I wouldn't know anything about that. What I meant was that he tried to protect her from a situation here.'

'Explain.'

'Well, we have a lad here, Travis Schultz. Look, he's a good lad, but just a bit, I don't know, slow. He never did well at school, poor attendance and so on. There was some suggestion he had a learning disability and I think, because of that, he was bullied as a kid. He left school as soon as he was old enough, just like Amy. He works here now, filling shelves and to be honest, I think that's about as good as he's likely to get. Anyway, Amy looked out for him. She felt sorry for him and often talked to him in the staff room. Not like the others, she genuinely cared.'

'And how does Kyle fit in?'

'Well, I think Kyle and Travis know each other from school.'

Riley interrupted. 'Travis and Kyle were friends a while back, sir, got into trouble stealing some spirits from the drive in bottle shop of the hotel. They both got off with a strict warning.'

Kym Collins continued, 'A few weeks ago, Kyle told Amy she should back off with Travis a bit. He told her he was unpredictable and had a short fuse, but Amy seemed to feel that he had a soft spot for her and would never hurt her.'

'So how do you know this?'

'Amy told me a couple of weeks ago.'

'One last question. Are you aware whether Amy, or Kyle or Travis for that matter, have been involved with drugs?'

Collins looked surprised and paused before answering.

'Look, I don't know but I'd be shocked. Maybe I'm naïve but I don't think they are the type.'

'Ok, thanks for that, Mr Collins. I think we need to talk with Travis Schultz. Is he at work today?'

'Yes, I'll get him for you. You can use my office. Inspector, I don't think...' He allowed his sentence to trail off.

While Collins was gone, Smith turned to Riley.

'He's another one you can add to your background check. I think we might need to know a bit more about Travis Schultz.'

While Collins was away, Smith surveyed the papers on his desk and the graphs on the walls. Despite the man's apparent lack of organisation, the store seemed to be performing well. A letter from head office sat atop one of the piles and congratulated Collins on the quarterly performance of the store. He noted a folder labelled "Performance Appraisals" and was about to open it, when the door opened.

Collins waved in Travis Schultz. Paul Smith offered him the seat he had occupied earlier and remained standing near the door.

'Thank you, Mr Collins. We'll try not to keep Travis too long; we know how busy you are.'

Collins withdrew, closing the door behind him, while Smith scanned Travis. He saw a young man in his late teens. His size and bulk, nearly two metres tall and around one hundred and twenty kilograms, would have made him appear much older, if not for his pimpled, ruddy face speckled with fine whiskers. He was dressed in the corporate uniform although it did not fit him well. His sneakers were well worn.

'Travis, my name is Detective Inspector Paul Smith and this is Sergeant Riley O'Brien. We would like to have a chat with you if that's all right.'

'I know Mr O'Brien,' Travis said. 'Are you here about Amy?'

'Yes, I understand she worked here with you.'

'She is my friend.'

'And you know her boyfriend, Kyle?'

'Yes, he's my friend too.'

'Do you know where he is now?'

'No.'

'Tell me about Amy.'

'She's nice.'

'In what way?'

'She talks to me. Most of the others don't. They think I'm weird.'

'Are you?' Smith asked. Riley looked up with raised eyebrows.

'I'm not weird, just different,' his voice rose a little, then in a quieter tone, 'I just don't catch on to stuff as quick as other people.'

'I'm told you have a short fuse.'

'What's that mean?'

Smith looked him in the eye. 'It means you can lose your temper quickly.'

Travis sat quietly looking at the floor.

'Do you?' Smith presses.

'I dunno.'

'When did you last see Amy, Travis?'

'When she left work on Friday night.'

'And you haven't seen her since?'

'No, sir.'

'What about Kyle?'

'I seen him on Saturday morning. He came into the shop to get some stuff for his mum.'

'Did you talk to him?'

'Yeah, just about stuff, nothin' special.'

'Did he tell you what he was going to be doing that day?'

'Don't think so. Don't remember.'

'Have you ever been involved with drugs, Travis? Pot, meth, anything?'

'No, sir.'

'What about Kyle or Amy? Do you know if either of them have?'

'Don't think so. Never seen them with any drugs.'

Smith opened the door.

'Ok, you can go now, Travis. We may need to talk to you again later, lad. Is that ok?'

'Yes, sir, thank you.' Travis lumbered out the door and into the storeroom.

Smith turned back into the office and closed the door.

'He's certainly big enough to do some damage, but I don't think he's our man. Still, do the check and let's see what we've got.'

'Sir, can I ask? You didn't mention Amy's pregnancy to either of them. Why not? Wouldn't it be useful to see if they knew?'

'Maybe next time. First, I want to know if she had told her parents. I don't want anyone else to tell them if they don't already know. If they do know, I wonder why they didn't tell you last night.'

As Riley drove back to the police station, Paul Smith looked out the window, thinking through the evidence they had gained so far. The drive was not long enough for him to have made much progress and as he walked through the door of the station, Constable Rachel Cross passed him a handful of telephone messages, one from his superior asking for an update, but most from enquiring media.

Chapter 16
Monday July 18 2016

Smith spent the next hour reporting up the line. He decided to leave responding to media enquiries until later. *In fact, they can wait for the next official release.*

Frustrated by bureaucracy and the need to keep the media appeased, he headed to the front door of the station and called to Rachel. 'Ok, Constable Cross, let's go for a drive.'

Rachel grabbed the keys to one of the cars parked out back and ran to catch up to Smith.

She drove through town, along Liverpool Road toward the home of Karen and Michael Richards.

'So, Cross, enjoying the force?' Smith asked. His tone was flat but inviting.

'Yes, sir, although it can be a challenge sometimes.'

'Glass ceilings, boys' club, that sort of thing?'

She looked across at him, wondering where he was going with this. She wondered if he was baiting her so she decided to play it conservatively.

'Not quite sure what you mean by that, sir.'

'Oh, come on, I know you were pissed off when I sent you off to get coffee yesterday. Just so you know, that had nothing to do with you being female. You just happened to be the junior officer there.'

Rachel was both impressed and annoyed. She was surprised that a chauvinist like him picked up what she had been thinking but annoyed because he still used his rank to get her to do a menial task.

'Sir, with respect...'

'I know, you still think it's unfair, female or not, that I sent you off when you could have been doing something more practical. You know what, you're right and I apologise. It takes a bit for us old farts to change. But a piece of advice for you – there's still a lot of us old farts around, so whatever you're thinking, don't always let it show. It won't do your career any good to show you're thin skinned ... especially, when you're a woman.'

Rachel grinned, exposing her perfect white teeth. 'Noted, sir.'

Rachel pulled the car into the kerb outside the Richards' house. They noted a van parked on the other side of the road. It was emblazoned with the logo of one of the commercial television stations.

'Great,' Smith exclaimed, 'the parasites are here.'

As they exited the car, a young woman in a tight grey skirt, buttoned jacket and high heels jumped out of the van. In her heels, she nearly stumbled as she ran to intercept the police officers.

'Can you comment on the investigation into Amy Richard's death, Inspector?' She thrust the microphone toward Smith. He recognised her from his press conference at the boat ramp.

'Not yet,' he answered brusquely.

'Can you tell me why you are at her parents' house?'

Smith looked at her with contempt as they walked to the door that Riley had knocked on just twenty four hours previously. He knew the reporter would wait as long as needed to get the opportunity to speak with one of the family.

A tall, fit young man opened the door.

'You must be Brock. I'm Detective Inspector Paul Smith and this is Constable Rachel Cross. Are your parent's home?'

'Come in.' Brock Richards stepped forward to pass them, car keys in hand.

Smith raised a hand. 'Actually, Brock, would you mind hanging around for a few minutes, I'd like to talk?'

'Why? I've got nothing to say.'

'Well, we might find that there is something you know that we don't and that might just help us. So, if you don't mind. Besides, you really don't want to be out there just now.' He motioned at the reporter standing patiently at the fence-line.

Brock turned and puerilely huffed back through the living room. 'I'll be out the back when you're ready.'

Karen watched Brock leave. 'I'm sorry. He's not dealing with Amy's death very well.'

Michael Richards burst through the back door, a concerned look on his face. 'What's up with Brock? Oh, hello,' he says as he sees the officers.

'Mr, Mrs Richards, I'm Detective Inspector Paul Smith and you may already know Constable Cross. We just want to follow up with some more questions in relation to Amy's death.'

'We told Riley pretty much all we know, Mr Smith,' said Karen.

'I'm sure, but maybe there might be some other little pieces of information that will help. Firstly, how did you cope with Amy's identification? I'm sure it was very difficult.'

It was Michael who responded. 'It was, Inspector. Have you ever lost a child? If not, you would have no idea how difficult it was. Anyway, have you found Kyle Hooper yet?'

'No, we have not. Not Amy's car or her phone either, but believe me we are doing everything we can. I'd like to just follow through on a couple of areas.

'Firstly, I just want to confirm. Amy did not come home at any time after you got home on Saturday night?'

'Of course not, don't you think we would have told Riley O'Brien that? We didn't see her again after about 11.30 on Saturday morning,' Michael fired back indignantly.

Paul Smith had expected a volatile response and he knew that in many ways the question was unfair. He had asked it consciously and watched Karen's face closely as Michael retorted. He was looking for any indication, through facial expression or otherwise that may have suggested that anything other than the truth was being told.

'Of course, I'm sorry. Now, let me just confirm also. As far as you know, Amy would have been driving?'

'Yes, Kyle Hooper hasn't got a license.'

'Now, Mr Richards, I know you don't like Kyle too much. Can you just tell me why?'

'His father shot through on him a while back, probably seven or eight years. He fell in with a bad crowd and didn't have a father figure to bring him back in line, so he got into some trouble.'

'Do you share that view, Mrs Richards?'

She looked at Michael before responding. 'Well, I don't really know. I have seen his mother around a bit. She seems a nice enough lady, but I think they are battlers. I don't imagine it's been the perfect environment to bring up a headstrong boy.'

'You think he's headstrong?'

'Aren't all juvenile boys, Inspector?'

'Do you know if Amy or Kyle ever experimented with drugs? Or maybe got more serious?'

Michael was first to react.

"No way would Amy get involved with drugs. She might have been rebellious but, no, she wouldn't have. Unless Kyle... are you suggesting she had been taking drugs?'

'No, I'm not suggesting that, Mr Richards, but you have to understand we are exploring every possible reason why someone would kill Amy.'

'Right. Well, I don't know for sure about Kyle and drugs, but I've made my thoughts on him clear.'

'Just a couple more questions. Can you tell me what Amy was wearing on Saturday night, Mrs Richards?'

'We didn't see her dressed to go out, of course. But her leather jacket is missing and I imagine she would have worn jeans and sneakers, like she usually does. I can't tell you what top she had on under the jacket.'

'Mr Richards, just for clarity, can you tell me what time you got home on Saturday night?'

'I'd say it was between about 11.30 and 11.45.'

'And you didn't go out again once you were home?'

Michael exploded. 'Of course not, what are you suggesting? I was with Karen all night,' He turned to Karen a mystified look on his face.

Smith was looking at her too. She was looking downward but with no obvious change in expression.

'I'm not suggesting anything Mr Richards, but you will appreciate we sometimes need to verify all the information we gather. Now, just on that, you hadn't told us that Amy was pregnant.'

'What?' Michael was visibly shaken. 'I don't believe you.' Karen covered her mouth, trembling.

'The post mortem shows that she was nine weeks pregnant. Can I take it then that neither of you were aware?'

Karen responded, 'We had no idea. She didn't tell us. Oh, god.' She burst into tears as she absorbed the full realisation of what she has been told.

Michael confronted Smith eye to eye. 'Well, we didn't know but I bet that bastard Kyle did. If he killed Amy to get rid of the problem, all I can say is that you had better find him before I do. I will fucking kill him.'

'Mr Richards, I understand your reaction but please leave Kyle to us. We will certainly be having a good talk with him once he is located. I know this is very difficult and I apologise if I have made you feel uncomfortable, but I'm afraid these are questions we must ask. Now, may I speak with Brock?'

Smith saw himself out the back door, with Rachel following. He found Brock Richards slouched on a sofa under the verandah. He was engrossed with his mobile phone, scrolling through Facebook posts. He didn't raise his head as the police officers approached him.

'I'd like to ask a few questions, Brock.'

Brock's eyes remained fixated on the phone.

'Would you mind putting the phone away for a moment, please?' Smith was calm but firm.

Brock looked at him with disdain, before jamming the phone into the back pocket of his jeans.

'Thank you. Brock, did you see Amy at all on Saturday?'

'Nope, she was still in bed when I left.'

'What time was that?'

'About ten.'

'Where did you go?'

'I had footy at Langhorne Creek.'

'What time did that finish?'

'Game finished about 5.00, had a shower, got changed, left about 6.00.'

'So, did you come back home after?'

'Nup, went to the pub for a while, then to a mate's place for a party.'

Smith appraised Brock, before continuing. He was clearly not wanting to elaborate more than he needed and his attitude verged on hostile.

'Brock, understand that we are trying to investigate Amy's death. Any help you can provide might be crucial. How long were you at the party?'

'I'm answering your questions, aren't I? I was at the party all night. Got back here after Mum and Dad on Sunday.'

'You slept there?'

'Yes.'

'So you had someone with you all night? We need to eliminate all avenues, so if you have witnesses for your whereabouts for the period we are interested in, we can move on.'

'Well, no I crashed in the car. I was pretty hammered.'

'What time did you leave the party?'

'No idea. Maybe midnight.'

'So, can you tell us whose house the party was at and where?'

'It was at Todd William's place, 11 Jamieson Road, Goolwa South.'

Smith looked across at Rachel to ensure she was writing the detail in her notepad.

'Thank you. How did you get along with Amy?'

'All right, I suppose. We didn't really move in the same circles much and I'm not home any more than I need to be.'

'Why is that?'

'Better things to do, I guess.'

'Was anything troubling Amy, do you know?'

'Not that I know of.'

'What about Kyle Hooper. Do you know him?'

'Only from school. He's a bit of a wanker.'

'Why do you say that?'

'Shit, I don't know. He never did much, you know, sports and stuff. He hung out with all the losers. Then since Amy's met him, she's gone a bit weird with hair colour and metal in her face and shit. I don't rate him.'

'So, these losers you mentioned. Would that include Travis Schultz?'

Brock scoffed under his breath. 'Yeah, he'd be one of them. Weird, that guy. Hey, what's he got to do with this?'

'Maybe nothing, Brock, but you know he works with Amy?'

'Yeah, she told me.'

'So, do you know of any issues between them or between Kyle and Travis?'

Brock looked surprised. 'Don't know what you're talking about, but as I said they're all losers.'

'Did any of these "losers" as you call them use drugs, as far as you know?'

'You must be kidding, man. I reckon they stayed well away from that shit.'

'Did you know Amy was pregnant, Brock?'

Brock emitted a guttural cackle. 'I'm not surprised. They couldn't even screw without stuffing it up. Nah, I didn't know.'

Smith wrapped up the interview. 'Ok, Brock, that's it for now but if you think of anything that might be relevant, please let me know. I can be contacted through the police station.'

The reporter they saw on their way into the house had taken warmth in the van in preference to the afternoon chill outside.

Smith waved and gave her the slightest smile as they got in the car. The van door stayed firmly closed.

Satisfied, Smith turned to Rachel, 'Is he always like that, Brock? Real attitude hasn't he?'

'I don't know him well enough, sir, but I hear he can be a bit of a surly type.'

'Ok, Rachel, I want you to do something for me if you've got the time. Otherwise, I'll get someone else onto it.'

'No, I'm sure it will be fine,' Rachel relished the opportunity to get involved in a real investigation. She realised she was beginning to warm to Paul Smith. 'I'll just need to clear it with Riley.'

'Good. I need you to get in touch with Todd bloody Williams and see if he can verify Brock's timeline. If he can't, then find the names of some other people that were there and ask them. I want to know what Brock was doing on Saturday night.'

'Will do, sir. Do you mind if I ask you a question? Were you deliberately trying to wind Michael Richards up in there?'

'Yeah, might seem a bit cruel, especially if he hasn't got anything to hide, but frankly, the quicker we can eliminate or confirm suspects the closer we are to finding the killer. As most detectives will tell you, the longer the investigation goes, the harder it is to solve. Michael won't be thinking it right now, but he will be grateful if we wrap this up by the end of the week. On the other hand, if it drags out a couple more weeks they will feel a heap more pain than I just put them through in there.'

****

While Smith and Rachel were interviewing the Richards, Riley was undertaking the background checks on Kyle Hooper and Carl Johnson that Paul Smith had requested.

His first call was to the Victor Harbor High School where Kyle attended. After a short wait he was connected with the school principal, Louise Stratton, and he quickly introduced himself and the purpose of his call.

'I'll help you any way I can, Sergeant. The news of Amy's death has sent a shock wave through the school.'

Riley was not the least bit surprised that Amy's identity was public knowledge, even though it had not been released to the media awaiting the formal identification by her parents.

'Ms Stratton, we have not officially confirmed that the person who died is Amy Richards, but you can reasonably assume that we have strong reason to believe it is her. Now, as you may know Amy had a boyfriend, Kyle Hooper, who I understand is a student at your school. Can you just confirm some of his details for me?'

'Sure,' she replied, 'and please call me Louise. I always find Ms so clumsy and apparently we shouldn't use Miss or Missus. Let me just pull out Kyle's file.'

Moments later she was back.

'Here we go. Kyle started year 8 in 2012, the same year as Amy. He is studying year 12 this year.'

'Can you tell me what his attendance record is like?'

'Let's see. This year, it's exemplary – he hasn't missed a day. He missed two for the whole of last year and, oh my goodness, thirty four the year before. That's some turnaround.'

Sensing Louise was about to offer some reason for the change, Riley interjected.

'Louise, you say Kyle hasn't missed a day this year. Is he at school today?'

'Well, I'm not sure. I doubt today's absences have been recorded yet. Just give me a moment to check with my admin manager.'

Riley heard her call out to someone followed by a muffled conversation. He couldn't hear the detail but it was clear he was not going to get a simple yes or no answer.

'Sorry to keep you waiting, Sergeant. It seems that Kyle is not at school today. We haven't received a call to advise us of his absence. For a younger student we would follow up with parents but, frankly, once students are in year 12 we expect them to be able to manage themselves effectively. It's part of their preparation for university.'

'That's fine, thank you. We can follow up with Mrs Hooper if necessary. Did you know Amy?'

'Only superficially. Nevertheless, I must say I am shaken by her death. As I understand, she was a nice kid that had lost her way a bit, but no-one deserves to die like this.'

'As I mentioned, we have not yet officially released Amy's name, so can I ask that you treat this conversation confidentially?'

'Of course. I'm sorry. It's still such a shock. You don't think Kyle's involved, do you?'

'He is just one person we need to talk to as part of our investigation, especially given his relationship with Amy. How well do you know him?'

'I have nearly seven hundred students here, Sergeant. While I would like to say I know them all well, I'm afraid I simply can't. However, if it would help, I can have Kyle's class teacher call you at the end of the next period. I'm sure he will help you much better than I'm able.'

'Louise, that would be really helpful and I appreciate your help.'

While he waited for the teacher to call back, Riley checked the database and noted that Kyle had no recorded convictions. He remembered that Kyle had got into some mischief three or four years before that had required some police intervention but his recollection was that it hadn't been too serious.

Checking the file, he saw two references to incidents involving Kyle. He read the first, a report for attempted theft – the incident that he recalled at the Corio Hotel involving Travis Schultz.

The second report was one that he hadn't been aware of and for that reason he took more interest in it. Police had been called to a disturbance in Strathalbyn, a town about forty kilometres north of Goolwa. It had involved two groups of teenage boys in January, only six months earlier. Kyle and Travis had been in one of the groups. The other group had included Brock Richards. Apparently, both groups had been at the same party when a disagreement occurred, details unrecorded, and the fight spread out onto the street. Of course, alcohol had been involved. According to the report, police were able to split the groups and send the respective parties on their way. The only injuries were to the hot-headed youngsters' prides.

Riley pondered the coincidence of the parties involved and dismissed that it has any relevance. Goolwa was a small town of just over two thousand and the boys all attended the same school, so it would have been unlikely that the boys hadn't known each other. The fact that they had all travelled to a party at Strathalbyn was also not unusual. He already knew they were very different personalities, so it was no surprise that they were on opposing sides of the argument.

He was about to put the file away when his phone rang.

'Sergeant Riley? It's John Tamblyn here. Louise Stratton asked me to call you – about Kyle Hooper, is that right?'

'Yes, thanks for calling me. I am just hoping you can tell me a little about Kyle. What sort of student he is, how he gets on with other people and so on.'

'Alright, where to start? Ok, look, Kyle is a great kid, but he hasn't always been. I've been his class teacher for the last two years and I have seen a remarkable change in him as a person. He's what I'd call a solid student without being brilliant. Is that the sort of thing you want?'

Riley responded, searching for more specific information. 'How does he fit into the school community, what's his relationship like with others?'

'Ok, I'm with you. Kyle is well liked. He has a reasonable circle of friends and I think he's known to be a friendly lad. I wouldn't say he's a leader, but I think he is loyal to his mates.'

'What about the teaching community? How would you say they regard Kyle?'

'Generally, I think they are impressed with how he's turned himself around. I'd say they all regard him as respectful and willing to cooperate in school activities. That's certainly my view and I think I'm pretty representative.'

'Has he ever been involved with drugs, do you know?'

'How would I know? I've got no idea what these kids get up to outside school. Shouldn't you blokes be on top of who's who in the zoo with drug use?

'Are you able to speculate why he's not at school today?'

'I'd say it's quite straight forward, wouldn't you? His girlfriend has just been murdered.'

'Well, that's not confirmed or official yet?'

'But you must have a reason for asking about Kyle then,' the teacher retorted.

'Ok, I take your point,' Riley sighed. 'The thing is, we haven't been able to locate Kyle. As you say, being away from school is understandable, but then we would expect him to be amongst people he's close to – family and friends.'

'In that case, I can't help you, Sergeant. '

'Ok, let's step back a bit. What do you know about Kyle's relationship with Amy Richards?'

'Oh, look, I know they are boyfriend and girlfriend. I can't tell you any more than that. I'm not privy to the conversations my students have with each other and I'm not sure I'd want to be. As I said before, I don't have any idea what kids do in their own time and it's not my job to know either, Sergeant.

'I tell you, though, I was shocked to hear that it was Amy that drowned yesterday. I taught her Australian History in years 8 and 9. Would you pass on my condolences to Michael and Karen?'

'Just a couple of final questions and I'll let you get back to your classes. Can you tell me what you know about Travis Schultz?'

'Travis Schultz? He was friends with both Amy and Kyle when he was at school here. He would have left around the same time as Amy, but I haven't kept up with what happened to him. He's a gentle giant, that lad, but I do worry about what the future holds for him.'

'Ever seen him lose his temper or become violent?'

'Not that I recall, although I imagine he could have lashed out when he was taunted by other kids. He's different, slow, and he copped a bit from the school bullies.'

Riley smiled. 'That's how he describes himself too – different and slow. Now, finally, what about Amy's brother, Brock? What was his relationship with Kyle like?'

'Ah, speak of the devil. Brock was one of the school bullies I was referring to. Hey, it was no secret that Brock and Kyle didn't get on. I suppose I could have mentioned earlier that Kyle was, I guess, a "protector". He often stood up for kids that were being picked on, especially Travis. Having said that, I can't remember anything that ever got out of hand at school.'

'Well, thank you, Mr Tamblyn, you've been very helpful.'

Riley hung up, almost with relief. His interview with John Tamblyn felt strained at times but he was unable to explain why. He turned his attention to Carl Johnson. His stomach tensed as he considered the potential complications, given Carl's relationship with Sally. He started by checking the database to see whether Carl had a criminal record. He was not surprised, but still relieved, that he didn't have anything recorded.

For completeness, he decided to check his Driver's License with the motor registration department to see what, if any traffic infringements, Carl may have committed.

He found, but again was not surprised, that there was no record of him at his Goolwa address. Riley figured that this wasn't necessarily an issue. While strictly speaking Carl should have updated his address with the licensing departments when he moved to Goolwa, it was possible he just forgot to do it.

However, Riley knew this wouldn't satisfy Paul Smith, so he lifted his phone and called the main motor mechanic in town. After confirming that he did in fact service Carl's car, he asked him for its registration number. The mechanic left the phone briefly to consult his files. Meanwhile Riley was entertained overhearing an inane conversation elsewhere in the workshop. The mechanic returned to the phone and told him the number.

Riley then accessed the database of the motor registration department and found that the car with the registration number given by the mechanic was a blue Mitsubishi Triton 4x4, as expected.

He was dumbfounded to see that the car was registered in the name of Callum Donald Johnston, 21 Sixth Street, Loxton, date of birth 8 February 1975. Now consumed by curiosity, Riley retraced the databases searching that name and found no recorded criminal convictions and relatively few traffic incidents over the previous 15 years. He then tracked down the details of the land owner of the Loxton address and after a further phone call learnt that the address had been unoccupied for around 18 months. He was flabbergasted. *What the hell was going on?*

As Riley closed out his revelation of what he suspected was Carl Johnson's true identity, Paul Smith walked through the door, followed by a seemingly self-satisfied Rachel Cross.

'What's up with you?' Riley murmured, as she leaned across his desk.

'He's alright,' she whispered, 'I could learn a lot from him.'

Riley shook his head as he rose and called to Smith.

'Could I have a moment, sir?'

'Sure, what have you got?'

Riley relayed his findings from his research.

Smith listened intently before responding.

'Ok Riley, let's have a talk with Carl or Callum or whatever he's calling himself today. I want to do it as soon as we can so why don't you phone ahead to make sure we know where he is? You remember I said I'd need to exclude you if this got too close to you personally. Just so you know, it's bloody near now, so make sure you stay objective, alright?'

'I'm very aware, sir. If it's any comfort, I need to watch out for Sally, too. I have a vested interest in making sure we sort this out, one way or the other.'

Riley looked at his watch and saw that was almost 6.00. He called Carl's mobile phone at intervals until after 6.30, the lack of an answer suggesting that his mobile was switched off. He briefly discussed his lack of success with Paul Smith and they decided they would meet at the station in the morning at 6.30 and go straight to Carl's house.

Before the team disbanded for the night, they quickly debriefed, covering the results of the day's activities. Of most concern was that they still had not found Kyle Hooper, Amy's car or either of their phones. Their list of persons of interest had grown but there was no overwhelming evidence pointing in a single direction.

Chapter 17
Sunday 27 August 1854

Alexander and Joe's return journey was uneventful. The tide favoured the small boat as it negotiated the mouth of the Murray comfortably.

Alexander and Joe discussed their good fortune on the way back but resolved that they needed to keep their discovery secret and that they would resist the temptation to make any financial commitments until they had actual cash in hand.

Nonetheless, they chatted about how they planned to spend their money. From Alexander's perspective, the direction was clear. He would invest in Johnston and Murphy, fully expecting a different outcome to last time he had partnered with a Murphy. He would be a significant businessman in the Goolwa, an equal partner with George Johnston and Thomas Murphy. He would be a man of influence and a provider for his wife and son.

Joe could not say with any certainty what his plans were. He restated his belief that the best thing he could do would be to go back to the goldfields or to return home to Wiltshire. With more discussion, he was shifting ground a little. He could see now that he could operate a small fleet of fishing boats on the river and the Coorong. He would stop fishing himself, of course, that was a mug's game. He would be the master of the fleet, employing other men to do the hard work while he did the trading. With the £500 he was expecting, he could have a sound little business. If he had a thousand, he would be one of the biggest operators on the river.

The dreaming of the men came to a close only when the wharf at the Goolwa came into sight. The last discourse on the matter was Joe exhorting Alexander to look after the necklace, not to be swindled in the selling of it and above all to make sure he paid Joe his fair share.

The sun was emitting its last feeble winter rays as they drew into shore. The men shook hands and Alexander made his way up the hill toward the little cottage, where he knew Rubina would be waiting for him.

He burst through the front door and paced through to the kitchen at the back. Rubina was at the stove, cooking up a broth for their evening meal.

'Ah, Alexander, I was starting to wonder if you would make it home for tea. How was the fishing?'

Before they had retired on their last night on the Coorong, Alexander had made sure that he set a couple of nets. He didn't want to arrive home with no fish after a fishing trip with a professional fisherman. They had been lucky and pulled in a dozen good size mulloway, the largest over ten pounds. By the time they had split the catch, Alexander had enough for several meals for his family.

Rubina watched now as Alexander emptied the sack of fish onto the kitchen table. She squealed with delight.

'Oh, the stews I will be able to make with this lot. They will be just like we had at home in Scotland. Ooh, I wonder if I could smoke them and make Cullen Skink.'

'Where is Donald, love?'

'Well now, he's around helping Mr Goode. Mr Goode has said he will give Donald an apprenticeship when he opens his new shop, so Donald is helping him unload his first consignment of haberdashery.'

'Good. I'm glad he is nae here right now. I have something to show you.'

He fished into the inside of his jacket and held the leather pouch in front of Rubina.

'What is it, Alexander?'

'That, my love is Albert's Folly. Rube, we are going to be rich.'

'What are you talking about, Albert's Folly? If there's any folly here, it's you. What are you on about?' Rubina was clearly frustrated.

'Sit down, love. I'll explain'.

Alexander proceeded to tell Rubina the story of the emerald necklace, how it became known as Albert's Folly and eventually passed into the hands of Catharine Delaney. When he explained how he and Joe Tripp had gone in search of the piece and found it, she put her hand to her mouth.

'You must go to the Goolwa Hotel at once. I hear Missus Delaney is leaving for Adelaide in the morning. Aye, she will probably have a decent reward for you, Alexander.'

'Nay, Ruby, that's not the plan. I'm going to Swan Hill with Francis Cadell in a few days. I'm going to leave them there and go down to Melbourne so that I can sell the necklace. I have to pay Tripp twenty five percent and we will have the rest.'

Ruby sank onto a kitchen chair.

'Alexander, you cannae do that. This does nae belong to you, 'tis Missus Delaney's.'

'Well, the way I see it Rube, they have finished searching the wreck. Delaney is claiming the loss from her insurance, so she's nought worse off. If Joe and I had nae gone in search of it, the necklace would still be lost and it would stay that way forever. This way, we win, Joe Tripp wins and Catharine Delaney is nae any worse off.'

'But, Alexander,' Rubina continued, 'this is nae right. The bible says so.' She was reluctant to persist with her objection; after all, it should be the man of the house who made all the big decisions. However, her morals and religious convictions now conflicted with this belief.

She tried one more time.

'Alexander, surely someone loses. The insurance company or someone. This feels like the devil's temptation. The Lord will punish us.'

'Dinnae talk rot, woman.' Alexander was becoming heated. He had never raised his voice to Rubina before, but he could see his dreams slipping away if he couldn't convince her.

'Look, Catharine Delaney's type has never done people like us any favours. How many people did we see forced out of Scotland, or worse still starved, during the famine? And why? There was plenty of food, it was just that wealthy landowners, like the Delaney's, would nae share it with the working class.'

'She's Irish, Alexander.'

'Does nae matter. It happened in Ireland as well as Scotland. Those people are the same wherever they are. I cannae abide the thought it would happen in this country too. Your cousin, Eliza, what happened to her?'

'The wee lass died. Her family could nae feed her and she fell ill.'

'Aye. And what about Duncan Seton's boys?'

'I know. They got shipped away to Canada after Duncan and Mary died in the famine.'

'Are you telling me that was all God's will?'

Rubina felt her resistance dissolving. The truth was that she actually knew that what Alexander was saying was true. The landlords in Scotland were the same as those in Ireland or in England. They didn't give a hoot about ordinary folk as long as they were continuing to make money and expand their holdings.

Despite that, she felt uneasy about Alexander's plan.

'Why would you partner with Joe Tripp, though? The man cannae be trusted, just like Paddy Murphy.'

The comment stang Alexander, but he was ready for the question, which he had played out in his mind dozens of times.

Quietly, he responded, 'I'll nae get caught like that again, Ruby. I know what Joseph Tripp is and this time I am prepared for it. He'll nae hoodwink me the way Murphy did.'

'And how will you make sure of that, Alexander Johnston?'

'Well, to begin with, I have the necklace in my keeping. And that's how it will stay until I have sold it. As well as that, I am handling the sale. Joe Tripp needs me.'

'You cannae carry it around with you all the time. You will be asking to be mugged. If nae by Joe Tripp, then by one of his associates or some other person of foul intent.'

'I ken that,' he said. 'That's why I am going to hide it. I just need to work out where.'

By now Ruby accepted that Alexander was not to be dissuaded. While she was still conflicted, she switched her thinking to making sure they protected the valuable gem and themselves, until Alexander was able to safely deposit the proceeds.

'I have an idea,' she said. 'You need to travel to Melbourne to sell the necklace?'

'Aye,' said Alexander, understanding that Rubina could provide a new approach that he may not have considered. 'I had planned to take out the gems, melt down the gold and sell them separately.'

'Good, good,' she said, 'now you need to be able to keep them hidden, nae just now but right up until you get to Melbourne.'

'Aye, what are you thinking, lass?'

'Well, I think you do as you say. Separate the gems and melt the gold. Then we will sew them into the lining of your best coat. That's what you will wear to Melbourne, is it nae?'

'Oh, my love, I knew you would come up with the best idea.'

Over the next hour, Alexander gently prised each emerald from its setting, putting them in a small pile on the kitchen table. After that he placed the gold chain and setting into a small pan and heated it over the hot coals in the kitchen fire. Once the gold was molten, he carefully poured the yellow liquid into a can of cold water. Sizzle and steam rose from the can but when it settled he could see that he had converted the chain into a single nugget of pure gold.

Meanwhile, Rubina unpicked the lining of Alexander's best coat, a mid-length dress coat, worn at the elbows and cuffs but otherwise still quite presentable.

When the gold nugget had cooled, they inserted it together with the twenty emerald jewels into the small length of unpicked lining. They spread all the contents so that they were evenly placed around the bottom hem of the coat.

'There, you would ne'er ken that they were there.'

'Grand, Ruby. Now what do you think I should do with this?' he asked, showing her the leather pouch stamped with Geo. Fotheringham.'

'You must hide it where it will never be found, Alexander.'

While Rubina re-stitched the jacket hem, Alexander set about concealing the pouch. First, he moved their bed out from the wall. Then using a hammer and chisel, he carefully forced out the smallest of the stones set in the mortar of the wall.

After removing the stone, he placed the pouch in the cavity before re-setting the stone to its proper place. He quickly made up some mortar and finished the setting.

He stood back, pleased with his work.

'When that's dry, no-one will be able to tell that it was nae part of the original wall.'

'Good, love.' Rubina hung Alexander's jacket on the hook behind the bedroom door.

They had just finished when Donald came through the front door.

'Oh, you're home, Donald. Just in time for some broth with us. Will ye set the table, please, love?'

Chapter 18
Tuesday, July 19 2016

It's 6.45 am and I hear the knocking on the door. I am just finishing brushing my teeth and about to hit the road to start my mowing rounds, so I'm not expecting anyone. Last night, Sally and I had gone to the movies in Victor Harbor and saw an over-rated rom-com that I'm sure she enjoyed a lot more than I did. At least it did serve the purpose of distracting me for a couple of hours.

I think she sensed that I had not taken Amy's death well. After coming a long way in developing a trusting, healthy relationship with Amy, selfishly I now felt somewhat bitter about that being taken away from me. Of course, I grieved for Amy and her family as well, but I couldn't get rid of the gloom for my own loss.

I had dropped Sally at her house on the way home. When I hear the knock on the door, I figure she must have left her purse or her phone in the car and called by on her way to work to pick it up. It's early for librarian hours but I don't question it.

I open the door expecting, and wanting, to see her, but instead I see a familial resemblance. It takes me a moment to realise Riley has come back again. He's accompanied by the detective he was with yesterday and neither looks pleased.

'Paul Smith again, Mr Johnson. Can we come in please, sir?'

I invite them into my living room and ask if they want a coffee. They both decline and I frown as I see that Riley is strangely quiet with his eyes focussed on the floor. I sense a change in their approach to me but have absolutely no idea where this is heading.

Smith breaks the awkward silence.

'May I have a look at your driver's license please, sir?'

I am about to ask why he would want that, when it hits me like a cricket bat and the reason for change of mood becomes overwhelmingly obvious.

I fish the plastic card out of my wallet and hand it to Paul Smith and then sink onto the sofa. He looks at it and turns it over in his hand. He then glances at me while he hands the card to Riley. He gives it scant attention before handing it back to me.

'Well,' Smith said, 'the person in the photograph on that license certainly looks like you but, oddly this license is in the name of a Callum Johnston. Care to explain, Mr Johnson or Johnston?'

My mind is racing and I can feel my heart beating so hard my chest feels like it's about to explode. *The biggest question is how much explanation do I give them?* I am churning over the implications of what I am about to say – if the rumours of my past, no matter how untrue, become public how will it affect my relationship with Sally and Riley and with the people of Goolwa. I know what it was like in Loxton. *Am I going to have it all re-surface? What will it mean for the investigation into Amy's death?*

'You're right, Detective Inspector,' I say as composed as I am able. 'I have been living in Goolwa under a false name and I suspect you are now going to ask me why.'

'Good observation. Why?'

For the next thirty minutes I explain the story of my life in Loxton, the school, the kayak squad, Emma Satchin, the accusations and my exoneration.

'Excuse me for saying, sir, but it seems to me that fleeing a town as an innocent man and taking up a new identity in another town is at best odd and at worst highly suspicious behaviour. There's not something else you need to tell us, is there?'

'No,' I answer solemnly.

'Just one more question and I'll caution you to answer this very honestly. If I find you're hiding anything else, I'll run your arse up a flagpole.'

Smith is looking at me through eyes of steel.

'Have you any connections with anyone in the drug trade?'

'Certainly not. Check my files. I'm absolutely clean and always have been.' *Where did that come from?*

'Ok, Mr Johnston, I expect we may want to ask you more questions later so make sure you will be available for us.

Of course I say I will be. *No matter how anxious, dismayed and utterly pissed off I'm feeling.*

Riley has not said a word during the whole exchange, but as Smith walks through the front door, he hisses at me through clenched teeth 'I want you to keep away from my sister. Understand?'

I am gob-smacked and open mouthed as I close the door behind him. I feel the old deep routed shadow closing around me, with the feeling that it's only time before the accusations start flying and my life in Goolwa will become a reflection of Loxton.

My day has started badly. *How much worse can it get?*

Chapter 19
Tuesday, July 19 2016

After they leave Carl's house, Smith got into the passenger seat of the police car and Riley hurried to catch him, hopping into the driver's seat moments after.

'Well,' Smith said, 'innocent of past indiscretions or not, he is still in our sights. I have to say that I'm a bit surprised, Riley, that you weren't aware of his background, given how close you are to him.'

His tone was more indicative of a mentor than a critic, but nonetheless the comment caused Riley to bite on his bottom lip. He held his tongue despite wanting to point out that none of Carl's background was his business other than because of his relationship with Sally. Smith sensed Riley's silence.

'You might think this difficult, I think we are at a point where I've got to make a call to exclude you from any part of the investigation relating to Carl Johnson. At least for the time being.'

'But, sir, I ...'

'No, you're too close, Riley, and we can't afford any stuff-ups. I'm getting a full check done on Callum Johnston, but I'll get it coordinated through one of the teams in Adelaide. We need to know what really happened in Loxton.'

Riley was about to protest further when a message came through on the police radio. It was PC Reid, advising that there had been a call from a volunteer at the Currency Creek Cemetery.

'The volunteer is a bloke by the name of Reg Parkinson. He says there's been a grave tampered with and he wants us to have a look. Probably just kids but he seems pretty excited by it.'

Smith turned to Sergeant O'Brien, 'I did warn you that there would be business as usual for you to deal with as well as this case. It's probably a good time for you to have a break from this anyway. How about you check out the cemetery incident, while I get the ball rolling on Johnston and follow up on the search for Kyle Hooper?'

Despondent and sulky, Riley drove back to the station, where he dropped Smith, before continuing out of town to the cemetery.

As he drove, he reflected on the conversation with Carl. While he felt disappointed in Carl's deception, he was building an understanding as to why Carl may have made the choices he did. Living in a small town had its challenges and reputations, professional and personal, could be destroyed in the blink of an eye. He didn't yet regret warning Carl off Sally, but he did resolve that he should take time to understand Carl's point of view.   After all he wasn't found guilty of any improper behaviour and Riley would not want to fall into the narrow minded attitudes of some in the community. Talking openly will be hard, though, now that his line of communication with Carl had been effectively cut off by Paul Smith's instruction. *Maybe once all this is over…*

The other issue, he pondered, was what he would say to Sally. She needed to know, of course, but he would need to be diplomatic in how he told her... *a problem for later today.*

He pulled off the Goolwa to Mount Compass Road onto the dirt road that led down to the cemetery. The day was fine with billowing white clouds providing a sharp contrast to the bright blue sky.   It was a beautiful winter day, with only a cool southerly breeze coming straight off the Antarctic providing a sharp chill.

He passed the firing range to his left and after a couple of turns in the road found himself in the car park of the cemetery. He saw a man aged in his late sixties waiting at the gate, but that was not where his attention was drawn. He was fixated by the orange Mazda 323 that he had parked next to.

Riley quickly checked the registration number against his notebook and confirmed what he strongly suspected. *Amy's car.* He climbed out of the police car, hastily pulling on a parka that he lifted from the back seat. He walked with a sense of urgency to the side of the Mazda and looked through the driver's window.

'I'm glad you're here, Sergeant. I'm Reg Parkinson. Here, the grave I want to show you is this way.'

'Just a moment, sir. What do you know about this car?' Riley continued peering through the car window and, wrapping his handkerchief around his hand, tried the door handle but it held firm.

'Call me Reg. The car was here when I arrived this morning about an hour ago. I haven't seen anyone else here – not surprising though, mid-week. Do you think it's connected to the vandalism?'

Riley realised that the discovery of Amy's car so far from her body had huge implications for the investigation. He contemplated calling into Paul Smith but decided he should first understand how the car might fit into the disturbance of the grave.

'So, Reg, show me this grave. What is it that you do here, anyway?'

'This way, it's in row two,' he indicated as he opened the gate for Riley. 'I usually come by once a week, just to check everything's ok, you know no vandalism, graffiti in the toilets and so on. I didn't expect to see one of our graves half dug up though.'

They walked over to the grave in row two and Riley saw a hole around thirty centimetres deep and a metre long by half a metre wide.

'Looks like they were intending to dig down to the coffin,' Reg commented.

The grave was surrounded by a low wrought iron fence, a single bar only fifteen centimetres above the ground, rusted to an earthy brown with the passage of time. Riley looked at the gravestone. While the stone was well worn, the inscription was perfectly legible.

IN MEMORY OF

ALEXANDER GEORGE JOHNSTON

BORN COCKENZIE SCOTLAND
11 NOVEMBER 1817
DIED 30 AUGUST 1854

TO DIE IS GAIN
ALL EARTHLY CARES FORSAKING
FROM TOIL AND PAIN
TO ENDLESS JOY AWAKENING

'Why would someone be digging up a grave that's over one hundred and fifty years old?' Riley questioned out loud.

He noticed that the adjoining grave had an identical fence and the same sized and shaped headstone. He read the words etched into the stone.

IN LOVING MEMORY OF

RUBINA MAY JOHNSTON

PRECIOUS IN THE SIGHT OF THE LORD
IS THE DEATH OF HIS SAINTS

BORN 14 APRIL 1822
DIED 31 AUGUST 1854
IN THE 33RD YEAR OF HER AGE

'Wow,' exclaimed Riley, 'Looks like husband and wife; they died within days of each other.'

'Yes, their son, Donald is buried over in row ten. Do you want to have a look?'

They walked over to row ten. Riley saw that Donald had at least enjoyed a longer life than his parents, dying in Goolwa in 1932 at the age of ninety one.

'At least he had some good fortune.'

'Well now, so did another Johnston.' Reg pointed back to row nine at one of the largest plots and headstones in this part of the cemetery. 'That's George Bain Johnston, famous river captain, he was.'

They walked to this gravesite and Riley observed how well maintained this one was compared to almost every other grave of the same era. The wrought iron fence around the grave was higher and more elaborate than most, and the monument stretched nearly three metres high. The ground within the border was covered with white gravel and was completely free of weeds.

Riley read George's inscription.

GEORGE BAIN JOHNSTON
OF GOOLWA, SHIPBUILDER

BORN AT COCKENZIE, SCOTLAND
29 NOVEMBER 1829
DIED 29 JUNE 1882

PIONEER NAVIGATOR OF THE RIVERS
MURRAY, DARLING, MURRUMBIDGEE
AND TRIBUTARIES

'So he's related to Alexander?'

'I believe they were cousins. I recall reading they were both connected to Francis Cadell.'

'Who looks after George's grave? It's pristine.'

'I do,' replied Reg, proudly. 'It's one of the most important plots in the whole cemetery.'

'Then why is Alexander's grave the one that's being dug up?' Riley asked.

'Beats me.'

Riley pondered for a moment. Ravens were cawing in the background as if encouraging him to hurry up with his business so they could get on with theirs. The breeze sent a chill through him as he wandered back to the grave of Donald Johnston, perturbed by a nagging thought. Like a lightning bolt had hit him, he stopped in his tracks. Reg, unaware of the ponderings of the young sergeant, walked on a further couple of steps before turning to look at Riley. He was unable to explain the expression on Riley's face but it was clear that it was not to be shared with him.

'Thanks, Reg. I've got to call the station. Was there anything else you noticed?'

'Nope, only that obviously the job wasn't finished and there's no digging tools in sight.'

Riley walked back to his car, mind confused but engaged with what he had found out in the last half hour. He called through to Paul Smith and provided a full update on the discovery of Amy Richards' car, the grave disturbance but more puzzling the apparent coincidence linking Callum Johnston, now Carl Johnson, with Alexander, Rubina, George and Donald Johnston, all long dead.

Paul Smith repeated much of what Riley had said to make sure he understood. 'So let me get this right, we now have Amy Richards' car and we have a grave disturbance that hypothetically may have a link to the man who is one of our emerging suspects.'

'Sir, I don't mean to question your intelligence, but did you recall Callum Johnston's middle name? It's Donald, the same as the son of Alexander Johnston whose grave is the one that's been messed with. Too coincidental isn't it?'

'That didn't escape me, Riley. Good work with this. Now, what I need you to do is secure that cemetery, I don't want anyone else to go in there. Also cordon off the car. I want to get forensics onto it as soon as I can. We've had no further word on Kyle Hooper's whereabouts. I'm now starting to wonder if he's a potential suspect or a second victim.'

Riley recoiled at the thought. He hadn't considered that as a possibility. He was brought back to earth as the Detective Inspector resumed.

'I'm going to get a full search of the cemetery kicked off in case the car and the disturbance of the grave are linked. That will take me about half hour, then I'll come out there and I'll be bringing a guest, our mysterious Callum Johnston.'

Chapter 20
Tuesday 29th August 1854

Two nights after his return from the Coorong Alexander was maintaining watch on Francis Cadell's paddle steamer, the Lady Augusta at the Goolwa wharf. The steamer had achieved notoriety 12 months before in a race along the Murray against Captain Randell's steamer Mary Ann.

In 1851, the Governor of the colony of South Australia was Sir Henry Fox Young and as a consequence of the gold rushes occurring in New South Wales and Victoria, he became concerned for the colony's economy and population growth. He, like many, believed that South Australia, with access to the mouth of the River Murray, was in a unique position to capitalise on the inland trade that would surely follow the development of towns along the river system.

To accelerate this development he offered a bonus to the first boat owner that could navigate from the Murray mouth to the junction of the Murray River with the Darling River. The boats were required to be iron clad steamers that were powered by at least forty horsepower and, due to the shallowness of the river, could draw no more than two feet of water when laden.

This challenge immediately appealed to Francis Cadell, George Johnston's sponsor. He had been a mariner for many years and had spent time in the United States studying river navigation. His eighty ton vessel was built in Sydney and eventually sailed through the Murray mouth, creating much interest on her maiden voyage. Cadell had cleverly named his boat the Lady Augusta after the Governor's wife, who together with the Governor and several other dignitaries sailed on that maiden voyage.

Cadell left the Goolwa on 25 August 1853, several months behind his competitor William Randell, who sought to claim the Governor's prize in his much smaller boat, the Mary Ann.

Francis Cadell and his crew passed the Mary Ann near the junction of the Murray with the Murrumbidgee River and from there the two boats sailed in very close proximity until the Lady Augusta arrived at Swan Hill just twenty three days after leaving the Goolwa.

Although neither of the captains had strictly met the conditions for the Governor's bonus, they were nonetheless rewarded, no doubt for proving that the river was navigable and endorsing South Australia's role as the route to the inland.

With the funds he had received, Cadell established the River Murray Navigation Company and under its auspices, the Lady Augusta continued to ply trade along the river.

The boat was due to leave for Swan Hill in two days and Alexander had ensured he was to crew on the journey, at least one way. From Swan Hill he intended to travel to Melbourne to sell the jewels and gold that he had extracted from Albert's Folly.

This had been more difficult to arrange than he had thought. Firstly, he had needed to find a plausible reason why he wanted only to crew the boat in one direction. After pondering this problem for some time, he eventually decided that his best course was to stick as closely to the truth as he could.

In the Goolwa Hotel earlier in the evening, he had noticed Francis Cadell and George Johnston in conversation about their upcoming journey.

Cadell was jibing George about his soon to be business that would be competing with Cadell's now thriving operation.

'Francis, there's plenty for us all. Soon this river's going to be full of boats carrying all manner of goods. Better for you if 'tis a friend you'll be a rival with.'

'I ken, George. I am just kidding you, my friend. I am very honestly pleased that you are taking this opportunity now; and Charles Murphy is a fine man. He will be a good partner.' Cadell was as jovial as George had seen him. Business had been good and even with the exodus of men to the goldfields, the Goolwa's port was busy and had become even more so with the opening of the railway to Port Elliot.

'Aha,' exclaimed Cadell, 'and here's your new partner. Is that right, Alexander? You'll be a fool nae to join this man. Come, let me buy you an ale to celebrate the venture.'

Alexander joined the pair, greeted with a slap on the back from Cadell.

'Francis, Geordie. Well, I wanted to talk to you about your proposal, George. And thank you, Francis, I'd be grateful for an ale.'

Francis Cadell left the men, walking to the bar to get Alexander's ale. His intuition had told him he should leave Alexander and Geordie to do their business for a moment.

'George, about the partnership,' Alexander started carefully. 'I'm keen to join you and Charles. Don't get me wrong, I always have been but I needed to get my affairs in order.'

'That's wonderful, cousin. Elizabeth will be delighted for Ruby, as well.'

'There is one thing, though Geordie. You see, some of my funds are tied up in Melbourne, so I need to go back there to make arrangements for their transfer here.'

'Well, 'tis no business of mine. We can wait a little longer.'

'I am hoping that I can leave the Lady Augusta in Swan Hill and go down to Melbourne from there. Do you think Francis will mind?'

'Ha-ha. Mind? Of course not, Alexander. Just dinnae ruin my business in the course of making yours, hey.' Cadell slapped him on the back and handed him the mug of ale. 'Here's to healthy rivalry.'

The three men drank together and shared stories from their Scottish heritage, before Alexander left the others to walk to the Lady Augusta. On his way out, he ran into Joseph Tripp.

The fisherman had been on the river fishing since the pair had returned from the Coorong.

'Alexander, I want to see you. Has anyone said anything about the necklace?'

Alexander looked nervously about.

'Tripp,' he hissed, 'this is neither the place nae the time to be talking about it. We have to keep it quiet. Dinnae ruin it for us both, man.'

'Nonetheless, we need to talk. I want to know what's happening.'

'You ken what's happening. Be patient and I'll let you ken when you will get your commission.'

'Alexander, I won't be brushed aside like some minnow. You will talk to me tonight.'

'All right, Joe. I'm on the Lady Augusta tonight, keeping watch before she sails. Wait until the hotel empties, after dark. Then come down to the wharf. We can talk then.'

He strode off before Tripp could engage him in further discussion. Aggrieved, the fisherman stormed inside, slamming the door behind him. Eyes turned briefly, but then turned back to look into the bottoms of beer mugs.

He ambled to the bar, where John Varcoe was working.

'Not a good day today, then Tripp?'

Scowling, Tripp looked at the innkeeper.

'None of your business, Varcoe. Give me rum. A bottle, not a glass.'

'Must have been a bad day. Everyone else is in good spirits here, Tripp. Don't you go spoiling it now.'

'Like I said, Varcoe. None of your business.'

Tripp took himself to a table in the corner, lifting the cork of the bottle on his way. He didn't have much time for John Varcoe, or anyone else in this godforsaken place and it was clear that, generally speaking, feelings were mutual. He was even having second thoughts about Alexander Johnston and whether he could be trusted with their fortune.

Two hours later, the hotel was almost empty; Tripp was still sitting in the corner although the rum bottle was now only quarter full. He pushed the cork into the neck of the bottle and made his way, somewhat unsteadily out of the front door.

Outside, the night was cold and Tripp felt the bracing wind bite into his face, temporarily sobering him. He still staggered and occasionally stumbled as he followed the path down to the wharf. No one else was about and he saw nothing until he sighted the lantern alight inside the Lady Augusta. When he reached the gangplank, he called 'Coming aboard, Alexander.'

The Scotsman had been mulling what he now knew was a problem with his partner in crime. He was sure that Joseph Tripp would want to protect his interest in the salvaged treasure. He was unlikely to be comfortable with Alexander disappearing to Melbourne for several weeks and having no say at all in the sale process.

'Come in, Joseph.'

The two men sat across the table from each other. Tripp pulled the cork from his rum bottle and took a long swig. Alexander eyed him carefully, realising that this was to be a difficult discussion.

'Alexander,' Tripp began, 'I'll be coming with you to Melbourne to sell the necklace.'

'There's nae need for that, Joe. I can do the business better on my own. 'Twill be foolhardy and suspicious if you come with me.'

'Why? Does anyone suspect we have the necklace? Where is the woman?'

'What woman?'

'The one what owns, or owned, the necklace. Is she still looking for it?'

'Nay, she's gone … to Sydney.'

'Then what's the problem? I want to be part of this, Alexander, and I int going to be cheated of what's rightfully mine.'

'Rightfully? 'Tis not rightfully ours, Joe. That's why we have to be careful. We cannae allow anyone to see that we are doing anything unusual. No one suspects anything yet and there's no reason for them to if we keep our heads.'

'Don't you patronise me, Alexander Johnston. I don't trust anyone in this town, you included.'

Alexander stood and walked toward the door of the cabin.

'Joe, you've had a lot to drink and you're nae thinking clearly. Why dinnae you go home, sleep off your belly full of rum and you'll see sense in the morning.'

With that, Tripp lifted the rum bottle and waved it vigorously at Alexander, contents spilling onto the floor of the cabin. He pushed up from his seat upending the heavy table in the process, then lurched toward Alexander. The Scot stepped outside the door so that as the big fisherman rushed at him, he clumsily tripped and fell heavily onto the deck outside. The rum bottle spilled from his hand and rolled toward the stern of the boat.

The comic movements of the big man exposed the alcohol that he had consumed and the loss of control that had come with it.

Alexander moved away from the doorway and bent over to help Tripp to his feet. The fisherman was quiet and confused, allowing Alexander to help him up.

When he rose he looked at Alexander through glazed, kaleidoscope eyes, before grabbing him around the shoulders and pushing him backward.

'You're like the rest of them, you are. Not to be trusted. Where's the necklace, Alexander? I want to see it.'

'It's nae here, Joe. Do you think I'd be that foolish?'

'No you're hiding it alright. From me as well.'

He still had hold of Alexander's shoulders and pushed him further back along the deck.

'Tell me where it is.'

Although Alexander was strong, Joe was a much bigger man and as hard as he tried to resist him, he felt himself being pushed aside. Eventually, Alexander had no more strength to fight and Tripp's strength prevailed, forcing Alexander off balance. As he stumbled back, his left foot trod on the rum bottle. He lost balance and staggered further backward until he felt his calf rest against the stern of the boat.

Alexander looked back at Joseph Tripp but he knew even at this stage that he could not control the backward momentum of his upper body. He attempted to grab at anything he could with his hands. He found only fresh air.

Tripp watched in a dumbed confusion as he saw Alexander fall over the stern. He stumbled to the edge and looked over the back of the boat. He saw Alexander laying broken across the rudder. There was no movement from the man that was his friend, his partner in crime, but ultimately the man he had been unable to trust.

Falling onto the rudder, Alexander hit his head and slipped into unconsciousness, his face buried in the murky water. The water was frightfully cold but he did not wake from his coma and lay face submerged until he drowned.

Joseph Tripp snapped from his drunken, dulled state and realised that he needed to leave the boat quickly. Just as importantly, he told himself, he needed to work out how he could still profit from the sale of the necklace. He turned toward the Goolwa Hotel for another drink, which he so badly wanted.

Walking up the hill, it occurred to Tripp that if Alexander did not have the necklace with him and he didn't believe that he did, then he must have hidden it in his cottage.

He thought about his next steps, but he knew he could afford no more mistakes, starting immediately. Instead of walking up the hill, he turned and walked down, not to the Lady Augusta but to his own boat, which he had moored just downstream from the wharf.

The night had suddenly become much colder, Joe imagined, and as he looked at the clear black sky above, pierced by a million stars that had witnessed his treachery, he realised he needed to stay very low for a day or two.

The stillness of the night made raising the sail futile, so he fitted his oars and slowly rowed his way from the sandy bank to the middle of the river. He could see that the Goolwa was now in darkness, although he could also see that the lamp inside the cabin of the Lady Augusta was still burning brightly.

He rowed steadily until he was only a few strokes out from the far bank on Hindmarsh Island. He followed it around toward the mouth of the river until he found a secluded inlet, far from the Goolwa and protected from the eyes of river traffic.

He set camp on the bank and lay, thinking about how his plans were coming unstuck and how he had just killed the only man who resembled anything like a friend in this town. As he lay, he felt the eyes of the sky staring down at him, judging, condemning.

He turned his head into his groundsheet so that he could no longer see the stars. At last he could think, albeit with a mind still curdled from alcohol and guilt.

Chapter 21
Tuesday, July 19 2016

I have just finished a job at Goolwa North when I see a call on my mobile phone from an unrecognised number. This isn't unusual given the nature of my business. Most referrals come from word of mouth.

However, when I answer, my heart drops. The caller is Detective Inspector Paul Smith. I had been dwelling all day on the implications of my visit from him and Riley O'Brien this morning. The more I thought about it, the more I became despondent about my future with Sally. *Would she forgive my secrecy about my true identity, particularly now that it was clear that I had lost her brother as a friend?* His warning to stay away from Sally made his position clear and I wondered if I would ever regain his trust.

I had come to the conclusion that I had to have the conversation with Sally before Riley did, so that I could put my side of the story in a way that I thought she might understand, even if she felt betrayed by my lack of honesty. I had been rushing all afternoon to get my committed jobs finished so that I could catch up with Sally as soon as she finished work.

'Mr Johnson? Paul Smith here.'

'Oh.' My surprise and dismay is obvious.

'Mr Johnson, I'd like to ask you to come and help with our enquiries. Can I pick you up from your home in, say, ten minutes?'

Help with our enquiries. Isn't that what they say when they think they have the bad guy?

'I'm just about to head off somewhere. Is this important?'

'I'm afraid it is, sir. I'll expect you to be waiting at the front of your house at, say, 4.15.'

Well, that makes it clear. He is giving me no option. I quickly pack up and drive home, wondering the whole time what more I can give them. I don't know anything that's relevant to Amy's death that I can help them with.

I pull up at the front of my house to find Paul Smith waiting with a young male officer I don't know. He motions me to the back seat of the police car and we head into the centre of town. There hasn't even been any small talk in the car and I am stunned when we drive straight past the police station.

'So where are we going?' I ask.

'I just want to show you something. I'm hoping you can clarify a couple of things for me.' *An obtuse answer that is surely intended to tell me nothing.*

Surprisingly, we head out of town and then turn left onto the Mount Compass Road. We just cross the rail crossing when the police officer slows the car and we turn right onto a dirt road. A signpost indicates we are going to the cemetery. Now I am completely bewildered.

We drive a further five hundred metres or so and we pass a shooting club and firing range on the left. *Never even knew they were there.*

We pull into the car park. I see three cars already parked. One is a police car and, to my shock, one of the others is Amy's. I walk toward the car, thinking through the implications of this discovery. Paul Smith grabs my elbow, not sharply, but enough to let me know he doesn't want me to go near the car.

'We'll be checking the car for fingerprints and any other forensic evidence,' he says.

He leads me through the gate and we turn to the left where I see Riley standing with an older man. I am bitterly cold. The cemetery is at the top of a hill and I can see clearly three hundred and sixty degrees across small valleys to the surrounding hills.

Although it's winter, I had been wearing just a tee shirt while I was working. The sun is starting its slide to the horizon and while the sky is fairly clear, the southerly breeze is cold and blows up the hill straight through me. Tall eucalypts and pines grow on the top of the hill and the rush of the breeze through the tree tops moans with an eeriness you'd expect in a cemetery. The place has charm but it is chilling in every sense of the word.

Even the ravens in the trees seem to object to our presence, cawing sharp protests to no-one in particular. In the background, I can hear the sound of a light aircraft taking off at the strip not far away. On a hill ahead, I see wispy, white smoke rising into the afternoon azure. It's most likely coming from a chimney on one of the houses on the hills ahead. What I wouldn't give to be standing in front of that fireplace right now.

Riley avoids eye contact with me and as we walk toward him, I notice that the grave he is standing next to has a shallow hole in it. He shakes hands with the older man.

'Thanks again, Reg, you've been a big help.'

I don't know who the man is and he shoots a curious glance at me as he walks toward the gate and out to his car.

Paul Smith stops and points at the grave.

'I'm wondering if you can shed any light on this, Mr Johnston.'

I note the use of my birth surname now and wonder if that signals a change in direction.

'What do you mean? Why would I know anything about this?'

'Is it coincidental that this man's name is Alexander Johnston and yours is Callum Johnston? What's more, his grave is dug over in the same place we have found the missing car of a girl that was murdered three days ago and that girl happens to be known to you.'

I am startled by the connections he has drawn.

'Fanciful thinking, detective,' I respond,' I have no idea who this is and surely our surname is not so unusual. Being a Smith, you must have come across dozens of other Smiths that you don't know and, for God's sake, this person has been dead for one hundred and fifty years.'

I think I have his accusation covered, but he seems unflustered.

'Let us show you something else.'

Riley leads us across a couple of rows farther from the gate. As we are walking, Smith asks, 'So what is your full name? Your real name, not your alias.'

'You already know that. But to humour you, it's Callum Donald Johnston,' I answer defiantly.

'What is the name on this grave?'

We have stopped in front of another old grave. I read the name and repeat it. 'Donald Johnston.' I am becoming rattled and I'm trying not to let it show, but my nerves and the cold wind now make me shiver uncontrollably.

'Donald Johnston is the son of Alexander and Rubina who we just met. So how did you get the middle name Donald? From your father, maybe?'

'My father's name was Angus James Johnston. Look I don't know anything about my family before my grandparents. I'm an only child and my parents were killed in a car accident fourteen years ago. As far as I know, they never lived in Goolwa. You are making connections maybe you shouldn't.'

'Well, we'll see about that. Sergeant O'Brien, I think we might do some further checking on Mr Johnston's family background.'

'Yes, sir.' Riley looks like he is actually starting to enjoy my discomfort, the hint of a smirk sneaking across his face as he makes a note in his notebook.

Paul Smith continues, 'You mentioned your grandfather. What was his full name?'

'I actually got my middle name from him. His name was Donald Johnston, Donald Bain Johnston.'

Then something odd happens. For the first time I seem to have got Paul Smith off guard. A flicker of his eye indicates that he is genuinely surprised. The snap of Riley's head as he looks up from his notebook tells me something significant has just changed the game, again.

'Come with us, please Mr Johnston. Riley, can you show us the way?'

We walk back toward the gate. If I think we are leaving the cemetery for the warmth of one of the police cars, I am very wrong. We stop in front of the tallest memorial that I can see. The plot is large and impeccably maintained, even though it is clear that it dates from the nineteenth century. My uneasy curiosity takes my eyes straight to the name on the epitaph. George Bain Johnston.

'Alexander's cousin,' Riley says.

Now it's my turn to be caught off guard. I see both Paul Smith and Riley O'Brien watching closely to see my reaction.

'Look, I have no more idea about what's going on than you do, but I can assure you I know nothing more than I have told you. I have done nothing that's connected to any of this.'

Smith looks at me silently for a moment, piercing my eyes with the stare of a cobra looking for the slightest movement before he strikes.

Finally, he takes a breath.

'Ok, Callum.' I can't help but notice he is sticking with my link to the past but now using a more familiar form of address.

'I think that's it for now. I think you see why you are a person of interest. You were one of the last people to see Amy Richards. She is dead. Her car is here and here we have a disturbed grave that belongs to someone who it strongly appears may be related to you, albeit a long time ago. See where we are going?

'So, what we are going to do now, is have one of the officers take you back to the station for fingerprinting. Then he will take you home. For your own sake, I would strongly encourage you to tell us anything you know that may be relevant to this case before we find out by other means. Also, please make sure you don't go too far without checking in with me first.'

I see him signal to the officer that had driven us to the cemetery and have a private word with him. He then strides across to Riley, who is now standing out of the wind in the covered shelter on the other side of the path.

My day has gone decidedly downhill. My mental state sits somewhere between utter confusion and total meltdown. I can't clear my mind to grieve for Amy while my life is under attack by the police investigation. I'm not sure that I am up to having a difficult discussion with Sally.

It's gone 7.00 by the time the police officer drops me home. Darkness is enveloping the town as much as it is me. I decide that I need a drink to calm myself down and to prepare for my talk with Sally. As I pour a triple scotch over ice, I check my phone and see that I have three missed calls from Sally. We hadn't arranged to catch up so I am comfortable I haven't already got her offside … *unless of course Riley has already spoken to her.*

I see that she has left a voice message and I warily press the keys to pick it up. I am relieved to hear her voice tell me that she has made late arrangements to meet up with colleagues for drinks, so she will talk with me in the morning.

I feel like I'm shirking the issue but relieved that I don't need to talk with her tonight. I will have at least one more night that she respects me. I down the scotch and pour another triple.

Chapter 22
Tuesday, July 19 2016

After Carl left the cemetery, Paul Smith stood with Riley O'Brien under the covered shelter. The light was gradually fading and although the wind had dropped it remained penetratingly cold.

Smith inclined his head back toward the graves and started walking in that direction. Riley followed him to the highest point in the cemetery, a position from which there was a full view of the surrounding hills and valleys.

'Who's that?' Smith said, pointing discretely to an adjacent hill. In the dimness, a figure stood at a fence-line looking toward them. Even from this distance, the figure looked bearish.

'I don't know,' Riley said, 'I wouldn't have expected us to be attracting attention just yet.'

'Maybe whoever it is has a reason to watch. What's over there?'

'There's a dirt road that services a couple of the farms in the area, but that's about all. Want me to get someone over there?'

Smith frowned. 'Don't think there's much point to be honest. It will be dark by the time we get someone there and I'll bet our snoop will be gone before we get close. Let's make sure we keep an eye out tomorrow.'

'Tomorrow?'

'Tomorrow, we turn this place inside out. I have the feeling we are starting to make progress, believe it or not.

'We have a girl who was drowned twelve kilometres away, but her car is here. Her boyfriend is missing – is he a murderer or another victim? Where her car is, we have a disturbed grave. Were she and Kyle digging up the grave? If not, who? It just happens that her kayak buddy, one of the last people she was seen with, has no verifiable alibi and it also just happens that he looks to have a strong link with the person whose grave has been tampered with. We also have evidence that our murdered lassie might have had an issue with one of her work colleagues, at least in the mind of her boyfriend and we haven't even scraped the surface of that possibility yet.'

'You want me to get onto that, sir?'

'Yes, let's start with a background check. Travis Schultz just seems like a gentle giant to me but you never know. I've got a very strong feeling that this place is where we are going to find at least some of the answers. I also need you to start planning for the search team to go over every inch of this cemetery. If there's a hairclip or a cigarette butt on the ground or a flea with its hair out of place, I want forensics to look at it. And get someone to watch this place overnight.'

As Riley was taking this in and writing furiously in his notebook, Paul Smith's mobile phone rang. He started walking toward Riley's car. Darkness had now shrouded them and there was nothing more that could be done there tonight.

'Smith here.'

'Oh, hi Paul. Ray Dennis here. Listen, I've got some more results for you following the PM on Amy Richards.'

'Anything of interest, doc?'

'Well, yes, actually. I don't think Amy was drowned anywhere near where her body was found.'

Smith stopped at the car, listening intently before opening the door. 'Why so?'

'We ran some tests on the water in Amy's lungs and, well, it's nowhere near brackish enough to have been on the sea side of the barrages. In fact there's not enough salt for her to have been drowned in the Murray River anywhere this side of the Victorian border.'

'So, where should we be looking, doc?'

'Well, there are some bacteria in this water but it hasn't been treated with chlorine. So I think you are still looking at a natural watercourse but one that has a reasonable flow of freshwater through it.'

'I think I know where to start. Thanks, Ray, anything else?'

'Just a couple of things. We found what looks to be hessian or rope fibres in Amy's ears and nostrils. She wasn't bound with rope, so I'm guessing she was wrapped in hessian or something similar after death.'

'That makes sense.'

'Also, just to confirm she was probably murdered in a different location, we have compared the material under the skin on her knees and legs with what is on the ground around the ramp. No match. If you suspect an alternative location, we can probably verify with a high degree of confidence pretty quickly.'

'Doc, you are worth your weight in gold. I'll be in touch. Thanks again.'

Smith got into the car. Thankfully, Riley had already started the engine and the heater was starting to provide some relief from the cold.

'So, Riley, Currency Creek, the creek not the town, is down from the cemetery, right? Tell me about it.'

'Ok. There's a path that runs down the hill from the cemetery that takes you to a track that runs alongside the creek. It's a popular walking spot on weekends, maybe not so much this time of year. The catchment area takes in most of the hills around here and the water flows from there down into the Murray.'

'So the water is pretty fresh?'

'Yeah, this time of year it flows down a little waterfall over to our left, right through. It is still just a creek, but the water flows pretty well.'

'Ok, our search area has just got bigger.'

Smith repeated to Riley the information from his call with Ray Dennis.

'I think it's entirely likely Amy was drowned in that creek. We need to search the area thoroughly from the cemetery down to the creek and along it as far as we need to. Also, we need to collect soil and stone samples to see if we can match them to what Amy collected under her skin. I think we are starting to get somewhere.'

They drove back to the station and spent the next hour planning the search to commence at 7.00 sharp the following morning. As they walked out the front door of the station, Paul Smith turned to Riley.

'Good work today. How about joining me for a steak at the motel restaurant?'

'I'd be happy to. I just need to make a phone call. Can I meet you there in ten?'

'Fine, I'll just drop back to my room and give my lovely lady a call. I'll see you soon,' Smith replied as he headed across the road to the motel.

Riley waited until Smith crossed the road before selecting Sally's number and pressing the call button.

'Hey, Riley,' Sally answered. 'You still working?'

'Sort of, I'm just going to have a meal with the DI.'

'Oh, how's that going?'

'Yeah, he's actually pretty good. I'm learning a bit. Listen, I need to tell you something.'

'Sure, what's up?'

'Sal, I want you to stay away from Carl…. for a while, at least. He's implicated in this case I'm working on.'

'The murder? How?'

'I can't go into details, but he's not all that you think he is. Just promise me, ok?'

Sally was frustrated. 'No, it's not ok. You can't just ring me and tell me not to see Carl without explaining why? What is it he's done?'

'Well, maybe nothing. I don't have any proof that he's done anything wrong but he hasn't been entirely truthful with us either.'

'Ok, enough. He hasn't done anything wrong, but you want me to stay away from him. You will have to do better than that. Have a good night, I'll see you later.'

Riley heard the call disconnect and wondered if making the call was such a good idea. He would try to talk to her later in the night or in the morning.

He trudged across the road to the motel, wondering if this was such a good idea either.

Chapter 23
Wednesday 30 August 1854

The morning after Alexander's death, there was a heavy mist in the air, reducing visibility to just a few feet. George Johnston and Francis Cadell walked down the hill toward the wharf, engrossed in discussing the arrangements for the forthcoming journey to Swan Hill.

'You know, George, a fog like this is murderous on this river. I know there were plenty worse back in Scotland, but this river is too shallow in places and you need to have your wits about you and your eyes open.'

'Aye, and the increasing number of boats on the river in the hands of inexperienced captains leaves me uneasy too. 'Tis nae so bad if you can at least see them coming, but on a dreich morning such as this, accidents are sure to happen.'

'Let's hope this is the last fog for the year. 'Tis spring in a couple of days, so there cannae be many more in the offing.'

The pair reached the bottom of the hill and walked along the wharf toward the Lady Augusta.'

'That's odd,' said George, 'the gangplank's down.'

'Perhaps Alexander has already been out to check the cargo in the barge. We'll ken soon enough.'

Francis led the way up onto the deck and opened the door into the cabin. Alexander was not to be seen and Francis looked curiously at George.

George shrugged and said, 'I'm sure Alexander would nae have just left the boat unattended.' He felt the extinguished lamp. It was luke warm. He shook it.

'Empty. I suspect it only expired when the oil ran out. This is peculiar.'

Francis Cadell picked up a cork from the table, smelt it and handed it to George Johnston who lifted it to his nose.

'Rum. Alexander does nae drink rum, only ale.'

They walked out onto the deck. From the corner of his eye, George saw a bottle lying on the deck at the stern of the boat. He strode over and picked up the near empty bottle. He examined the contents.

'An opened bottle, left uncorked with an inch of rum in the bottle and no Alexander. This does nae bode well.'

'It does nae, George. Let's look around the wharf.'

They disembarked and walked along the wharf, Francis to the bow of the boat, George to the stern and the barge tied behind.'

After seeing nothing unusual at the bow, Francis walked back toward the barge where George was checking under the tarpaulins covering the loaded cargo.

As he came out from the last section, he heard Francis call.

'George, you'd best come here.'

As he stepped from the barge he saw Francis looking down into the water lapping at the stern of the Lady Augusta. He stood next to the river boat captain and looked down. He saw what Francis had seen, the body of Alexander Johnston lying across the rudder of the Lady Augusta, his face submerged in the murky water. George was stunned into silence until Francis spoke.

'I'll get some men to go out in a boat to bring him in, George.' He saw some of his crew now approaching the Lady Augusta, about to start the preparation for the upcoming journey. He beckoned to a burly man at the front of the group.

'Seamus, here. I have something I need you to do.'

The man approached and looked into the water where Francis was pointing. Seamus crossed himself.

'Holy Mother of Christ. Who is it?' George gave him a withering stare, before answering.

'Alexander Johnston. Now, will you give the man some dignity and get him out of there.'

In a gentler tone, Francis said, 'I understand it's a shock, Seamus. Can you get a couple of men and take a boat around to get him out? Then I imagine George will want you to take Alexander to Alfred Bates, the undertaker. Yes, George?'

George turned to Francis. 'Aye, yes, I suppose. But I should go and see Rubina.'

'I'm very sorry, Captain Johnston,' said Seamus before hurrying off to organise the recovery.

'George, let's go back on deck for a moment. I want to discuss something with you.' Before George could reply, Francis was walking toward the gangplank.

Once they were on deck, Francis picked the rum bottle from the deck, where George had laid it.

'George, it may be too soon to jump to conclusions, but I think that poor Alexander has been the victim of foul play. He's an experienced sailor. He's nae going to fall from a moored boat on a fine night. Then this,' he said, pointing at the bottle,' is nae Alexander's.'

'Then, whose?'

'As I said, we cannae say for certain, but Alexander has been seeing too much of that oaf, Tripp, of late and he is a heavy rum drinker. I dinnae trust the man and I think it would be prudent for the police to find out what he was doing last night.'

'Yes, I suppose. But there is no police trooper in the Goolwa. PT Brackenridge is based in Port Elliot.'

'I ken, but John Varcoe was a policeman before he became a publican. I'm sure he will start proceedings until Brackenridge gets here.'

'I need to tell Rubina, Francis. She must hear from me before she hears it through town gossip. Will you talk to Varcoe? I'll see you later, after I see Rubina and then Bates.'

George rushed away to the sound of oars splashing as the men rowed a small boat around to the stern of the Lady Augusta.

Before he walked to Alexander and Rubina's cottage, he called by his home and told Elizabeth what had happened. Elizabeth was, of course, shocked and distressed for her dear friend, Rubina. George did not need to ask her to accompany him and in just a few moments they were on their way to Newacott Place.

The fog had lifted and the winter sun had begun to warm the town, heralding an early start to spring. On reaching the door to the little cottage, George paused momentarily and looked at Elizabeth. She put her hand on his arm and squeezed gently. He gave the door a firm knock.

Rubina opened the door and smiled broadly.

'Elizabeth and George. How wonderful. I thought you were Alexander getting home, but for the life of me I dinnae ken why I expected him to knock on the door of his own house.'

As she spoke, she sensed the seriousness in the countenance of her visitors.

'My, whatever's wrong? Come in, come in.'

Elizabeth and George entered the living room. Donald came through from the kitchen behind.

George started, 'Rubina, Donald, you should sit down. I have some bad news.'

Elizabeth rushed to Rubina and wrapped her in her arms before helping her into a chair. Rubina looked with piteous eyes to Elizabeth while Donald stood frozen, staring at George.

'I'm afraid it's Alexander. He's had a terrible accident.'

'Is he……' Rubina pleaded.

'I'm sorry, my dear, yes. He fell over the back of the Lady Augusta.'

'Impossible. Alexander would not fall.' She broke into fits of sobs. Elizabeth handed her a handkerchief, which she put to her eyes.

'Ruby, 'tis too soon to say exactly what happened, but Francis and John Varcoe will start an investigation with suitable haste. Donald, are you alright, lad?'

Donald stood silent, rooted to the spot. George walked to him and the boy buried his face into his chest, still unspeaking.

An hour later, George left the cottage. He had told Rubina that he would make all the necessary arrangements for Alexander's burial. Elizabeth naturally stayed with her dear friend and Donald, consoling them as best as she was able.

George spent only the time with Alfred Bates that was necessary to ensure Alexander's proper burial. He gave a final message to the builder, carpenter and undertaker not to rob the body of its clothing or other personal items. George was only too aware of the practice of undertakers to profit from burials through thievery.

'I will know, Bates, and if I find that you have stolen from my cousin, I will see that you are brought to account,' he said with enough menace that the undertaker had no doubt that he meant every word.

George rushed to the Goolwa Hotel where he hoped he would find Francis Cadell and John Varcoe. He knew he should get back to Newacott Place as soon as he could to comfort his cousin's family, but he also felt that he had an obligation to make sure that if a crime had been committed, the guilty party faced the full force of the law.

Varcoe had served as a police constable in Adelaide before becoming a publican and still worked closely with PT Edward Brackenridge on matters in the Goolwa district if the Police Trooper was not around. Because he was based in Port Elliot, that seemed to be most of the time.

George had no misgivings about this. He knew John well and had confidence that he would enforce the law equal to any trooper in the colony. Nonetheless, George needed to know what was going on. He had not mentioned to Rubina the suspicion he and Francis had shared in relation to Alexander's death. Until he was sure that there had been foul play, he felt she would be less pained by the belief that Alexander had simply had a terrible accident.

'George, what are you doing here?' asked Francis. 'You should be taking care of your family.'

'And I will, Francis, but I need to ken that something is happening.'

John put his hand on George's shoulder.

'I know, George, and I would feel the same if it were my family affected. Cadell here has told me what you found this morning and your fear that Alexander's death was not an accident. From what I have heard, I share that belief.

'I have sent a dispatch to Brackenridge and expect to hear from him by return tomorrow. He may even come himself. In the meantime, I have selected the best of my men and Francis has added a couple of his to start a search for Joseph Tripp. Mind, now, we don't have proof he was involved, but we should talk to him to find his whereabouts last evening and so on.'

'Thank you, John. 'Tis as I had expected you might have arranged.'

'So, there's nought for you to do here. Go to your family and we will let you know if we find Tripp.'

'John's right, George. Please give our sympathy to Rubina and Donald. Let them ken we will help them in any way we can.'

Evening was approaching as George left the hotel. The day that had started with a cool fog and developed into a pleasant pre-Spring day was transforming to a cold night. The wind was shifting to the south and drizzle fell lightly from the grey clouds that now cloaked the sky. The bleak outlook matched George's mood.

It took only a couple of minutes to reach the cottage. He found Elizabeth pouring broth into bowls and Donald slicing a loaf of bread. Rubina sat in a chair in the corner, her eyes staring into her lap.

'Oh, George, I'm glad you're back. We are just about to share some dinner.' Elizabeth walked to him and gave him a light peck on his bearded cheek.

Rubina looked up at him, her eyes reddened.

'The arrangements are made, George?'

'What? Oh yes, the funeral. Aye, aye of course.' George cursed himself for confusing Rubina's question, thinking she was aware of the search for Tripp. 'Bates will build the coffin tomorrow and I expect we can arrange the burial for Friday or Saturday.'

'Thank you, George. You and Elizabeth have been so good. I'm nae sure I could have managed.' Her eyes returned to her lap.

Elizabeth grasped George's arm.

'I have suggested to Rubina that she and Donald should stay at our house tonight.'

Rubina lifted her head sharply.

'I'll nae leave this house. Alexander built this for us and I am nae about to leave it now … out of respect for my husband.'

'Very well, dear, I dinnae want to upset you. But what about poor Donald? He needs someone to comfort him too and you are in nae state to do that. Would you like us to take Donald home for the night.'

Donald looked to Elizabeth, nodding.

'Mam, why dinnae you come as well?'

'I have told you why, son, and I'll nae be changing my mind. I do think it is right that you go with Elizabeth, though. She and George will be better company than me tonight.'

Donald retreated into the shell that had trapped him since he had learned of his father's death. While he felt like he should stay to look after his mother, he had no idea how he could do it. Sullenly, he withdrew from the room and decided it was less confronting to let the others make decisions for him.

The four ate their broth quietly. After dinner, Elizabeth cleaned up while Donald gathered his night clothes and George stacked enough wood to keep the fire overnight. Before George, Elizabeth and Donald left, the family shared a prayer for Alexander's soul and said thanks to God for granting them a man who had loved and provided as best as a man could do.

After they left, Rubina sat in her chair and in the dim light of her oil lamp read and re-read the letters that Alexander had sent to her from the goldfields. The pain she felt would not pass, even for a moment, the memories of the life they had shared consuming her.

The promise of a better life in a new country, the opportunity given them in the goldfields then taken away and then Alexander's risky venture with the necklace had brought her to this miserable night. Perhaps God was telling her she had been too greedy, expecting too much from life, that she should have known her station and stayed in Cockenzie. She was reminded of a saying her mother had often used. *Whit's fur ye'll no go by ye!* – *What's meant to happen will happen.*

She would have to decide what would be best for Donald now.

Wearily, she took herself to bed, dreading the aloneness, even though as a sailor's wife, she had slept alone more often than with her husband.   Surprisingly, she fell to sleep almost immediately. Fatigue defeated her desire to adore and revere her lost love every moment for the rest of her life.

While sleep came quickly, it soon became fitful, Rubina's mind awakening and taunting her as she re-lived the events of the day. She tossed and turned as the wind rose outside and the shadows flickered with the half-moon light.

She could hear the creaking of the timbers and the rattling of the front gate. She wondered how she would manage the house on her own, to finish off the unfinished elements, now that Alexander was gone. Donald had not yet acquired the skills and she couldn't pester George, dear friend though he was.

She remembered that one of the unfinished jobs was the fitting of a bolt on the back door. Alexander had bought the bolt but had not had the chance to fit it. They had agreed that it would be a necessary security, with him travelling up and down the river so much and now that they had built one of the few permanent homes in the town, it may be perceived that they had other wealth.

She would ask George to have the bolt fitted in the morning. Suddenly feeling vulnerable, she got out of bed and walked to the kitchen. Her large carving knife sat on the bench under the window. She looked out the window then picked up the knife, returned to her room and placed it on the bedside table.

She pulled the covers around her, knowing that she would not sleep and she lay, watching the shadows dance across the front window.

By early morning, Rubina was drifting in and out of sleep. If anything, the wind had lifted and occasionally she was woken by the sound of a gust picking up and dropping a sheet of iron on the back shed. Each time, she'd reached for the knife and waited, hand outstretched, until she was satisfied that there was nothing amiss.

Just as she slipped into a deeper sleep, she was again woken by a crashing sound. She told herself that it was the same piece of iron shifting in the wind but reached toward the knife anyway. As she did, she heard another noise, a different noise. Startled, she opened her eyes wide, waiting for another sound. It came. The noise of the back door being opened, its bottom scraping on the wooden floorboards – another minor repair Alexander had meant to fix.

This time, she grabbed the knife firmly in her hand and slowly raised herself to sit at the side of the bed. She could not hear any sound other than the wind outside. She looked to the door of the bedroom and saw a shadow move across. This was different to the shadows before. The others had danced across the windows and walls, while this one moved slowly, almost gracefully.

She was sure someone was in her kitchen. She lifted the knife above her head and made her way slowly to the door of her room. Once there she could see into the kitchen, moonlight shining in through the window above her bench.

Rubina saw the movement near the back door and spun around.

'Who's there?' she called.

As she turned, she saw the silhouette of Joe Tripp filling the doorway. The man looked massive in the near darkness, much bigger than he did in the light of day. Rubina was stricken with fear and clenched the knife even tighter, her hand shaking uncontrollably.

'Now, no need for that missus. I dint come to harm you.'

'What do you want here, at this hour?'

'Is the boy here?' Tripp's eyes darted around the room.

'He's nae here. What do you want of me, Joseph Tripp? Have I nae suffered enough grief?'

'No, No, Rubina. I int here to harm you. Alexander was my best friend. I just want the necklace.'

Rubina was stunned and lacking any comprehension as to what the man was talking about. 'The necklace?'

Tripp's tone became cold and callous.

'You know what I mean, woman. Tell me where it is and I'll be on my way.'

Realisation hit Rubina as she connected the pieces of the puzzle. The necklace, the emerald necklace, Albert's Folly, Alexander's plan, the partnership with Joe Tripp.

Rubina now knew why Alexander had died. She now knew with certainty it wasn't an accident. She now knew that the man who had killed her husband, the man she had loved, was here in front of her, threatening her.

She ran at him, screaming, flailing the knife at him.

Joe Tripp had not anticipated a confrontation and if there had been one he would have reasonably expected that he would be the dominator. He lifted his hands in self-defence, enough to protect his head and body, but his forearms took a heavy blow from the knife and blood spurted freely from a nasty gash.

Before Rubina could strike again, he grabbed her wrists and held them high above her head, the knife well away from his body. He looked into her face, before twisting her around and bringing her arms down and across her body, so that she was helpless in his firm hold.

Rubina was not spent, however, and threw her head back sharply. Standing at normal height she would normally have pushed her head harmlessly into his chest, but Joe had his head down and she crashed heavily into his nose. She felt the sinew collapse under the force of her skull.

Tripp released his hold on her and lifted his hand to his profusely bleeding nose.

Rubina was not a tall woman, but she could not have been described as petite, either. Alongside Alexander she had looked squat and broad. She also had no fear at that moment. She wanted to kill the man that had hurt her more than anyone else in her life. She rushed at Tripp again shrieking a blood curdling scream.

This time Tripp was better prepared and instead of raising his hands in protection he skilfully grabbed Rubina's right wrist with both hands. He did not lift her hands above her head, but pushed the knife-wielding hand down before pulling it up again.

The blade entered her body on the left hand side below the rib cage and with massive strength Tripp pushed further upward looking directly into Rubina's widening eyes. As the knife entered her heart, her body slumped against him. He released his grip on her and allowed her to slide silently to the floor.

He stood against the wall, breathless. This was not the way he had meant for it to turn out. Now he had killed his only friend and that man's wife, all in the cause of greed. He looked down at Rubina, lifeless with blood pooling around her, soaking into her night gown and onto the floorboards.

Tripp stared the reality in the face. Alexander was dead. Rubina was dead. Nothing could change that now. What he could change was his future. He could still become a wealthy man, wealthier now that he did not have to share the spoils. He just needed to find the necklace.

It was near dawn. Lighting the oil lamp, Tripp started methodically, checking each drawer, shelf, tin and pan but found nothing. He worked his way through each of the rooms looking for secret hiding places. He felt around the chimney place inside and out. Still nothing.

His desperation grew as the time passed and the orderly search of each piece of furniture became a frenzied, turning, ripping, hurling of anything in the cottage. Clothes were strewn about on the floors of the bedrooms. Food, pots and pans littered the kitchen floor, much falling on and around Rubina and her congealing blood.

Eventually, Tripp saw that dawn was approaching and the question was now not so much about how he could find the fortune as how he would escape the crime scene before he was caught. He envisaged hanging from a noose and decided that he had to give up on the necklace, for now at least.

He stumbled out the back door of the house. The town was still quiet, although he could hear roosters crowing behind the stables at the Goolwa Hotel.

He crept silently down to the river where he had moored his fishing boat. The wind was still whistling up the hill, cold and unfriendly. At least, Tripp thought, he would be able to raise his sail and be away from the town well before the townspeople of the Goolwa were out.

He jumped aboard his boat and cast off. Within seconds he had the sail set and moved out to the middle of the river. *Should he head to the Murray mouth and the Coorong or up river?* He decided on the latter which would present more options for his escape.

He faced the boat to the north and allowed the sail the full face of the breeze, gathering speed as it passed the wharf and headed away from the town. He did not even glance back, knowing he would never return to the Goolwa. It caused him no sorrow. He had no love for the town or its people ... even Alexander, who was the closest he had to a friend, was there no more.

He kept a good pace for several miles, strenuously working the sail and the tiller, finally arriving at the mouth of the River Finniss. He was exhausted and decided to turn the boat into the tributary. It was narrower here and although boats used the waterway, there was far less traffic than on the Murray.

He took the fishing boat into the narrower stretches of the river, at last finding a section thick with reeds. He dropped the sail and used his oars to push the small craft into the reeds as far as he could. It was now light and he looked toward the shore and then out to the river. Satisfied that he could not be seen from either, he lay and slept. In a few hours, invigorated, he would head north by foot and try to disappear.

Chapter 24
Wednesday July 20 2016

Another morning, another clatter at my front door.

I am still in bed when the incessant knocking wakes me from a deep sleep. As I get to my feet, the explosion in my head reminds me how much scotch I drank last night.

As I stumble out of my bedroom, I see in the mirror the face of someone I don't know. My "fashionable" three day growth today couldn't look less flattering. My hair is unkempt and my eyes look like they will fall out of their sockets if I am shaken hard enough. The last thing I need right now is another visit from Riley and Smith.

I had drunk myself further into misery until somehow, sometime I dragged myself to bed. It had achieved one result however – I slept soundly without the sense of foreboding I had carried all day yesterday.

The knocking on the door is still driving knives into my brain as I open the door and see Sally standing there.

'How come you took so long to answer, Carl? Oh, shit, you look terrible.'

I can't even answer. I walk back inside and then find myself rushing to the toilet, where I drop to my knees and vomit violently into the pan.

It is five full minutes before I pull myself back onto my feet and splash my face with cold water. I don't look any better than when I woke, but at least I can open my eyes.

I throw on track pants and tee shirt before heading back to the living room. Sally is sitting on the sofa. She has made herself a coffee and I see another cup with strong black coffee on the table, two painkillers stationed right next to the cup.

'Thanks,' I mumble.

'So, what's going on, Carl? I have seen you bad before, but this is ....'

'I know, sorry,' I say. I pick up the pills and swallow them with the coffee. 'Have you spoken with Riley, then?'

'He rang me last night and said something about you not being truthful with us. Then he started again this morning but said he couldn't tell me any details because of the case he's working on. We had a terrible row and I told him I would find out for myself. Now, talk.'

I sigh and sit down next to her on the sofa.

'Riley's right. I haven't been entirely truthful with you. Mainly, I haven't told you the whole truth about me. Let me start by saying my name hasn't always been Carl Johnson.'

She sits in bewilderment as I unravel my past, from my life in Loxton and the Emma Satchin issue right through to my change of identity and relocation to Goolwa.

'But, 'she says, 'I don't understand why you had to conceal your real name. If you were exonerated, surely there's nothing to hide from.'

'I know it seems stupid now. But at the time, I felt like there were people in Loxton that would never trust me – somehow there would always be this doubt. It just seemed simpler to disappear and to start again somewhere else. A new name, new job, the works. Believe me, I didn't mean to deceive you and I certainly didn't want to. The truth is, I didn't know you would come along and then when you did, it was too hard to undo my lie. I'm so sorry.'

Sally looks at me and takes my hand.

'If that's the worst of it, I can get over that as long as you promise never to hold anything from me again.'

'Well, there's more.'

She releases my hand and looks into my eyes, fearing some dreadful revelation, like there could have been more incidents involving teenage students.

'It's about Amy.'

I tell her how the uncovering of my identity revealed the coincidence of my name, right down to my middle name, being linked with the tampered gravesite. The fact that I was Amy's coach and that her car was found at the cemetery only further implicates me.

'So, are the police treating you as a suspect?'

'Well, I'd say so. They've told me not to leave town and I have to admit, if I was them I'd suspect me on the basis of the evidence, even if it is all circumstantial.'

Sally frowns and puts her coffee cup on the table.

'Do you really think that wiping yourself out with booze is going to fix it?'

'Well, last night I did. Not the smartest plan, I guess.'

'So, what do you intend to do about it, just give up?' Her Irish temper was just starting to kick in.

'Sally, I don't know what to do. Riley is totally pissed with me. I was so scared I would lose you and on top of that I could foresee Goolwa turning on me just like Loxton did. Just like then, I feel so helpless.'

'Right,' she says. 'What you are going to do first is sober up. Second, understand that I am here for you. I love you and I'm in for the fight with you. Just don't bullshit me again, is that clear?'

'Yes,' I answer meekly. I feel pathetic.

'Next,' she continues, 'you are going to sit down with a clear head and work out how you can clear your name. Remember, they have to prove you are guilty, so if you're not that can't happen. What you can do is see how you can get them to the conclusion that it couldn't have been you that did it. For god's sake, Carl, you have to pull yourself together.'

I realise that, of course, she is right and it is only the fragility of my own personality that is keeping me in this hole. Sally's strength and encouragement gives me the resolve to shoo that black dog away and fight back to clear my name.

'I'm going to come back after work and by then I want you to have a plan of action, ok?'

I nod.

'I love you,' she says tenderly, taking my face in her hands, 'and I am here for you but you need to help yourself.' She kisses me on the lips. 'I have to go.'

I stand, feeling a lot stronger, although my head is still thumping.

'Drink lots of water,' she says as she heads toward the door.

'Sally' I call. She turns. 'I love you too and thanks for being you.'

She smiles as she goes out the door. I decide my first action is to take a shower, set cold as long as I can bear.

Chapter 25
Wednesday July 20 2016

It was 7.00 when the cavalcade of police vehicles arrived at the cemetery car park. Officers recruited from local stations, plus a few from Adelaide, unloaded their vehicles with wet weather gear, boots, rubber gloves and anything else deemed to be useful for a thorough search. A forensics team had set up a small tent to allow evidence to be properly sorted and catalogued.

Within a few minutes, a second group established itself in the car park at the start of the walking trail. Across the creek they could see the marquee of the reception centre.

Paul Smith undertook the briefing of the cemetery team while Riley O'Brien ran a parallel session with the second group.

The day was fine but cool. There was no wind to speak of and a mild frost had covered the ground with a thin white layer.

The cemetery team started from the gate, fanning out through the gravestones. The grid had been methodically laid out and they expected that every square metre of the cemetery would have been examined by day's end.

The group on the walking trail was much smaller and worked two abreast, due to the narrowness of the trail. A third member in Wellington boots worked along the water's edge and where necessary trudged through the water to collect items of interest.

Another small team was tasked with collecting soil and stone samples from various spots in the search zone. These were to be used by forensics to match with the material taken from under Amy's skin.

Following a suggestion from Ray Dennis earlier in the day, this team would also take water samples from the creek for comparison with the water in Amy's lungs.

Paul Smith and Riley had set up their headquarters under the shelter in the cemetery. Any items of particular interest were to be brought to the shelter before being dispatched to forensics.

It was midday when both teams returned for lunch, comprising an assortment of sandwiches and hot tea and coffee. The teams returned with masses of items picked up on the search, each accompanied with a tag describing where the item was found. So far, there had been nothing at all that appeared related to the case.

A few minutes later, an officer arrived with a car load of crates filled with items taken at the creek. The water and soil samples were unloaded first and delivered to the forensic team. Smith quickly reviewed the other items collected and again saw nothing of special interest.

The cemetery team had almost completed its search, so Smith pulled aside four members of the team and briefed them on the search that he wanted undertaken between the cemetery and the walking path. He called Riley across and asked him to join this group.

'We've not had any luck yet, but I think we can be confident that we haven't missed anything. If that's the case we have narrowed down where anything is likely to be, if that makes sense.'

'That assumes there's something to find, sir. How do we know if there is anything?'

'Experience has taught me that there is always likely to be something. We just need to persevere. Make sure the team stays alert, we can't be far off.'

Riley headed to the back of the cemetery with the team. The day was not warm, but the sun had been out all day and there was no wind. On another occasion, this would have been a pleasant afternoon pastime.

The team crossed the stile at the cemetery boundary and started walking along the narrow trail leading down the hill. Two of the team were spread out into the long grass on the side of the trail, prodding bushes and poking at the ground.

It took less than ten minutes for one of the team to call out.

'Over here, Riley. I've got a spade.'

Riley walked over to the man, slipped on rubber gloves and picked up the spade. In itself it was not of much interest. It looked just like any standard garden spade that could be bought at a hardware store. Riley knew, however, that this may have been the same spade used to dig Alexander Johnstone's grave site. Time and tests would determine whether it was a breakthrough or not.

'Good work. Ok, guys, keep working down the hill and keep your eyes peeled. Who knows what else could be here.'

Riley turned and headed up the hill with the spade. He arrived at the shelter and saw that Paul Smith had been watching him as he made his way through the cemetery. He was smiling for once.

'So, this looks promising?'

'Yes, let's hope so. We found it part way down the hill, so if it's the one used to dig the grave, he or she must have dropped it there for a reason. '

'Maybe. Perhaps he was chasing someone – Amy – or maybe he just dumped it there, but god knows why. My bet is on the first option. Riley, get that to forensics. I want to know as soon as possible if we have a fingerprint match to Amy or Carl Johnson, for starters.'

Paul Smith's mobile phone rang.

Leaving Smith, Riley took the spade to the forensics tent and was about to head back to the hillside search team when Smith motioned for Riley to wait. He was on the call for less than a minute.

'That was the coordinator of the team down below. They have found a body in a cave.'

'That would be the old copper mine. Who is it?'

'Well, I'm guessing that it's Kyle Hooper. Do you know where this mine is?'

Riley nodded.

'Let's go then.'

They walked through the cemetery across the stile and down the hill, passing the two search teams still combing the areas. They don't speak with them other than to encourage them to stay alert.

At the bottom of the hill, Riley led Smith left onto the walking trail. A few minutes later they found two of their searchers standing at the side of a narrow path winding up the hill.

Riley and Smith walked up the path and into the mine. A lamp had been placed inside providing sufficient illumination but that didn't stop Smith from hitting his head on the ceiling of the shaft.

'Shit!' he exclaimed before moving on.

At the end of the entry, the shaft turned right and became higher. At the end of the shaft, a woman in yellow overalls was bent over a prostrate body on the floor of the cave.

'Been dead for a few days, sir,' she declared, 'and I don't think we need to look far for the weapon.' She held up a plastic bag holding a fist sized rock covered in dried blood.

Smith looked at the face of the victim, handkerchief over his nose.

'Bit of a mess, Riley, but does that look like Kyle Hooper to you?'

Riley retched as he hesitantly bent over to look at the bloodied face. He stood and even in the artificial light he looked pale.

'Hard to say for certain, sir, but I'd say it's him.'

'Ok, let's get out of here. Thanks, Shelley. You'll take care of bringing him out when you wrap up here?'

'Yes, sir.'

'Thanks. Oh, can you get some fingerprints off him too? We want to compare them to some that could be on a spade we found a few minutes ago. Ok, Riley, let's go back up top. We have some not so pleasant work to do.'

The pair made their way up the hill. They stood alongside the same bench seat that Amy and Kyle had occupied when their cemetery visit had started so innocently. Of course, they were fully unaware of this as they briefed the senior officers coordinating the teams on the significant finds they had made. While they were standing, Riley spotted a glinted light over Paul Smith's shoulder.

'Sir, sorry to interrupt, but our sticky beak is back.'

Smith wheeled around and stared, before turning back. He surveyed the officers in their vicinity.

'Rachel,' he called out and as she looked back, 'we have an onlooker on the hill over there. Take someone with you and find out who it is if you can. Do you know how to get there?'

'Yes, sir, that's just off Frome Road out of Currency Creek.'

'Good, go. Call me when you have something.'

'Riley, we are going to see Vicky Hooper.'

They drove through Goolwa and out to Goolwa North, pulling up outside Vicky Hooper's house. As they stopped, Smith's phone rang. It was Rachel Cross who told him that the person who had been watching through binoculars had gone by the time they arrived. Smith hung up and told Riley they would follow up on that tomorrow.

Vicky opened the door at their knock and invited them inside.

'Inspector Smith, have you found Kyle? I still haven't heard from him and his phone is still off.' The lines on her face seemed more furrowed than when Smith had first met her.

'Mrs Hooper, I'm afraid I have some bad news for you. We have found another body and unfortunately, we think it might be Kyle.'

She sank heavily onto a chair and covered her face with her hands. Smith allowed her a minute before he continued.

'We located a body in an old mine off the walking path at Currency Creek. The death appears to have taken place around the same time that Amy Richards was drowned.'

'Oh, my god. That means it is Kyle, doesn't it?'

'We will need you to identify the body, when you're up to it, but yes, we believe it's Kyle. It's highly likely that both he and Amy were killed on the same night.'

'But Amy was drowned near the barrages, wasn't she?'

'We no longer think that. It's more likely she was drowned in Currency Creek.'

'Why? They are just kids. They wouldn't hurt anyone. Why?'

'That's what we are trying to find out, Mrs Hooper. Would you like Sergeant O'Brien to fix you a tea or coffee?'

'No. no. Thank you.'

'Mrs Hooper, Vicky, can I just ask a couple of questions that might help our investigations.'

'Yes, of course,' she whispered, holding her handkerchief to her face. 'Forgive me, Chief Inspector. I feared the worst, of course, but it's still come as such a shock.'

'I'm sorry we need to do this at this time. We will try to be as quick as we can. Both Kyle and Amy were friends with Travis Schultz, I believe?'

Vicky looked up at the policeman and without tone, she responded, 'Well, I think Kyle more than Amy, although I know Kyle wasn't that happy that Amy and Travis worked together.'

'Why, if Kyle and Travis were friends?'

'They were friends, Mr Smith, a little while ago but they sort of fell out a few months ago.'

'Do you know why?'

'At school, Kyle was like Travis's protector. Trav was bullied a lot because he's, you know, a bit different. Anyway, there was a party they both went to in Strath and they ended up getting into a bit of a fight. The police got called to break it up.'

'Yes, we've read the report on that. But I understand no-one got hurt and they all went their own ways.'

The pain of the questioning showed in Vicky's face but she summoned all the strength she could. She took the handkerchief away from her face and answered very deliberately,

'That's true, but before the police arrived, Travis had got into a punch-up with Amy's brother, Brock. Kyle was busy with one of Brock's friends. Apparently at some point, Travis pulled out a knife and threatened to castrate Brock. Kyle didn't even know Travis had the knife, but he was able to talk him into handing the knife to him. Brock wasn't any too happy and called Travis a 'retard' and told him and Kyle he was going to get even with them. So with that Travis and Brock started the fisticuffs again. That's when the police arrived and broke it up.'

'What happened to the knife?'

'Kyle threw it into the bushes when the police came. After that day, he started steering clear of Travis. I think he felt he didn't know what he was capable of. What's all this got to do with what's happened?'

'Maybe nothing, but we need to explore every avenue of enquiry. Now, would you like for me to arrange someone to be with you?'

Vicky lowered her head and lifted her handkerchief back to her face.

'No, Mr Smith. It's always just been Kyle and me. I'll be alright.'

'Ok, we will see ourselves out. I'll contact you again tomorrow to arrange for someone to pick you up and take you down to formally identify Kyle. Please feel free to bring someone with you if you'd like.'

'Thank you,' Vicky said as she looked away and closed herself into her own world.

As they left, they heard her sobbing uncontrollably.

'Riley, can you arrange for Rachel to drop in on her tomorrow morning? I think she's going to need some support, even if she's not asking for it.'

They got back into the car.

'Ok, can we go to the Richards' house now, please, Riley. I want to talk to Brock.'

Just a couple of minutes later, they were at the front door of the house. Karen Richards opened the door, the trauma of the last three days clearly evident in her face. She was in the middle of reluctantly throwing together an evening meal for the family.

'Hello, Mrs Richards. Is Michael at home?'

She called Michael and he came through into the living room just a few seconds later.

'Mr Smith, Riley. Do you have some news?'

Smith responded, 'We just wanted to let you know that we have learnt a little more about Amy's death. We now don't believe she was killed at the boat ramp.'

The air in the room was thick with tension, no doubt the consequence of Smith's last interviews at the house.

Smith continued, 'We now believe she was drowned in Currency Creek.'

'What makes you think that?' Michael Richards asked.

'Well, several factors point to it, including the fact that we found Amy's car in the car park at the cemetery. I should also tell you that we believe we have found Kyle Hooper as well.'

'So, what's he had to say?'

'Not much, unfortunately. You see it looks like he was murdered as well.'

Smith watched Michael's face for any change of expression. He saw genuine shock.

Karen let out a gasp.

'We believe that Amy and Kyle went to the cemetery, perhaps for some alone time, when they interrupted someone, who we think may be responsible for their death.'

'Who?'

'Well,' Smith said, 'there are several possibilities that we are looking into, but right now, I want to talk with Brock, if he's at home.'

'You can't think Brock has anything to do with this?' Karen asked defiantly.

Michael Richards showed his angst, doubts storming his mind. He silently led the policemen to the back shed, where Brock was drinking a beer and polishing his car.

'Ah, Brock,' Smith said, 'Can we have a word?'

Brock looked both the policemen up and down before replying.

'Told you all that I know, didn't I?'

'Kyle's dead,' Michael blurted.

Brock put his beer down on a table. 'Fuck.'

'I want to ask about a little altercation you had with Kyle a few months ago, in Strathalbyn,' Smith said.

'That was nothing. Anyway, it was me and Travis dickhead rather than me and Kyle.'

'Yes, we have heard the story from Kyle's mother. Correct me if you disagree, but I understand that Travis produced a knife which Kyle was able to talk him into handing over. Then you told them both you would get even with them.'

'Yeah, well, that's right, but you know, that was just in the heat of the moment. Anyway, Travis had the knife, why aren't you talking with him?'

'Oh, we will be, Brock. But, you see, now that Kyle is dead, we have more reason to be interested in your activities too.'

'Well, you can fuck off. It's my sister that's been killed here. You've got no right to be coming around accusing me of shit.'

'Brock is right, Smith,' Michael erupted, 'I want you to leave now and let this family have some peace.'

'Thank you, Mr Richards. We may need to talk to you both later, but that's it for now. However, we have found a piece of evidence that we think might be useful, so we'd like you both to come into the station for fingerprinting tomorrow morning. It may help us eliminate you as potential suspects.'

Riley sensed the jaws of both the Richards men drop in disbelief as he walked away.

When they are back in the car, Smith rubbed his eyes.

'Well, that was intense. Certainly neither of them had any time for Kyle but I don't know that either was capable of killing Amy. Tomorrow morning, let's go see Travis and maybe bring him in for fingerprinting. Can you chase up the background check on Travis tonight? I'd like to read up a bit on him before we talk to him.'

Chapter 26
Thursday 31 August 1854

Elizabeth Johnston was anxious to get going. She had felt uncomfortable leaving Rubina on her own, but she also respected her right to be alone if that was what she wanted. She wondered what she would do if the roles had been reversed.

She imagined that if George had met his death, she would feel like her life was over as well. She knew, or at least she thought she knew, how Rubina must be feeling. If it were George, not Alexander, Elizabeth knew she would just want to hide herself away. She would want no sympathy, no mixing in society. It would all mean nothing if George was not part of it.

Although Elizabeth was several years younger than Rubina, the two had become inseparable since being reunited at the Goolwa. Their shared faith had guided them, had given them strength when their men were at peril, at sea, on the river or in the goldfield. Above all, faith had given them the strength to persist in this country which was more uncivilised, more brutal and less forgiving than their native Scotland.

She had cooked porridge for George and Donald and was waiting for them to come to the table. George arrived first, dressed, as always, ready for business. Her pride in him grew every day and she admired how she, and Rubina, would be able to rely on him to ensure that Alexander's burial was properly and respectfully conducted.

'Good morning, my love,' she greeted him. 'Is Donald about?'

'Aye, he'll be with us shortly. I think he is finding this all very difficult, but he's a fine lad.'

'He is, George. But you realise, dinnae you, that you have a responsibility now that he has nae father.'

'I do and I am glad you see it, Elizabeth, although I should never have doubted your providence. He is a quiet boy and has nae yet shown his true feelings, but I fear he has a rocky path to traverse in the coming years. Still, 'tis good that Alexander has accumulated some funds that will help provide for the boy.'

'Indeed, but was he nae to go to Melbourne to withdraw them? You will need to do that for Rubina now, George.'

'Aye, all in due course. The will must be read first. We will ensure they are looked after until that can be settled. In any event, we have postponed our departure to Swan Hill until after Alexander's funeral, so there need nae be haste. Now, will you be calling on Rubina this morning?'

'Of course, George. I will leave presently, as soon as you have gone. What about Donald? Shall I take him?'

George closed the door, lest Donald overhear.

'I think nae. I have spoken with Thomas Goode. I think it best the boy be occupied so as nae to become too encumbered by grief. Goode is happy for Donald to work at his store and he has undertaken to make sure he is well looked after.'

'I suppose 'tis for the best. He must learn to become a man more quickly now. Very well, I shall go on my own. I have baked some bread. I'll stop and have breakfast with Ruby and perhaps bring her here for a while, if she is willing.'

George kissed his wife on the cheek and left the room to talk with Donald. He found him sitting on a chair facing the fields at the back of the house.

'Donald, how are you, laddie?'

'Fine, sir. That is, I'm nae sure.'

'It's alright, Donald. You can say as you feel with Elizabeth and I. We both understand that this is very difficult. You dinnae ken how you should be feeling and you cannae control how you do. You ken your mother is suffering, but you can do nought for her.'

'Yes, sir, I dinnae ken what to do.'

'You must do simply what you think you should do. You cannae always do as everyone else wants, so you have to do what you feel is right. You may nae get it right all the time, even with your mother, but you must be satisfied with yourself. One thing you can do is to realise that you are now the man in your household.'

'Yes, sir.'

'So with that responsibility, you should be treated as a man as well. From now, you should call me George instead of sir. Is that alright?'

'If you think that's best ….. George.'

'Good lad. Now, today,' George said softly, 'I think you should go to work with Mister Goode. He is waiting for you. Dinnae worry about your mother. Elizabeth will make sure that she is well cared for. Now, if you get yourself ready forthwith, I'll walk you to the store.'

Elizabeth was taking the bread from her oven as George and Donald left. While she knew that George was right, she also knew that Rubina would be pining to see Donald. She would cross that bridge when she came to it. Her biggest task would be to comfort Rubina in her grief.

She hastily wrapped the warm bread in a cloth and put it into a basket. She quickly checked her hair in the mirror in the parlour, tucking an errant strand behind her ear. As she closed the door behind her, she looked to the sky and was grateful that the wind that had gusted all night had not brought rain with it. Thankfully, the roadway was clear of puddles and her boots would stay free of the mud today.

She hurried onto Cadell Street and almost immediately ran into Mary Varcoe.

'Oh, Elizabeth, good morning. What a terrible misfortune for Alexander. Are you to see Rubina now?'

'Hello, Mary. Yes, I expect she is waiting.'

'Well, don't let me hold you, my dear. And give her our love.'

'Thank you, Mary. I will.'

She was relieved that she had not been unduly delayed by Mary Varcoe, but she had no sooner turned the corner when she was confronted by Agnes McNaught. Known as the biggest gossip in the Goolwa, as well as the most spiteful, Agnes was not to be deterred, immediately grasping Elizabeth at the forearms, so that she could not continue. Elizabeth released an exasperated sigh.

'Ooh, Elizabeth, I am so glad to see you. 'Tis true then, about Alexander?'

'I'm afraid so. I really must go to Rubina. She is waiting for me.'

'I shall come with you, dear. You will need help. That poor woman will be too much for you to handle on your own.'

'I really don't think she will ....'

'Nonsense, Elizabeth, she does nae know what she needs. That poor woman, come let us go.'

Agnes turned and strode purposefully toward Newacott Place. Elizabeth hurried after her, desperately searching for a way that she could convince Agnes to stay away.

Despite Elizabeth's entreaties, Agnes continued marching forward, unrelentingly toward the cottage. Elizabeth was only just keeping pace with her and by the time she had got near the front door, Agnes was still half a stride ahead and had started rapping with determined knuckles.

When there was no response, Agnes called in a loud, shrill voice. 'Rubina, 'tis Agnes and Elizabeth. We have come to keep company.'

There was still no sound from inside the house. Elizabeth went to the front window of the sitting room and peered through. It was dark inside and she was unable to see any movement. Meanwhile, Agnes, a large framed woman, tried to open the front door, rattling it with such force that it appeared for a moment that she would shake it off its hinges. The door held firm.

Elizabeth went to the bedroom window and was able to see that Rubina's bed was unmade. She turned to Agnes, only to see that she was no longer there.

She realised that Agnes must have walked around to the rear of the cottage to try the back door. Before Elizabeth had rounded the corner of the house, she heard the most terrifying, piercing scream she had ever experienced. She dropped her basket and lifted her dress above her knees running as fast as she was able to the rear of the house.

She reached the back door, but was unable to enter. Agnes had fallen to her knees and was gasping, hand over mouth. Elizabeth smelt a strong metallic odour and for a moment wondered where it was coming from. She leaned past Agnes and peered into the kitchen. The sight horrified her. There she saw Rubina, lying on the floor surrounded by thick crimson blood, her nightgown stained in the same colour. Rubina's eyes were transfixed, staring blankly at the ceiling. From her abdomen stuck only the shaft of what Elizabeth knew was Rubina's carving knife.

Elizabeth screamed and fell to the ground alongside Agnes. It was she, however, that regained her composure first. She lifted herself to her knees, then her feet and she again peered into the room.

Household goods were strewn all about the place – plates, pots, pans, almost every item that Rubina owned. Furniture was tipped over and there was barely room to step.

Elizabeth turned her attention to Agnes and helped the big woman to her feet. She walked her to a bench near the back shed and sat her there.

'Stay here, Agnes. I will get help.'

Agnes sat speechless, still gasping. Elizabeth left her and hurried back toward Cadell Street. There she encountered John Varcoe, talking with Thomas Goode, the storekeeper.

'Mister Varcoe, you must come. Rubina Johnston has been murdered, in her own home.'

Varcoe looked at her, then at Goode.

'Thomas, go find George and tell him to come to the house. But dinnae say anything to Donald.'

Goode rushed away, toward the wharf, while John Varcoe held Elizabeth by the elbow and they hurried back to Newacott Place. When they got there, Agnes was wailing, still sitting on the bench perspiring profusely, although the day was still cool.

'Oh, Mister Varcoe, 'tis dreadful. I was first to find her, she was ...'

'Very well, Agnes, I will get your statement soon. You just rest there while I look around inside.'

Varcoe entered the back door and tried best he could to avoid stepping in the pooled blood. He looked briefly at Rubina before moving through to her bedroom, followed by the sitting room and finally Donald's bedroom next to the kitchen. Apart from the blood that desecrated the kitchen and of course Rubina's body, each room was the same. No item was in its intended place. It was clear that the house had been thoroughly ransacked.

John Varcoe left the house, walking to where Elizabeth was comforting Agnes McNaught. Elizabeth herself was distraught, but nonetheless sought to quieten the older woman who was now rocking back and forth on the bench, continually chanting, "that poor woman, that poor woman."

Her ample breasts were heaving and it was all Elizabeth could do to stop her from dragging her down on top of her.

Varcoe addressed her sternly.

'Come now, Agnes, leave Elizabeth be. Rubina was her cousin by marriage after all.'

'I'll not be spoken to like that, Mister Varcoe. I was the one who found the bloodshed. Have you no sympathy for a poor woman who has been shocked out of her wits?'

At that moment, George Johnston rounded the corner and immediately took Elizabeth in his arms. Varcoe was relieved that he could get away from Agnes's tirade and instead focus on the important matters at hand.

'Oh, George, it's just awful but I'm alright, really I am,' said Elizabeth. 'Why dinnae you take a look with John, while I get Agnes home? Come now Agnes, let's go and have a cup of tea to calm our nerves.'

'I must stay. Mister Varcoe will want to interview me, I am sure.'

'Agnes, Elizabeth is right. Go home and rest and please, discuss this with no-one. I will come to talk with you this evening, but first I must send for the troopers and help George with Rubina. And let's not forget Donald.' Varcoe did not wait for a reply but took George by the arm and started toward the door of the house.

Reluctantly, Agnes heaved herself from the bench and allowed Elizabeth to guide her back to Cadell Street, again chanting her pity for poor Rubina.

George stood looking in horror at the carnage inside the house, his eyes widened at the sight of Rubina. He looked around the room at the disorder, frowning in bewilderment.

'I dinnae understand, John, who would do such a thing? Murder a defenceless woman and then this.' He swept his arm around.

'George, this confirms our suspicion that Alexander's death was not accidental, don't you agree? Clearly, whoever killed Rubina was looking for something, something I'll wager he couldn't get from Alexander. It looks like Rubina could not or would not give it either, so after he killed her, he had to find it himself. The other rooms are the same as this.'

'Tripp?'

'Most probably, I think. When Francis raised it with me, I recalled that Tripp had purchased a bottle of rum the night that

Alexander died, the same as the bottle found on the Lady Augusta. What I don't have an answer to is what he was trying to get from Alexander and Rubina, if that was the reason for killing them.'

'I dinnae ken if I can help much with that, John. I ken Alexander had funds tied up in Melbourne. He had a good find in the goldfields. He was to have gone to Melbourne from our next voyage to transfer the money back here so he could invest in our partnership, but for the life of me I dinnae ken what the nature of the investment was. I'm sure Rubina would have ken but that's of little comfort now.'

'Do you think Donald will know?'

'Unlikely, but I shall ask him in due course. Has there been any trace of Tripp?'

'None, of him or his boat. I am sure Brackenridge will organise a more thorough search, especially now.'

'Well, I must find Donald. The poor boy has now lost his father and his mother in the space of two days. I shall find it difficult to tell him what has happened today. He will take it hard.'

'He is very fortunate to have you and Elizabeth, George. Don't you worry about this. I will arrange for Rubina to be taken to Alfred Bates quietly and without attention. I will also post men here to keep out any would be looters until Brackenridge arrives.'

The two men parted, George for the first time in his life feeling like he was unable to control what was happening to the people he loved. With a heavy heart, he made his way to Thomas Goode's store to find Donald.

Chapter 27
Wednesday July 20 2016

After I have my shower, I dress into comfortable jeans and a sweater, put on a pair of sneakers and take a brisk walk for ten minutes. The air is crisp and cool and by the time I am home, I feel that my brain will be able to function with some degree of clarity.

I grab a two litre bottle of water from the fridge, take a couple of large swigs and set it on the kitchen table. I throw a couple of pieces of bread in the toaster and sit down to make a list of the contacts for the jobs I am going to cancel.

By the time I have spread my toast and eaten it, I have finished my calls. I am clear of all commitments until Sally gets back later in the day.

Now for the hard part – what am I going to do about the predicament I am now in? I am trying to stay in a positive frame of mind and reflect on Sally's advice. I need to work on a solution that proves that I couldn't have killed Amy.

I decide to start by reviewing the evidence that points to me as a suspect. Firstly, I knew Amy well and had seen her just hours before she was killed. In fact, it is likely I was one of the last people to have seen her alive.

Next, Amy's car was found at the cemetery, where a grave has been disturbed and it appears the grave belonged to a long lost relative of mine. *Maybe I need to check that is right.* I mentally note that while Amy's car is there, her body was actually found over ten kilometres away. *How could that be?*

I then think about other things that might incriminate me and decide the only thing is that I don't have a provable alibi for the timeframe in which Amy was killed. An added complication is that I have been living under a false identity, but that can hardly be construed as evidence.

As I contemplate the evidence of my guilt, I realise that the connections are, at best circumstantial. I am starting to feel more comfortable that I can't be falsely accused. But I still have the nagging memory of Loxton and how truth does not necessarily equate to justice.

This thought is enough of a spur for me to continue my own rationalisation. I turn my mind to one question; *if it isn't sensible for me to be considered the killer, who else could be considered?* I know I don't have access to the same evidence that the police do, but I need to stretch my mind.

Kyle immediately comes to mind. He had seen her after me, I think. *But why?* Maybe he was unhappy about her pregnancy and she had put pressure on him. After all, he is still missing. *That seems to make some sense.*

If Kyle could have been angry about the pregnancy, isn't it possible that Amy's father Michael could have been too? She was very worried about his reaction and she had intended to tell him soon after I last saw her. *But surely not?* Being an angry and disappointed father is a long way from killing your own child.

I am seeing the futility of this rationale. I can't prove or disprove either scenario and I frankly have trouble believing either could be real.

I leave the table and go to the refrigerator. I need to clear my mind of my current thought patterns and come back at the problem from a different perspective. I grab a Pepsi can and pull the ring tab. The cold fizz of the sweet liquid seems to send a message to my brain to refocus.

As I walk back to the table, I start to ponder. Amy's body was found by the boat ramp. Her car is at the cemetery – *why?* There is a one hundred and fifty year old grave that has been disturbed there - *why? Is there a connection between the car and the grave – there must be, but why was Amy's body so far away?* I conclude that either she was killed at the cemetery and her body moved or she was killed at the boat ramp and her car dumped at the cemetery. Either way, the coincidence of the disturbed grave is too much to ignore.

Surely, then, that has to be my starting point. *Why was Alexander Johnston's grave tampered with?*

Who was he? Is it strange that his wife died so closely after him? Is there any connection to George Bain Johnston, the famous and well respected ship builder and river captain?

I think I know what I need to do. I need to understand why someone wanted to get to Alexander Johnston, who also happens to be a significant link to my implication.

I run to grab the laptop out of my bedroom. I really feel like I am on a mission and can avenge all the past wrongs thrown at me by other people's mis-judgements. I must have knocked it onto the floor in my drunken stupor last night and as I pick it up, I check myself. Stop playing the victim, I think. *What you do now, you do because it's in your control.*

Returning to the kitchen table, I hit the resume key, only to find out the machine is as dead as a door nail. *Damn, what did I do last night?* I retrieve the power cord from the bedroom and plug it into a socket in the kitchen. It takes a minute for the laptop to boot up and I head straight to Google.

In the search panel I type Alexander Johnston. I find references to a film director, a British colonial official and numerous connections available through LinkedIn but not the person I'm looking for. I refine the search adding Australia and then Goolwa, but to no avail.

The closest I get is a reference to George Bain Johnston. Maybe Alexander Johnston of Goolwa just wasn't important enough to warrant a Wikipedia reference. I do the same with Rubina and then with their son Donald Johnston. Again, my search is fruitless. I decide to turn back to George.

At last, I have a bit of detail around one of my namesakes buried at the Currency Creek Cemetery. As I look at George's photo, I smile as I see a mild family resemblance. He has curly dark hair similar to mine except his has a much bigger kick across the forehead. Unlike mine, his beard has several months' growth, not three days. I try to imagine him without the beard and I swear I can almost see my grandfather.

As I read, I learn with growing respect, the contribution that my forebear (well, maybe distant forebear) made to exploring the River Murray and developing trade along the river through building paddle steamers. I learn that he was strongly associated with the famous Francis Cadell, also a respected River Murray pioneer. With mild pride, I see that he was reputed to have saved at least fourteen people from drowning.

He also bought several plots of land in an area of Goolwa now largely heritage protected and known as Little Scotland. On these plots, he built cottages for the families of the men that worked for him. I wondered if one of these might have been Alexander and Rubina Johnston's house.

By the time I finish reading the several references to George Johnston, I feel like I have been thumbing through the family albums. Regrettably, I see no reference at all to Alexander.

It is now one in the afternoon and I wonder where the time has gone. I realise I haven't eaten since my toast early in the day, so I get up and stretch before going into the kitchen to make a cheese and tomato sandwich.

Strangely, I don't yet feel frustrated by my inability to learn more about Alexander Johnston. Somehow, George's story has served to remind me that these were very different times, when things were tougher, needs were fewer but people were more courageous and adventurous.

As I eat, I contemplate what my next step could be. In thinking about simpler times, I suddenly realise that I have relied on Google and Wikipedia to give me answers to my questions. I guess I'm not alone in that, but I had, of course, overlooked the only option that was available in simpler times – the printed word.

I am kicking myself that, here I am, my girlfriend a librarian, and I have overlooked probably the best resource I could have available to me – the library. Sally had often talked to me about the depth of information held in the Alexandrina Library, stationed in the main street of town. She had raved to me about the files maintained in the 'History Room'. I had listened to her talk about it with mild amusement, wondering when or why anyone would have a need to delve into dusty old books and records from a time no longer relevant. I feel mildly embarrassed that it had taken something like my current situation to make me appreciate it.

I suddenly feel weary. Sitting at a computer screen all day after a night on the booze is something I am not accustomed to.

Looking at my watch, I see that it is two thirty, probably two and a half hours before Sally will drop by to check on my progress. I am pleased with where I have got to, but I need to re-invigorate myself so that I can explain my theory lucidly and coherently to her. Then I need her help tomorrow to do research at the library.

I decide to go for a paddle and load the kayak onto the roof racks. By three o'clock, I am putting the boat into the water near the barrages.

I head toward town. The water is flat and I am paddling into a mild head wind – perfect conditions. I focus on technique and find that it is an effective means of clearing my mind of the concentration I have put in over the past few hours.

As I pass the wharf and head under the Hindmarsh Island Bridge, I realise that I am starting to push myself harder, my grab on the water with each stroke driving me forward in a steady rhythm. I allow myself thirty seconds of maximum effort, before stopping short of breath on the other side of the bridge.

I turn the kayak and rest for a couple of minutes. Physically, I am feeling good, the cobwebs well and truly cleaned out. As I paddle steadily back, I resist the temptation to push myself again. Instead, I start putting together my rationale for focussing on the disturbance of Alexander's grave and hypothesising on what that could possibly have to do with Amy. There are so many unknowns, but I remain convinced that finding the truth about the grave will lead me to Amy's killer.

I pull up the car at my house and am surprised to see Sally's car there already. Glancing at my watch I see that it is now just after four. She must have finished work early. She is inside, sitting at the kitchen table with a coffee.

'Want one?' she says.

'Love one,' I say as I peck her on the cheek.

She walks to the kettle.

'You know I'd think you've been out all day if it wasn't for the laptop on the table. How has your day been?'

'Productive, thanks to you. I'll fill you in on what I have been up to.'

She puts my coffee mug on the table and pulls up a chair next to me as I open up the laptop.

I explain to her how I have exonerated myself, how I have found it difficult to come up with a plausible suspect with the information available and how the tampered grave is the link that seems to tie everything together.

Sally has said nothing while I have been talking.

'So, what do you think?'

'The thing I am most happy about, Carl, is that you have finally got some balls. That is the biggest step. What are you going to do next?'

'Well,' I say, 'I have started already.' I show her what I have learnt about George Bain Johnston, but also the lack of any reference to Alexander. 'So, I was wondering if you could help me at the library tomorrow. Your History Room might have something that Google doesn't.'

She laughs. 'I can guarantee it. Luckily, I have tomorrow off, so I am all yours, sweet. What we should do though is get Sue to help us.'

'Sue?'

'Sue Geisen. She's a volunteer in the History Room. We have a few and they know their way around those old documents like you wouldn't believe.'

'What would I do without you, Sally?'

'Ok, man up, sunshine, we have a big day tomorrow. Now, I have a question for you.'

I look at her, puzzled.

'Are you going to keep calling yourself Carl Johnson or will it be Callum Johnston?'

'Oh, I reckon Carl. That's what everyone here knows me as. Callum Johnston reminds me of a different time when I wasn't happy with the world and the world wasn't happy with me.'

'Bring out the violins,' Sally sings. 'Look, I really don't care, but I don't want you to be afraid of your past. Promise me that once this is all over, you will reconsider. Whether you are Carl or Callum, I will still love you – if you do decide on Callum, I just need to decide if I'll call you Callum, or maybe Cal.'

She laughs again as I wrestle her off the chair onto the floor. We lay together in an embrace and suddenly, I actually feel happy.

Chapter 28
Wednesday July 20 2016

It had been dark for a couple of hours as Paul Smith gathered the investigative team around him. He had ordered in pizza and several bottles of soft drink.

He was surrounded by Riley O'Brien, Rachel Cross and Shelley Harrison. Phil Reid was at the front desk entering some routine paperwork into the computer.

'Why don't you join us in here for some pizza, Reid,' Smith called through the door. The lanky form ambled through the doorway and headed straight to the pizza cartons folded open on a table in the middle of the room.

'Hope none of you mind anchovies,' Smith said, 'a pizza's not right without them, I reckon.' He seemed remarkably upbeat.

'Ok, guys, we made some progress today. Not good for poor Kyle Hooper, but at least we are starting to get some leads. I'm assuming you're all across the latest?'

They all nodded, including Phil, who Riley had earlier pulled into a preliminary briefing with Rachel.

'Good. Ok, Shelley, anything new from your team.'

'Well, sir, most of the stuff picked up today is rubbish, so nothing new from that today. That leaves us with the spade, the rock we think was used to kill Kyle and the water, stone and soil samples.

'We won't have anything back on the samples until tomorrow. They have gone down to Adelaide to match with the control materials. On the spade, I'm afraid the prints we've been able to lift don't match Amy or Kyle and, for that matter, not Carl

Johnson either. So, unless they were wearing gloves, it wasn't handled by any of those three.'

'But you still have viable prints, right?'

'Oh, yes, sir, we sure do. From the size I'd say they are male, and probably a big bloke, but I can't tell you more than that.'

'What about Kyle? He's on his way down to Ray Dennis?'

'Yes, sir, but with their workload, he's not going to get to him until around midday tomorrow. I'm not sure what we will learn from his PM anyway, it's pretty obvious how and when he died – at least, it's highly probable.'

'Yeah, sure. Riley, tell me about Travis Schultz.'

Riley put down the pizza slice he had just picked up, wiped his hands on a piece of paper towel and flicked open his notebook.

'Well, most of this we already know. He wasn't a very good student and left school early. He's worked at the supermarket ever since. Both the school and Kym Collins at the supermarket said he's a good kid, maybe a bit slow. He does have a bit of a temper apparently, he's put up with a fair amount of teasing and bullying over the years. Sometimes he snaps and cuts loose. Nothing too serious, other than the incident with the knife earlier this year.'

'Which we can't ignore,' Smith piped in.

'Right. Anyway, he has been friends with Kyle Hooper for a long time, certainly from school, but Kym Collins also said he could see there has been a problem recently. Again probably due to the knife incident.

'Amy's been a pal with him of late but Collins didn't think there was anything odd about that. She was apparently a bit of a lost soul herself so it's not unnatural they'd get on.

'What was interesting was what came out of my check of Travis's driver's licence check. Not a single demerit point, so no problem there.'

'So, why interesting?' asked Rachel.

'Well, guess where he lives?'

Blank faces looked back at Riley.

'He lives in a farmlet, just off Frome Road, on the other side of the creek from the cemetery.'

'Ah, he may be our snoop,' said Smith.

'That's what I thought, too.'

'Ok, Riley, as planned you and I will go visit Travis tomorrow and bring him back for fingerprinting. Now, Phil, we have asked Michael and Brock Richards to also come to get their fingers inked tomorrow. Let's all be alert if they are here at the same time.

'Rachel, your turn. Have you been able to talk with anyone from the party about Brock's movements on Saturday night?'

'Well, sir, I did manage to talk with Todd Williams, the lad whose place the party was at. He was a right prat too. Anyway, according to him, he couldn't remember what time Brock left the party, but he thought he was pretty drunk. I've been able to track down three other people who were there until late, a Caitlin Jessop, Tom Sprigg and Josh Miller. They all said they thought he left at about 11.00. Tom and Josh agreed with Todd that he was intoxicated, but Caitlin said he wasn't that bad and that he was trying to hit on her until he left. None of them could tell me whether his car was parked there the whole time.'

Smith rubbed his chin.

'Alright, nothing substantial yet. I can tell you, I'm getting a bit tired of Brock Richards though, even if it is his sister that's been murdered. Actually, I'm not sure how much he cares.

'Anyway, good work today, guys, but we are back at it tomorrow. While I think of it, Riley, we will lose the extra support from the Adelaide team on Friday, so is there any chance you can spare one of your team to sit out at the cemetery for a night or two? I'll see if I can organise some more back up - we don't want to have the area messed up for a couple more days yet.'

Riley looked across to Phil, who had just stuffed a mouthful of pizza into his mouth. He shrugged.

'Why not? I have no social life. '

'Thanks, Phil. I'll make it up to you later.'

****

The gravedigger was concerned but not anxious.

Earlier in the afternoon, news had spread quickly all the way from Goolwa to Victor Harbor that police had set up a search cordon around the Currency Creek Cemetery. Late in the day, he had overheard a couple of school kids talking.

'Hey, the cops have found another body. Guess who it is?' one had said.

'Beats me, I'm still blown away by Amy Richards getting killed. Oh shit, it's not Kyle Hooper they found is it?'

'Dunno, for sure, but it makes sense. He's been missing a couple of days. Get this, though. They found the body in the old copper mine.'

The gravedigger had listened intently without wanting to look too obviously interested.

He accepted that the police would find Kyle's body sooner or later. By extension, he figured they would have worked out that Amy was not killed at the boat ramp. They must have identified the car by now as well.

He wondered what this meant for the grave. *Could they have connected it to the murders?* He decided that it must have raised some curiosity by now, but there was nothing to connect the desecration of the grave to the murders.

He was not concerned that the police would come knocking on his door at any moment armed with an arrest warrant. There was nothing to implicate him in the teenagers' deaths.

He was satisfied that everything was still okay. He just needed to stay patient and wait for the attention to blow over. Then he could go back and finish what he started. After one hundred and fifty years, the treasure wasn't going anywhere soon.

Nevertheless, he decided, there was no harm in having a look to see what was going on at the cemetery. As long as he kept his distance and remained invisible.

Chapter 29
Monday September 4, 1854

It was a fine spring morning as the procession made its way out of the Goolwa to the cemetery. In the planning of the township of Currency Creek, initially considered as a capital for the new colony, provision had been made for the burial of its citizens. Despite the Goolwa's population surpassing that of the township, its cemetery was the preferred final resting place for the region's residents.

The reason why was simple. It was situated on the top of a hill, from where there was a clear view east to the river and across to the surrounding hills in every other direction, giving a sense that it was the closest place to heaven in the district. The tall pines attracted the slightest breeze and carried the whispers of the deceased in unintelligible but comforting murmurs.

The horse and dray carrying the coffins of Rubina and Alexander rounded the bend on the narrow dirt track leading to the cemetery, coming to a stop at the small wire gate. Other wagons, mostly pulled by horses but a couple by bullocks had followed at a respectful distance and now drew up close by. The first was occupied by George and Elizabeth Johnston, with Donald seated between them. The boy had been glum during the ride, staring silently ahead and ignoring Elizabeth's efforts to comfort him by placing her hand gently on his arm.

Alfred Bates alighted from the leading dray and went to the back to lower the back tray. Donald could now clearly see the two wooden boxes but still sat unmoving.

'Just wait here for a moment,' George said.

He walked to Bates.

'You'll find everything in order, Mister Johnston.'

'Then you will nae mind if I look, will ye?'

He lifted the lid of Rubina's coffin enough to see how she was presented. She wore her church dress, one she had made only a few months before. There was no evidence of the vicious death she had suffered.

George walked around to the other side of the cart, lifted the lid to Alexander's coffin and peered in. He lay peacefully. He had a pair of breeches on together with his best jacket, a little worn at the elbows and cuffs, but otherwise very fine.

'Well done, Bates. Thank you.'

He walked back to his dray and helped Elizabeth to the ground. She had made the arrangements for the selection of clothes for Rubina and Alexander, so George whispered in her ear. 'You have chosen wisely, my dear, they look as well as could be possible.'

George then made sure Donald alighted before walking back to where Bates stood. Occupants of the other wagons were now walking toward the gate and George approached a number of men to assist him carry the coffins into the cemetery. When he had seven as well as himself, they started the process of sliding and lifting them, Rubina first.

Donald moved into the first group and pushed Seamus O'Leary away.

'I want to,' he said.

'Very well, lad,' said O'Leary in a gentle tone, 'I'll follow alongside in case it gets a bit heavy for you.'

The two groups walked solemnly into the cemetery to the second row of gravesites. It was clear where Rubina and Alexander were to be buried, fresh holes having been dug the previous day.   Two men stood back, away from the congregating mourners, cigarettes hanging from the corners of their mouths as they lent on their shovels.

Donald, George and Elizabeth stood closest to the graves. Behind them were many of the townsfolk that had known Rubina and Alexander, crews from the steamers that now worked the river and members of the Wesleyan congregation.

Francis Cadell was there of course, together with all the crew from the Lady Augusta. Their trip to Swan Hill would now be delayed until the end of the following week to allow a proper time to show respect for the deceased. John and Mary Varcoe had closed the Goolwa Hotel for the morning so that they could attend the burial, but they would return later in the day for those that wished to share a solemn drink in memory.

Similarly, Thomas Goode had closed his store and was there with his wife. They had reluctantly brought Agnes McNaught and her sister Charlotte, the pair having professed Agnes's tragic misfortune in finding Rubina for the whole of the journey from the Goolwa.

Police Troopers Edward Brackenridge and Douglas Graham had ridden from Port Elliot immediately on receiving news of the second suspicious death and stood to the rear of the mourners, hats in hand.

Reverend James Thorne was to conduct the service. As he stepped forward to speak, two ravens perched in the tree behind cawed at the intrusion into their habitat. The good minister looked up at them before turning back to face the congregation.

'My friends, we are here today in the presence of God, to commit Alexander and Rubina Johnston to his ever loving care.'

Ten minutes later, the service was over. The ravens had remained silent while the minister had spoken. As soon as he finished, they resumed their cawing before taking to the sky and drifting across the hill down into the valley on the northern side of the cemetery.

Donald had been silent and stoic during the service and now stood somewhat bewildered, uncertain as to what he should do next. Elizabeth stood close by his side and smiled and acknowledged each person as they came forward to give their condolences. After the first half dozen had spoken with Donald and shaken his hand, he began to accept his role and spoke more comfortably with each person about the virtues of his parents – his father's skill as a sailor and his ability to provide for his family and his mother's godliness and love for her husband and son.

Once he was satisfied that Donald was capable of managing the situation, George moved away from the graves to where John Varcoe was deep in conversation with the police troopers.

Brackenridge and Graham were only known to George by sight. Varcoe had worked closely with the pair on a number of matters and as the town's publican had needed to confer with them on the behaviour of some of his patrons on many occasions. He introduced them to George as he put his hand on his shoulder.

'Tripp's boat has been found, in reeds in the Finniss.'

'What about Tripp?'

'No sign, I'm afraid. The boat was found by a landowner looking for stray cattle, but Tripp was nowhere near.'

George turned to the troopers. 'What do you think? Is Tripp the killer?'

It was Brackenridge who spoke. He stroked his mutton chop whiskers before speaking.

'Captain, normally I would be reluctant to make a judgement too soon, but in this case it appears quite straightforward. His disappearance certainly has not helped demonstrate his innocence. Nonetheless, we must keep an open mind. We are still not clear on the reason that Tripp would have to kill not only Alexander but also Rubina Johnston.'

'Surely, 'twas to get his hands on Alexander's papers relating to his investment.'

'That is speculation, sir. Do you know the nature of the investment?'

'Nay, I'm afraid I dinnae.'

'The boy?'

'He has told me he does nae. It would nae usually be a father's custom to keep a boy informed as to his business.'

'Quite,' continued Brackenridge, 'but you get my point. Without knowing what Tripp, or another person, was looking to steal, it is difficult to be steadfast that it was the motive.'

'But surely, the state of the cottage.'

'Possibly the result of the struggle.'

George could not let the matter rest.

'I think that unlikely. Every room was disturbed and that does nae concur with it resulting from a struggle. Besides, we ken Alexander was to go to Melbourne to liquidate the investment.'

Varcoe intervened, 'George, all of that contributes to the likelihood that Rubina and Alexander were murdered so that the killer could get to that investment, whatever it is. Tripp's implication in the murder is possible, maybe even likely. The thing is there is no clear proof.'

'John's right, Captain Johnston,' said Brackenridge, 'when we find Tripp, we will be much more certain. What's going to happen with their son?'

'Oh, he will live with Elizabeth and me until he is of age. We will make sure he is brought up well and he has the cottage, so he will nae be disadvantaged financially. Thomas Goode has said he will keep him on at the store. The boy will be fine.'

At that moment, Elizabeth joined the men. The troopers doffed their hats.

'Gentlemen, this is my wife, Elizabeth. Elizabeth, these are Police Troopers Brackenridge and Graham.'

'Ma'am,' the men said in unison.

Elizabeth inclined her head slightly toward them.

'Gentlemen, I am sure you have been discussing the bringing to retribution the murderers of Rubina and Alexander, so I won't press you any further. However, George, dear, I am quite certain that Donald has suffered enough today. May we take him home, now?'

'Of course, my love.'

George turned to the policemen.

"My wife is, of course, quite correct and I shall leave you to follow through with your investigations. I do beseech you, however, to keep us informed and to ask for any assistance you may require. Gentlemen, John.'

George took Elizabeth's elbow and walked her back to Donald, the three then walking out of the cemetery to their dray.

As they left, the ravens again took up their position in the pine tree, pleading for the other mourners to leave.

Chapter 30
Thursday July 21 2016

Riley arrived at the police station at 7.30. He had got the cold shoulder from Sally when he got home the previous night and it was playing on his mind. Although he tried to make some form of peace following their earlier row, she had avoided any conversation with him. He had told her that Kyle Hooper's body had been found in the old mine near the cemetery. While she was taken aback, she had simply told him that she didn't want to discuss anything about the case with him until he had taken Carl off his list of suspects.

They had parted in icy silence this morning. He was about to walk through the front door of the station when his mobile phone rang. He had hoped it was Sally looking to reconcile, but instead he saw Paul Smith's name on the screen.

'Morning, sir, just coming through the door now.'

'Don't worry about that, Riley, I'm just finishing off my breakfast in that little café down the road. Come and join me down here.'

Riley walked the couple of hundred metres and saw Smith sitting at one of the outside tables on the footpath. He was hungrily engorging a serve of poached eggs on toasted ciabatta bread and looked up at Riley as he approached.

'Grab yourself a coffee and put it on my bill. I'll have a double shot large latte. And make them both take-away.'

Riley walked to the counter where a young waitress waited to take his order. She smiled at him as he thanked her. He was humoured at the increased attention he had received from the young women in the town since he returned in a uniform. He remembered that Rachel also commented on the increased attention she received as a female in uniform, but in her case it wasn't always welcomed.

By the time he sat at the table opposite Smith, the older man had put down his cutlery and was dabbing his mouth with a napkin.

'They do a great breakfast here, you know. I can see I'll have to bring my wife down here for the weekend one time, if for no better reason than this breakfast.'

'Nice thought, sir, but unless she's an Eskimo, I suggest you get a table inside. It's freezing out here in winter.'

'Oh, is it? I hadn't noticed. I've been thinking through this case. You know, we made a lot of headway yesterday I think. At least we now know what happened to Kyle and we have narrowed down where the murder took place. What we are still no closer to is knowing who our killer is. If anything, the number of suspects just seems to be growing.'

'So, who's top of your list now, sir?'

'Well, 1 think it could be one of a few. Michael or Brock Richards, Carl Johnson or Travis Schultz, I suppose are the prime candidates. The only one we have ruled out is Kyle Hooper. The problem is, they probably all had the time when they could have killed Amy and Kyle, but I am struggling to understand why.

'Seems to me that the gravesite is still in the mix, but maybe it's coincidence that it has been tampered with. We can't even be certain it happened on the same day. If you discount that as a factor, then I struggle to see how your Carl Johnson could be involved, even with his secrecy about his past. Maybe, it's someone else altogether. Was it random? Shit, I thought we were getting closer, but in some ways, I feel like it's slipping further away.

'Anyway, do we know where Travis is this morning?'

'He's not rostered on for work, sir, so I'm hoping he will be at home.'

'Ok, let me go fix up the bill here while you get the car.'

Five minutes later, Riley was parked out the front of the café. He glanced up and saw Sally's car pulling out of the service station on the opposite side of the road and drive toward, then past, him. He waved, but she either hadn't seen him or was ignoring him. He watched in his rear view mirror as her car rounded the corner on which the library was located.

Strange, he thought. *It is unusual for her to be up earlier than she needs to be on her day off and, in any case, if she isn't working today, why is she there now?* He convinced himself that he had the days of her shifts confused or maybe she wasn't going to the library. His train of thought was broken as Paul Smith opened the door and climbed in beside him.

'Ok, let's go.'

Riley drove back past the police station, heading out of town, again toward the turn-off to the cemetery. However, instead of turning off, he continued down the dip into the valley where Currency Creek was nestled. Crossing over the creek, they passed the reception centre on the left. It comprised a grand old building from the 1850's that originally served as the Currency Creek Inn.

The building itself had been quite dilapidated until about twenty years ago, when a new owner painstakingly restored the main building and the out-buildings to their former glory. Vines had been planted to take advantage of the growth of wine in the region and the facility now served as a premier reception centre.

Immediately past the centre, Riley slowed and turned left onto Frome Road. It was a dirt road that gently rose and fell with the hills that followed the creek, or vice versa. They passed a house on the left and one on the right before Riley again slowed, approaching an old wire gate at a track cutting back toward the creek. On the right as they entered was an old rusted combine seed drill and as they surveyed the paddock it stood in, it seemed surprising that this machine could have sowed the origins of the generous green crop of oats.

The track led down to an old run down stone building nestled behind a large gum tree that was probably older than the building. On either side of the track were mounds of rubbish of varying configurations. Here there was a pile of tractor and truck tyres, there a pile of wood scraps, next a forty-four gallon drum, continuing in the sea of weeds all the way along the track.

On the side of a house was a storage shed, inside which were round bales of hay. The shed itself was open on three sides, large and well maintained, so the hay had remained in good condition.

The house, on the other hand, was in a poor state of repair. Sheets of iron roofing covering the front verandah had either been removed or blown off. Whichever was the case, they had not been replaced. The guttering that remained attached to the roof was rusted through and the iron sheets on the roof appeared as though they would allow rain to enter the house in multiple locations.

The windows and doors had deteriorated and a screen door at the main entrance hung loosely on one hinge, with most of the fly wire detached from the frame.

The track rounded the corner of the house and as Riley slowed to park, he saw two 4x4 utilities parked next to the house. However, they couldn't have been much more different to each other.

One was a late model Isuzu, painted bright red with chromed bull bars and roll bars. It was clear that it had been recently cleaned and polished with a decent coat of black applied to the tyres. The second car was an old Toyota Hilux that was infested with almost as much rust as the house. One of the tail lights at the back of the car was broken and the rear tyres were almost bald. Riley made a mental note to come back at a later date and run a check over the whole vehicle for defects.

As they got out the police car, Riley and Smith couldn't help but hear raised voices coming from the back of the house. As they turned the corner, they saw two figures pushing at each other, one of them falling to the ground.

'What did you do to her, you freak?' the man still standing yelled. He had his finger pointed at the figure on the ground, who seemed to have given up offering any further resistance. Striding toward him, he made to kick him in the mid-drift, when Riley called out.

'Enough, Brock, back off.'

Smith walked up to Brock Richards and stood close enough to intimidate him.

'Ok, you, go stand over there and wait. You and I will be having a little chat in a minute.'

Riley helped Travis to his feet and walked him over to an old kitchen chair standing alongside a water tank.

'Riley, just go over and keep an eye on hot head over there while I have a chat to Travis, will you? Now Travis, what was that all about?'

'I don't know Mr Smith. He just pulled up and went crazy at me. He said I did something to Amy. I never did. I wouldn't.'

'Ok, let's just leave that for a minute. Where are your parents, Travis? Are they home?'

'I don't have a mum. She died when I was little. Dad's at work.'

'Right. Sorry to hear about your mother. When's Dad going to be home?'

'Friday next week.'

'Friday next week? What do you mean?'

'He does Fly In Fly Out for the mines. He left Monday last week for three weeks.'

'So you stay at home by yourself?'

'Yeah, of course. I'm alright. I can look after myself.'

'Yeah, I'm sure you can Travis. So, tell me what do you do at night time? What did you do last Saturday night?'

'Usually I just watch TV or play video games. Sometimes if it's not too dark, I go for a walk. I can't remember what I did on Saturday night but I probably played games.'

'You were on your own?'

'Yes.'

'Alright, how do you get to work – in the Hilux out there?'

'I've got my license.'

'Yes, I know. Look, you might want to get the tyres and a few other things looked at on the car, but that's not what we are here for today, Travis. I want to ask you about a couple of other things. First, I want you to tell me about a fight you had with Brock a few months ago. Do you remember that?'

'Yes. It was at that party at Strathalbyn.'

'That's right. Tell me what happened.'

'I don't really remember that good. We were at a party and Brock and his friends picked a fight with me and Kyle. Then the cops, I mean police, came and broke it up.'

'What was the fight about, Travis?'

'I dunno. Those blokes were teasing me, I guess. They always have, right from primary school.'

'So you cracked?'

'I s'pose. I pushed Brock and then he pushed me back and then Kyle came to help me.'

'Now, I hear that you pulled a knife. Is that right?'

Travis flushed with embarrassment and lowered his eyes to the ground.

'Travis?'

'I was sick of it, Mr Smith. It's always me they pick on. Anyway, Kyle took the knife off me and told me I was stupid. I didn't like him saying that to me. He's my friend.'

'So what happened next?'

'The cops came and Kyle threw the knife away. Then we all went away.'

'Did Kyle say anything more to you about it?'

'He told me why it was wrong to do it and I could get into real trouble carrying a knife around. So I don't do it anymore. But then Kyle didn't want to see me much after that. He said I had to grow up.'

'This is really important, Travis. How did you feel about Kyle after that, especially when you were working with his girlfriend?'

'He's still my friend and so is Amy. She told me that if I wanted to be Kyle's friend I had to show him that I have grown up and that I don't do things like that anymore. That's what I have been trying to do.'

Smith dropped to his haunches and looked Travis in the eye.

'Now, I want to know this too. Have you been watching what's been going on over there?' He pointed toward the creek and cemetery.

'Nuh.'

'Travis, it's ok if you have. It's not against the law, I just need to know.'

'I was just watching.'

'I know, that's ok.'

'Was that Kyle that you took out on the stretcher yesterday?'

Smith was flummoxed.

'How did you know?'

'Amy's been killed and no one knows where Kyle is. I know he wouldn't hurt Amy, he would protect her, so I thought maybe who killed Amy probably hurt Kyle too. Is he, you know, dead?'

'I'm afraid he is, Travis. But we really need you to help us. Can you?'

Travis nodded. His face lost all expression, his eyes glazed over and his shoulders slumped. Smith patted him on the back.

'Ok, what I want you to do is to come back with Sergeant O'Brien and me to the police station so we can take your fingerprints. First, I just need to talk with Brock over there and then we'll get going. I'll get someone to drop you back here after, ok?'

Travis nodded again.

'Good lad. You go sit in the back of the police car and wait for us.'

After Travis had trudged around the corner, Smith walked to where Riley and Brock were standing. It was clear that not many words had passed between the two.

'So, Brock, mind telling me what that was all about?'

'Well, he's trouble. He must be involved in Amy's death otherwise you wouldn't be here.'

'That's interesting, Brock, because if my memory serves me right, we have been to your house at least twice, so what does that say?'

He looked at the ground, sullenly.

Smith raised his finger to Brock's chest. 'Now look, you, young man, are really trying my patience. I am telling you now to stay away from Travis Schultz. If I find you harassing him again, I'll have your arse. Is that understood?'

'Yes.'

'Anyway, as it turns out, now that you are here, you can come back to the station and get your fingerprints taken. That will save you having to come back later.'

Brock started walking back to the red 4x4.

'Aah, not that one, Brock. You're going to be chauffer driven this time. Back seat of the police car next to Travis please.'

Riley smiled as Brock protested, 'but my car.'

'Don't worry, I'm sure it will be fine here, Brock,' Riley said. 'We'll drop you back here after and then you can go home and remind your dad to come in for his fingerprints.'

It was Smith's turn to smile.

They drove to the station in silence where the two juveniles undertook the fingerprinting process without further incident.

Riley grabbed Phil Reid.

'Phil, can you take these two back to Travis's house. Just make sure they don't kill each other on the way. And make sure Brock leaves before you head back.'

Chapter 31
Thursday July 21 2016

I am alert and enthusiastic. Since Sally told me she would help me in the library, I have been excited with the prospect of researching the past of my predecessors. The gloom and despondency that I had been feeling has dissolved. It is replaced by a steely determination to clear my name.

I know that I have this confidence only because Sally has stood so steadfastly alongside me in my dark moments. Now, we are going to work together to solve this mystery and I feel we are undeniable.

I had woken at 5:30 and couldn't get back to sleep. I didn't want to kayak – I worried it would take my focus away from the matter at hand; and it was still dark. I threw on old track pants, a sweater and sneakers and headed out into the dark winter chill for a jog. I didn't know where I was heading so I just ran, ending up on the bikeway running parallel to the beach. I hear the slosh and crash sounds of incoming waves just over the sand hills and I fall into a steady, rather than exerting pace that matches its rhythm.

Sucking in the cold fresh air, I impulsively headed up a steep sand hill. I was fully aware that the conservationists would have been aghast at me trampling the coastal vegetation. In the moment I was carried away by the need to test myself, to go where I hadn't been before and to stretch the boundaries of my accepted limits.

As I think on it now, I realise how self-absorbing it all sounds. If I was hearing it from someone else's mouth I would think them a pompous arse. *Still here I am.*

My run up the sand hill had certainly tested me. By the time I reached the summit, I was spent. I doubled over, gasping, my eyes locked onto the sand beneath my feet. I stood on top of the hill, feeling a sense of seclusion. Even though I was only a few hundred meters from the road, I was completely alone.

I turned and trudged back down the hill, now feeling a sense of guilt that I had disturbed in some way the fragile environment. As I jogged back home, I reminded myself not to take life so seriously.

I had arranged to meet Sally for breakfast at the café on the main street, just a few metres from the library. I park my car next to the library and stroll around the corner. I am just in time to see Detective Inspector Smith jump into the passenger seat of a police car. As it pulls away from the kerb, I am grateful that I haven't had to converse with him.

It's cool outside so I go inside and sit at a table next to the front window. I only wait a couple of minutes before Sally comes through the door. As always, she looks radiant. Her almond eyes sparkle as she leans over to kiss me.

'Ready to come into my world, mister?' she says.

'Ready, willing and able.'

While we eat breakfast, we review what we know and especially what we are hoping to learn from events one hundred and fifty years ago.

'It just seems to me,' I say, 'the fact that Alexander's grave has been disturbed around the same time Amy was killed and so near to her car must mean something.'

'Oh, Carl, of course, you don't know yet. They found Kyle's body yesterday.'

'What?' I exclaim.

'They found him in the old mine shaft next to Currency Creek. I'm sorry. Riley and I really haven't been talking the last couple of days, so I don't know any more.'

'Sally, you can't let this business get between Riley and you. It's not worth it.'

'I know. We'll be alright once this is all over. I know he's just doing his job. Anyway, what do you think Kyle's death means?'

'Well,' I start, 'Let's assume he didn't kill himself. If he did, then the whole mystery will unravel very quickly. I just don't think that's very likely. The other scenario is that Kyle was murdered too and if that's the case, I am even more convinced the grave is connected.'

'Do you think that Kyle and Amy were digging the grave?'

'Who knows? In any case, it probably doesn't matter. If they were, someone found out about it and killed them. Otherwise, maybe they found someone digging it and it was worth killing them for.'

'It's all a bit far-fetched, isn't it?'

'Maybe, Sal, but hopefully, today will lead us closer to the answer.'

After we finish breakfast, we walk to the library.

It is very quiet, as I guess libraries are. Sally's colleague is busy going through book returns and re-placing them onto shelves.

'Hi Jean,' Sally pipes, 'Is Sue in yet?'

Jean looks at her watch. 'She'll be in around ten. Anyway, what brings you in on your day off, my lovely?'

'Can't stay away,' Sally laughs. 'No, just kidding. Carl's doing some research into some of his ancestors from around here. We might start with some of the general reference books out here until Sue gets in.'

Sally leads me to a section specialising in local history.

'It's probably worth us spending some time here rifling for general clues and then Sue will be able to refine our search into specifics once we have some idea what we are looking for.'

She pulls a book from the shelf and passes it to me. "Early History of Goolwa" I read on the spine.

'Why don't you start looking through that one while I see if there are any others here that might interest us?' Sally points over to a desk and quickly turns back to the shelf.

I sit at the desk and thumb the book open to the contents page. Unfortunately, it seems to be categorised by subjects of interest – Chapter 1 First People, Chapter 2 Sealers and Whalers, and so on. I decide instead to try my luck in the index, looking first for Alexander Johnston. I can't believe my luck, there is one reference to him on page 121.

I hastily flick through the pages and see his name jump back at me. I read the paragraph:

"George Johnston had intended to enter into business with his cousin, Alexander Johnston in 1854. However, his plan had to be shelved when Alexander drowned, apparently in suspicious circumstances in August of that year. Adding to the intrigue, Alexander's wife, Rubina, was murdered in their home the day after his body was pulled from the Murray River.

George went on to form a business partnership with Charles Murphy and they became one of the most prolific and successful builders of river boats along the Murray."

I read backward and forward looking for more information. A few minutes later, I am disappointed that this is the only reference to Alexander.

Nonetheless, I have now learnt that there is a high probability that Alexander and Rubina did not die of natural causes. This now raises a new and interesting question – if they were murdered, why?

Sally returns with an armful of books. Excitedly, I show her the reference to Alexander and Rubina and their untimely demises.

'Wow that is strange. Anything else in there?'

'Not yet, I'm going to go back and read the whole section on George Bain Johnston. There seems to be more detail around him.'

'Ok, I'll start on the other books.'

I read more about George and develop an understanding about this highly respected captain and river boat builder. He was a deeply religious man with high ethics and a sense of care for his workers. He even bought land and built cottages for them in the area now known as Little Scotland.

It's 10.00. The time has passed by quickly but we have finished browsing all the books we selected.

'Well, I haven't come up with anything at all on Alexander. George was quite the man though, wasn't he?' Sally stretches her arms upward. 'You know, I can see some of his facial features in you. You both have the same hair and gentle face.'

'Not that you can see his face with the beard he's got,' I respond. 'I wish I could see a picture of Alexander. I wonder what he was like.'

'I see Sue's just gone into the History Room. Let's go.'

I grab the books and we enter the small room in the corner of the library. Against three of the walls are shelves containing more books, all dedicated to the history of Goolwa, the region and the state. Against the final wall is a large compactus unit, stacked with manila folders, each neatly labelled and stuffed with letters, photocopies, photographs and assorted material collected over decades of diligent work by volunteer historians.

In the centre of the room is a large table with eight chairs seated around it. I look at the centre of the table and, under the glass top, I see maps dating back to the mid-nineteenth century. One of them shows the intended layout of the Currency Creek township when it was proposed as an alternative capital city for the state.

At the head of the table sits a pleasant faced woman, I guess in her early fifties. She is groomed impeccably and clearly likes to look professional. I suspect she is a perfectionist in every aspect of her life. She smiles with twinkling eyes that invite engagement even though she is talking on her mobile phone as we enter. She lifts a hand politely, to indicate she won't be long. I don't know why but I can sense already she will be a great help to us.

Sally sits at the table, while I wander up and down, examining the books on each shelf. I am staggered by the resources available.

Sue says her farewells and places her phone on the table.

'Sally, my dear, what on earth are you doing here on your day off? I'd have thought you would have had lots of exciting things to be doing rather than being here.'

'Hi Sue. This is Carl. Carl, Sue.' Sue and I shake hands. I feel her surveying me while Sally continues.

'Carl's looking to do some research on a distant relative of his, Alexander Johnston.'

Sue reflects for a moment. 'That's not a name I really know. Of course there was George Bain Johnston and his wife Elizabeth. They had a son, also named George, who was a captain as well and I'm pretty sure one of his grandsons, another George, was a very good footballer. He was known as Blue and actually won a Magarey Medal.

'I'm just trying to think of any other Johnston's. I recall a Donald, but can't tell you anything about him.'

'Alexander was George senior's cousin, we believe,' I say.

Sue removes her reading glasses and holds them pensively to her mouth as she walks to the compactus.

'There's been a bit of interest in George Bain Johnston of late. I guess he was an important figure back then. Ah, here we go.'

She slips a marker in between the files and extracts a large manila folder, labelled George Bain Johnston. She hands it to me with the care she might use if she was handing me a baby.

'Why don't you start going through this one while I see what else I can find. What else do you know about Alexander?'

'Only that he and his wife are buried in the cemetery at Currency Creek.'

I start thumbing through the documents, amazed at how much has been collected concerning George. The work of the historians in tracing relatives, letters, photographs, official records and so on simply astounds me. I find title deeds for a property that George had purchased from Young Bingham Hutchinson in 1857 for £25. There are letters from his great granddaughter, Betty Groth and numerous newspaper articles spanning fifteen decades extolling the virtues of the man.

While I am fascinated to learn about George Bain Johnston, I am frustrated that I have found no further record of Alexander and Rubina.

Sally and Sue have been working their way through other files relating to 1850's Goolwa without success.

'Maybe there would have been more on Alexander and Rubina if they hadn't been murdered so young,' I say, exasperated.

'Murdered?' asks Sue. 'Are you sure?'

I show her the paragraph in "Early history of Goolwa".

'I wonder,' Sue mutters as she moves around the room.

She returns with a book, green cover, with embossed gold lettering on the spine.

She gently opens the old book to the title page, "SA Murder Trials 1851 -1899" and then turns the page to the contents. Running down the list she stops at an entry.

'Here, look.'

The line reads *"Double Murder at Goolwa 1854 ..... 48"*

She turns to page 48 and there it is.

For the next thirty minutes, while Sue and I listen intently, Sally reads the details of the trial of Joseph Tripp, who was accused of the murders of Alexander and Rubina Johnston.

The trial focused on Tripp's relationship with Alexander and Alexander's drowning after falling overboard from the PS Lady Augusta on the night of 30th August 1854.

Central to the case was Tripp's disappearance after the murder of Rubina in her home just a day after Alexander's death. Initially it was thought that Alexander had fallen from the boat and drowned, although most of his relatives and acquaintances had believed that highly unlikely for an experienced seaman. The theory of accidental death was also brought into question by the discovery on the deck of the Lady Augusta of a near empty rum bottle. While Alexander never drank rum, it was known to be Joseph Tripp's favourite beverage.

Tripp had fled Goolwa but was arrested a couple of months later in the copper mining townships then known as the Burra Burra.

The trial should have been a short affair after Tripp confessed to the killing of Alexander and Rubina. The bizarre twist, however, was the demented ramblings of Joe Tripp, testifying that the deaths were the result of a dispute over an emerald necklace known as Albert's Folly. Tripp had insisted that Alexander had hidden the necklace, which the pair had recovered from the wreck of the barque, Mozambique, in his house. He had claimed that Alexander intended to cheat him of his proceeds from the sale of the salvaged jewel.

Intrigued, Sue bursts out, 'So, where was the necklace?'

I shrug as we read on, to discover that, despite a thorough search of Alexander and Rubina's house, no sign of the necklace was ever found. The story closed with the tragic death of Joseph Tripp, hanged in his cell on Christmas Eve, 1854. A post script noted that the whereabouts of "Albert's Folly" was never determined and to this day, no-one knows whether Joseph Tripp had been telling the truth.

'Oh, my god, what a story,' Sue exclaims, 'In all my years here, I have never heard a story as bizarre as that one.'

'Agree, I wouldn't have imagined we would find this,' Sally adds.

I sit silent, trying to assess what it all means.

'We need to know where they lived,' I say.

'Who?' Sally looks at me, quizzically.

'Alexander and Rubina. I want to see where this so-called necklace was supposedly hidden.'

'Carl, it's at the start of the chapter on the trial proceedings, look,' says Sue, flicking back a few pages.

'Here, Alexander and Rubina Johnston, of 2 Newacott Place, Goolwa.'

'I have to look at the place.'

'Carl,' Sally says, 'you can't just barge into someone's house to look for something that's been missing one hundred and fifty years. You don't even know that it really existed.'

Sue joins in the protest, 'The thing is too, Carl, that even if they lived at that address, it doesn't mean the house is still there. If there is a house there now, it's quite likely the original has been demolished and a new one built since 1854. In those days, a lot of the men working here simply lived in canvas huts while they built their houses before their families joined them. We don't even know for sure that Alexander had a house.'

I am undeterred. 'Don't forget that Rubina was already in Goolwa, so maybe the house was actually built or at least in the process of being built. The trial suggests that a house was there at the time.'

We sit in silence for a time.

Finally, I stand.

'Sally, I really need to see if this house is still standing. If it is, we can decide what to do from there. Sue, thanks so much for all your help. We could never have found all this out so quickly without your help.'

'Carl, it's been a pleasure and just a bit exciting. Good luck with uncovering what happened. Let me know what you find, hey.'

'Oh, actually, it's not Carl, it's Callum, Callum Johnston, but I'll explain all that properly to you sometime soon.'

As I walk out the room, I can feel Sue's mouth agape and Sally's eyes in the back of my head.

'Carl, what was that all about? Am I supposed to call you Carl or Callum?'

'I'm sorry, Sally. That was a bit impetuous. I suddenly felt ok about reverting to Callum, but maybe I did get a bit carried away.'

'No maybe about it, but I'm happy you are feeling good about being Callum the person as well as the name. But perhaps, just to avoid confusion, you could stay as Carl until this is all sorted out.'

'Good idea,' I say as we walk out the front door of the library. 'Now, Newacott Place is just down here isn't it?'

Chapter 32
Thursday July 21 2016

We walk behind the Goolwa Hotel, taking a couple of back streets before finding ourselves on a road that is barely wider than a laneway. Most of the houses in the street are narrow, but the majority are from an era significantly later than the 1800's. My hopes drop. On closer observation a couple of the houses look like original constructions although they have been added to over the years.

When we find number two, my heart skips a beat. It is still there. A vehicle is parked out the front loaded with building materials – timber of varying dimensions, iron roofing sheets and bags of concrete.

I start to walk through the front gate.

'Carl, don't you think it would be wise to get the police involved before you just waltz in there?'

'I'm not intending to cause trouble. What's the problem?'

'I just think it would be worth avoiding any issues.'

'Ok,' I say, reluctantly, 'see if you can get Riley to come out, but if he's not here in thirty minutes, I'm going in anyway.'

Sally calls Riley and explains why we are at the house, asking him to join us. Riley arrives fifteen minutes later and he's not happy. He is still smarting from the rebuke Sally gave him when he suggested she stay away from me. On top of that, he is uncomfortable that Sally and I have been meddling in the investigation into Amy's death. If that isn't already enough to get him worked up, we have dragged him away from the station at short notice to follow up what he is thinking is a harebrained theory.

It's fair to say, we haven't started well. As we meet Riley outside the cottage, he glares at me. Before he has time to raise any form of protest, Sally thrusts the book, "SA Murder Trials 1851 -1899" in his face, already opened at page 48.

For five minutes, Riley listens intently without saying a word, allowing Sally and me to tag team in a detailed explanation as to why we now think it is worth looking at the house.

Finally, Riley speaks. 'Well, I think your theory is far-fetched to say the least and I wish you would leave the policing to the people that should be doing it. As it happens, though, you are very lucky. That car belongs to Peter Higgins, who I know pretty well through the footy committee. It looks like he's working on the place and I'm sure he won't mind taking us through.'

As we approach the front door, it suddenly opens and I see a man carrying the front end of a large wooden beam. At the other end of the beam is a woman who is clearly struggling with the weight she is carrying. Riley steps through the door and takes the end from her. After manoeuvring the timber around the doorway, they place it on the ground at the front of the house.

'Peter Higgins,' says Riley, 'This is Carl Johnson and, of course, you already know Sally. Cheryl, are you ok? Come out and meet Carl.'

Cheryl Higgins comes out the door and shakes Carl's hand.

'Why are you lifting weights like that, Cheryl? You'll do your back in.'

'Oh, Riley, I've been doing hard work like this for years. Anyway, we just have the one big piece. What brings you here?'

'Long story,' says Riley, 'Can we go inside?'

Cheryl leads the way and we find ourselves in the centre of what appears to be a living room undergoing major transformation.

'Wow, what's going on here?' asks Sally, 'This looks like some pretty significant interior refurbishment.'

Peter points to old wooden chairs around the edge of the room. There are only two, so Sally and Cheryl sit, while the men remain standing.

'We are turning this old girl into a B and B,' Peter says. 'It's owned by a couple in Adelaide who aren't afraid to spend a dollar, so we've been basically gutting it and re-building.'

I look around the room. A new wooden floor has been put down, the doors and frames have been sanded back and all the walls have had minor patching. I look up to the ceiling and see that it has been removed and bare light globes hang from the rafters.

'Are you doing this through the whole house?' I ask.

'Yes, pretty much, although this is the oldest part of the house. Most of the back was added over the years, so it's a bit easier to work with.'

Riley whistles. 'Looks like it's a big job. This will keep you busy for a while.'

'Just as well too,' Peter says. There's nothing else going on in town at the moment. If it wasn't for this job, I think I'd be stacking shelves at the supermarket. Anyway, I don't think you said what you were here for, Riley. What's up?'

'Pete, as you know, Amy Richards was drowned on the weekend. I don't think there's any secret that we suspect foul play.'

'Go on, I'm not seeing a connection.'

'Sure it's a bit of a long shot, but just take this in for a minute. We have now worked out that Amy was drowned at Currency Creek, not in the river at all. We also found her boyfriend, Kyle, in the old mine shaft near the creek. He was murdered too, we think.'

Peter and Cheryl are looking at Riley, eyes wide open.

'So, all that on its own doesn't mean much in terms of us being here. The thing is that there has been a grave disturbed at the cemetery and we think it happened around the same time as the deaths.

'The grave that was disturbed belongs to a man called Alexander Johnston. He and his wife once lived here. In fact, Alexander probably built the original house.'

Cheryl is about to talk but Riley lifts his hand.

'Nearly there. I know you are still wondering why that brings us here. It's possible that Amy and Kyle were killed because they disturbed the person that was tampering with the grave or maybe someone saw them tampering with it. The next connection is that Carl here believes that the reason why the grave was disturbed is because of something that happened back in the 1850's'

Cheryl looks at me. 'And what do you have to do with this, Carl?'

'I believe I am distantly related to Alexander Johnston and I was also Amy's kayak coach, so I have become, what you might call, a "person of interest".'

The silence is palpable, so I continue.

'I have found that Alexander Johnston and his wife were also murdered. I'm looking for a connection between their deaths and the digging up of the grave. I am hoping you will let us have a look around their house, even though I know they lived here so long ago.'

Again, I am surrounded by a suffocating silence. Eventually, it is Peter that speaks.

'Man, that all sounds a bit bizarre to me. But, hey, go your hardest, have a look around.'

'I appreciate it, Peter, and I know it's a long shot, but I'm just hoping I can learn something.'

'You understand that the house has changed a bit. The walls are probably the only original part of the house. I think it was built in the 1850's, but I wouldn't even be sure that Alexander built it even if he lived here. In those days the settlers lived in canvas huts like they had on the goldfields until they were able to build proper houses later. If he did build this house, it would have been one of the first in town.'

'I know,' I answer, with a sense of *déjà vu* following the debate at the library. 'But I'm relying on some records that suggest the house, rather than a hut, was searched by police shortly after the death of the Johnston's.'

We walk through the other rooms of the house. There are two rooms behind the main living room that appear to have been built at or around the same time. The kitchen, bathroom and laundry, together with another two bedrooms are further back and were almost certainly added much later.

As Peter Higgins described, the only part of the original home are the walls. They are made from limestone rocks, on average the size of a soccer ball, bound together by a soft, but obviously effective mortar. In places, repairs have been made to the walls to replace soft or crumbling mortar.

As we get to the back of the house, we walk out into the back yard, where a neat, but plain garden is laid out and a small shed is sited in the back corner.

Riley and Sally follow me out, while Peter and Cheryl stayed inside.

'There's nothing here, Carl,' Riley says, 'Let's go and leave these people to it.'

'You're right,' I say, 'I don't think we can learn anything further. You know what we need to do next?'

Riley looks at me enquiringly. 'What?'

'We need to dig up Alexander's coffin.'

'What? You're crazy. Why do that?'

'Think about it, Riley. If the necklace was hidden and it's not here, as Joseph Tripp thought it was, where was it hidden? Maybe it was buried with Alexander.'

'You don't know that!'

Sally jumps in. 'You know what, Riley, you're right. We don't know, but it's plausible and could be a logical explanation why someone has already tried to dig up the grave.'

'You will have to get Paul Smith to apply to have the body exhumed,' I urge.

'There's not enough evidence to justify that. Smith will go off his tree.'

'Riley, you have to try to convince him. You can't deny there is a link between the grave and the deaths. If you can find out why the grave was being tampered with, you are closer to solving the murders.'

Riley stands silent.

'Please, Riley,' Sally urges, grabbing him by the arm.

'Ok, ok, I'll talk to Smith in the morning, but in the meantime you two stop playing detective, please.'

The three of us walk back through the house.

'Find anything of interest?' Peter Higgins asks,

'No,' I say, 'but to be honest, I'm not sure what I am looking for.'

'Well if there's anything we can do, let us know. We know the Richards pretty well and we'd like to see this sorted out for their sake.'

'Thanks. Just let us know if you come across anything unexpected.'

We leave the Higgins to their refurbishment and briefly say our goodbyes to Riley out in the street.

Sally and I walk back to the library.

'So, what do you plan to do now, Carl?' Sally asks.

'You know, I haven't passed my condolences on to Amy's parents yet. Somehow it wasn't right while I felt like I was being thought of as a suspect. I'd like to go and see them, I think.'

'Do you want me to come with you?'

'No offense, but I reckon it would be better if I went on my own. Do you know them well?'

'No, not that well. I was just going to be there for you, but if you are comfortable on your own, I agree that would be better. Ring me later to let me know how it went?'

'Sure,' I say and lightly kiss her cheek. 'You have a good night and I'll call later.'

Sally gets into her car and waves, smiling as she drives off. Again, I am reminded just how lucky I am to have her.

Moments later, I am heading down Liverpool Road toward Amy's parents' house. It's not a conversation I am looking forward to but I know I need to do it.

Chapter 33
Thursday October 27 1854

The aboriginal men had been watching the stranger for at least two hours, but he didn't know it.

Billy Wonga and Jacky Waria were men of the Ngadjuri (or peppermint gum) people and knew the land well. They had been brought up near the springs at Appilla, but as the pastoralists had settled more and more of the land, their food sources were driven out of their country. Echidnas, bilbies, wallabies, wombats and bandicoots were difficult to find and the land that had good water sources was occupied by the pastoralists. Their people had needed to adapt or move, else die. And many did die, from typhoid, smallpox, diphtheria, tuberculosis, syphilis or a dozen other ailments brought by the white man.

Those aboriginals that tried to keep access to their land were often murdered, a more practical solution for the settlers than attempting to share the limited resources.

By the 1850's the pastoralists had problems of their own. The hired stockmen and even their own sons were leaving the district for the goldfields. As it turned out, the Ndagjuri men quickly learned the skills to become very good shearers, well sinkers and roustabouts.

So it was for Billy and Jacky. They had found work at Mannanarie Run, a sheep station owned by William Marchant. The property had been started as a cattle station when William's brother, Thomas, had taken an occupation license in 1847.

After Thomas was killed in a horse riding accident, William took over the property, obtaining a new lease in his own name. It was his decision that the land would be better suited to sheep, especially with better returns available from wool. With access to Ndagjuri men that were skilled in sheep handling, the property prospered and grew rapidly.

Billy and Jacky had come to this part of the run to check on a mob of sheep. They had seen the man camping nearby the previous night and were not overly concerned. He looked to be unarmed and they assumed he was just another traveller passing through. With no horse, however, the man would probably be dead within a week if he continued north. They had become accustomed to the strange ways of the white fellas even if they could not understand them. He already looked in bad shape. His clothes were ripped, his hair dishevelled and his face badly burnt by the sun.

They had tied their horses behind a large gum tree on the side of a rise. From the hill top their concern grew as they watched the stranger catch and kill one of the station's sheep.

As aboriginal men, they knew that they could not arrest the man. In fact, chances were it would be them hanged should the man be harmed.

'Better get the boss,' Jacky said. Billy returned to his horse and rode the rough track to where William Marchant was building fences with four men, eight miles away.

It was three and a half hours later when the party of three men, William Marchant, a stockman named Henry Jones and Billy Wonga, returned. Jacky met them at the hill top above where they had seen the man camped. After tying their horses, they walked toward the opening, each taking a compass point to encircle the man.

The sheep carcass lay in the remains of the fire. The man had eaten well and now lay sleeping in the afternoon sun.

William Marchant walked up to the prostrate figure and gave him a sharp kick in the buttocks. Startled out of his sleep, the man looked up. He lifted a hand to his face, the sun shining directly into his eyes.

'Get up,' said Marchant.

The man shook himself and rose to his feet. He looked pitiful – filthy and contemptible. Marchant looked at him scornfully.

'That is my sheep you've stolen.'

'I'm sorry, sir. I was hungry. I dint mean no harm.'

'Why didn't you come to the homestead? We wouldn't have sent you away in the condition you are now.'

The stranger did not answer.

'Why are you out here on your own? This land is no friend of an ill prepared traveller.'

'They've been following me. I get away from them every day, but they find me. Every night, they just stare at me. They're waiting.'

Marchant looked around at the others. Henry Jones shrugged, while the two aboriginal men looked on uninterested.

'Who are?'

'The stars, sir. They look down on me, judging me, but they don't understand. They don't know what really happened. So, I have to keep moving, get away from 'em'

'You don't want anyone to know where you are. Is that it?'

'I ... er, that is... I have had some trouble, sir. If you'll let me be, I'll just be on my way and cause you no more inconvenience.'

Marchant looked at the other men before answering.

'If I let you go, you are going to starve. There's nothing north of here that will provide for you. And there's the matter of the stolen sheep.'

'I can work for you, sir, for no wages, just keep; a roof over me head, is all.'

'What skills do you have?' Marchant was losing patience.

'I can work hard at anything. I was a fisherman before.'

'I think not. Henry, tie him up. Billy, he can ride back to the quarters on the back of your horse. We'll hold him for the troopers there.'

The man made to run but his emaciated condition was no match for the strong embrace of Henry Jones.

By nightfall, Henry and Billy had ridden back to the homestead, William Marchant and Jacky returning to the fencing crew. Henry took the man to the shearing shed and tied him in one of the pens as a makeshift jail.

Later, an aboriginal woman came with damper and a lamb stew, accompanied by Billy who brought hay for him to sleep on and a bucket for his toilet. The woman released the ropes securing the man to the shed wall while Billy stood guard, rifle in hand. He watched as the man ate greedily, even though he had eaten plenty earlier in the day.

After he had finished, the woman re-tied him. Billy waved his rifle at him.

'I think you're in big trouble, Mister.'

The man was quiet.

'The troopers gunna be here tomorrow. They come last week and said they'd be back on Friday. They'll take you away. Maybe hang you too.'

'They can't do that without a trial. Anyway, they won't hang me for stealing a sheep.'

'Yeah, but what else you done, Mister? That's what they hang you for.'

Tripp looked at Billy suspiciously.

'You know. How?'

He thought about the stars. They had been watching him ever since the night on Hindmarsh Island. Watching, haunting. Even on a cloudy night, he knew they were there, spying on him, waiting for him to falter.

People said some blackfellas had magical skills. *What if this one spoke to the stars? That's how he knew. They sent him.*

'You done a bad thing, Mister. That's why they gunna hang you.'

'I dint mean it. It was an accident. I dint mean to kill Alexander and she attacked me with the knife. She dint have to die.'

'They gunna hang you, Mister.' As Billy left, Tripp was at least grateful he was under cover for the first time in weeks. The stars wouldn't haunt him tonight. He actually felt better for having told Billy.

He knew they would catch him eventually. He knew they were probably going to hang him. But he had been living in hell for two months anyway. At least he could stop running and eat proper meals for the rest of his days.

He settled to sleep and, for the first time since he had left the Goolwa at the end of August, he was not troubled by nightmares.

The following morning, troopers McIntyre and Blake arrived at Mannanarie Run homestead. They had been attending to a property dispute between two pastoralists to the east and arrived at the homestead in the hope of a hearty breakfast.

The woman who had taken food to Joe Tripp the night before was walking from the shearing shed to the house when she saw the troopers. She led them to Henry Jones who was, with Billy Wonga, preparing to re-join Marchant and his men.

'Ah, I'm glad you have arrived before we set off.' Henry shook hands with the men. 'We have a thief in the shed. He stole one of Mister Marchant's sheep.'

'And a murderer,' added Billy.

The troopers turned to Billy. Henry swivelled as well.

'What are you talking about, Billy.'

'Told me last night. He killed two people, he said, a man called Alexander and a woman.'

The troopers accompanied Billy and Henry to the shed where Tripp had just finished his breakfast. The sight that beheld them was as pathetic as when Marchant and his men had detained him, despite the solid meals he had consumed over the last day.

'For God's sake, can he be washed before we take him? Maybe while we have some breakfast. And will you lend us a horse for him, Henry?'

Tripp was surprisingly relaxed and upbeat as they set out on the journey from Mannanarie Run to Clare. Less than an hour after departing, he began chatting as freely as a man in the company of his closest friends.

'A man feels the better for a good wash and some solid food in his belly, don't you think? That Marchant raises a tasty breed of sheep on that run, I'll allow him that.'

Trooper McIntyre was in no mood for conversation. This fool of an Englishman was going to occupy them for the best part of three days. Blake, however, was in the mood for entertainment to relieve the boredom, especially as his partner was so subdued.

'So, you stole one of his sheep. Why?'

'Hunger, friend. That beast was my first full meal in weeks.'

'Harsh country, this, for a vagrant. What brought you this far north?'

''Twas as the blackfella said. I killed a man and his wife in the Goolwa. 'Twas a terrible accident but they'll not believe me. I don't have any friends in that town now they're dead.'

Blake was confused. 'Who?'

'Do you not listen, man. Alexander Johnston and his wife, the two I killed. Alexander was my only friend.'

'And yet you killed him? Why did you confess to Billy after all this time?'

'No, no, I dint tell him. He already knew …from the stars.'

McIntyre could contain his silence no longer.

'What the hell are you talking about, fool?'

'The skies are witness to my crimes. That blackfella talks to the stars and they told him. But as I say, I int no murderer. I dint mean to kill them.'

The first night they camped, the air was warm and still. Not a cloud sat in the sky, the moon not even partly risen. The sky was raven black, twinkling stars perforating it with the eyes of a million birds. As the night wore on and the campfire embers dulled, Joe Tripp became increasingly sullen.

The troopers had tied him lest he try to escape, but they were woken abruptly shortly after midnight by the panicked ranting of their prisoner.

'I've told them, what more do you want of me?'

He was on his knees screaming into the sky.

'For the love of God, will you let me be! 'Twas not meant to happen. What can I do for them now?'

Blake grabbed Tripp and wrestled him to the ground. He lay whimpering.

'Think I'll stand watch for a while. Get some sleep and you can take over in a couple of hours.'

The next day their conversation as they rode was tentative. Tripp did not speak of his own accord and barely responded to questions from the troopers. That night was a repeat of the previous, with Tripp tormented by the watching stars in a black sky. Again the troopers rotated watch, eerily disturbed by the man in their custody.

They reached Clare late the following day, the troopers glad to be able to lock him in a cell. They would be more satisfied when he was out of their jurisdiction altogether. Charges were hastily prepared, accusing Tripp of the two murders. In order to be rid of him, no charges were laid in relation to the local issue, the theft of William Marchant's sheep.

On reading the charges and the interview records of the troopers, the town magistrate had no hesitation in committing Tripp for trial at the Goolwa and authorised the immediate transfer of the prisoner as soon as arrangements could be made.

By mid-November, Joseph Tripp was locked in a cell awaiting trial. Police Trooper Edward Brackenridge had transferred his station to the Goolwa temporarily, anxious that the trial was conducted as soon as possible and Tripp hanged in accordance with his crimes.

After reading the notes sent by Troopers McIntyre and Blake, Brackenridge sat across a desk from the bound Tripp. Although he had not known the man well, he had previously dealt with him on a matter of drunkenness. He was shocked to see his deterioration and notwithstanding the restoration of a reasonable diet, the big man had lost a considerable amount of weight and his skin sagged on his face.

Brackenridge had asked John Varcoe to join him in the interview. Resources were scarce and he had been unable to have a second trooper accompany him. Varcoe entered the room and sat next to the trooper. He too was shocked at Tripp's appearance.

'Tripp,' he said, acknowledging his presence.

'Oh, Mister Varcoe. No chance of some of your fine rum, I s'pose?'

It was Brackenridge that spoke. 'I understand you have confessed to killing Alexander and Rubina Johnston. Is that right?'

'Well, now, Constable. Yes, 'tis true I was there when they died but their deaths was accidental. I dint mean for it to happen.'

'Why don't you tell us the whole story, right from the start and we will decide if it's accidental?' He wanted Tripp to talk and was convinced the man would end up tying his own noose. He glanced across at Varcoe, who was wearing a frown.

For the next quarter hour, Tripp narrated how he and Alexander had concocted the scheme to find and then sell the emerald necklace.

Brackenridge motioned to Varcoe and they left the room.

'What do you know about this, John?'

'Well, it's true that an Irish woman, Catharine Delaney lost a very valuable emerald necklace when the Mozambique was wrecked. Supposedly made for Queen Victoria, it was. But I know nothing of any plan of Alexander's.'

'Was the necklace recovered, then?'

'Not to my knowledge. There was a whole trunk of her jewellery that was not recovered but the necklace was the item she seemed most concerned about.'

'Very well, let's see what else Joseph Tripp has to say.'

Over the course of the next two hours, Tripp told the men about how they had found the necklace and Alexander had taken it into his keeping. Increasingly agitated, he related how Alexander was going to cheat him, leading to the confrontation on the deck of the Lady Augusta.

'You were drunk that night, Tripp. I know because I sold you the rum and I saw you drink most of it. Later, the bottle was found on the deck, so we know you were there.' Varcoe glared at him. 'Are you sure you are not fabricating this story? Alexander Johnston was a good and honest man.'

Tripp scoffed.

'Think what you like, Varcoe. I've confessed my sins to the stars and they know the truth. They told it to the blackfella lad.'

Varcoe looked at Brackenridge, puzzled. The trooper handed the notes transferred from Clare for Varcoe to read.

'Tell me about Rubina Johnston. Why did you kill her?'

'I just went to get the necklace from her. Alexander must have hidden it in the house, but the stupid woman came at me with a knife. I had no cause to kill her.'

The interview descended into Tripp's ramblings about the necklace and the taunting of the night skies until he was caught at Mannanarie.

Afterward, Brackenridge and Varcoe conferred.

'The man is clearly mad,' said Brackenridge.

'Or he is making out to be. What manner of rot is this story about the necklace? Alexander was a good man and a cousin of George Johnston. I won't believe he would have been involved in a scheme such as this. He will hang!' he exclaimed, shaking his finger at the door between them and Joe Tripp.

'John, I know this is difficult for you, as it will be for George Johnston, but is it not true that Alexander was to travel to Melbourne to get funds for an investment? Could it not be that he was going to sell the necklace?'

'I won't believe that, Edward, and neither will George.'

'Is the house lived in?'

'No, it's still much the same as the way it was left by that murderous thug. Donald won't consent to its sale or even its clean up and George does not want to distress the lad.'

'Good. Then, we shall look tomorrow for this elusive necklace. If, as Tripp suggests, it was hidden there, it should surely still be there. See if George wishes to join us.'

The next morning, the three men entered the little cottage in Newacott Place. As John Varcoe had said, little had been attended to since the night of Rubina's death. Furniture, clothing and crockery littered the floor. Where Rubina's body had lain, the floor was now stained a dark brown.

'It's fortunate you have not cleaned this up, George.'

'If we had, Edward, we would have dispelled this preposterous story of Tripp's already. I'll wager we will find nothing.'

Brackenridge lifted a chest to an upright position. 'George, we must do this to pursue every line of investigation. We have no other motive behind Tripp's actions.'

'I know, let's get on with it. I confess I dinnae ken what investments Alexander had that Tripp may have stolen. And you have found nae evidence of stolen documents on him?'

'No.'

The three men worked methodically through the house. By the time they had finished, they had checked every movable item, searched the fireplaces, the ceiling space and even lifted the floorboards. Having finished in the house, they searched the outside shed just as thoroughly.

Finally, they stood at the back door, perplexed.

'There, nothing. Are you satisfied, Edward?'

'I am satisfied that there is no necklace in that house or in that shed. But I am confounded by Tripp's story and why he would have killed Alexander and Rubina.'

'So, what now?'

'Well, George, Tripp has confessed to the killings and despite his protestations, they are murders. He will be committed for trial, and I would expect that will take place before the end of the year.'

'Let us hope that his ramblings dinnae confuse the trial. He must hang for this.'

Varcoe patted George on the back. 'On that, we all agree, George. Come, let me fetch you an ale.'

Chapter 34
Friday July 22 2016

It was again early when Riley walked to the front door of the police station. He had not had a day off for ten days now and although he was enjoying the challenges that this investigation had thrown at him, he felt drained. He knew his temper had grown short and he had taken it out on Sally again earlier in the morning.

She had made the mistake of reminding him to approach Paul Smith about exhuming Alexander Johnston's body. What she didn't understand was the process that would need to be followed for that to happen. That actually wasn't what was most concerning him. The real problem was that he had no idea how he could convince Paul Smith to make the application.

Sally didn't know that worrying about this had troubled him much of the night and he still had no idea how to approach it. So when she had reminded him, he had snapped. He winced as he recalled how he had spoken to her. It was out of character for him to lose control like that.

'For god's sake, Sally, why don't you just butt out of police business. You two are actually starting to interfere with the investigation and maybe that makes you feel good, but you have no idea what you are doing. You will end up ruining my career if Smith thinks I'm allowing personal issues to interfere with my job.'

However, the more he thought about it, the more he accepted that the police investigations were going nowhere, regardless of what Smith had been saying. What's more, he had actually started to wonder if there might be some validity in the theory that Carl and Sally had put together. The investigation had certainly not yet identified the link between the disturbed grave and the murders. *Assuming there was one.*

Before he entered the station, he did a quick about turn and strolled a few metres along the footpath. As he did, he pulled his mobile phone from his pocket and called Sally. She was still at home and answered coolly.

'Hey Sal, I just wanted to have a quick chat. Listen I know I was a bit short with you this morning. I think this case is getting to me and I have to admit I'm feeling a little uncomfortable trying to keep my policing away from my personal side with you and Carl.'

'Riley, I know and I understand. I'm sorry, but Carl and I just need to do what we can to clear his name. You know you have him as a suspect, which I can't accept. I don't believe he would ever do a thing as horrible as that and it worries me that you do.'

'See, here's the thing. It doesn't matter what I believe. For me to do my job properly, I have to be a part of the investigating team. As a team, we have to explore all the options until we get the answer. Until we find the killer or clear Carl, he is going to be a potential suspect. Believe me, I don't want it to be Carl but if it is I would never forgive myself if I didn't protect you. Look, he and you need to let the facts speak. If he isn't guilty, that will come out. We can't charge him without evidence.'

'You know, Riley, I said pretty much the same thing to him the other day. Maybe we aren't so apart on this. Will you still talk to the Detective Inspector, though, please?'

'Yes. I've lost a lot of sleep over this but I do see where you're coming from. There seems to be some link between the grave and the murders, I get that. I just need to be able to sell it to

Smith. I'm not promising anything but I will try. I'll let you know.'

'Thanks. I love you, Riley.'

'I love you too. Let's make sure we keep talking.'

After disconnecting the call, Riley walked into the station and passed Phil Reid at the front desk. He also looked exhausted.

'Jeez, you look done, Phil.'

'Bloody cold, out at the cemetery all night. I'm going to make sure to take some warmer clothes tonight. Very uneventful, though. Just going to get some sleep now before I go back out later on.'

'Thanks, Phil. Take it easy. I'm hopeful we will have some other resources coming through starting tomorrow night.'

He walked through to the meeting room at the back, where he saw Paul Smith talking animatedly on the telephone. Once he hung up, Riley walked into the room.

'Morning, sir.'

'Morning, Riley. Just heard I have to go back to Adelaide this afternoon to report to the powers that be. I'll need to leave here at about 1.00, so I think I might stay in town tonight so I can say hello to the wife and kids. I reckon I might take my son to his school footy match in the morning and get back here tomorrow afternoon.'

'Ok, sir. We'll keep the wheels turning here.'

'Yes, good, and let me know if anything important comes up. I got the results from our fingerprint matching against those on the spade. Nothing, absolutely fucking nothing. No match to

Carl Johnson, Brock or Michael Richards or to Travis Schultz. Who the fuck used this spade?'

'So, you don't believe it was any of them?'

'Well, we can't be sure. Whoever it was could have worn gloves, I suppose. But then, whose fingerprints are on the spade?'

'Sir, I have another issue. I spent some time with Carl Johnson and my sister, Sally, yesterday afternoon.' Riley outlined the research that Sally and Carl had shown him, their visit to the house in Newacott Place and the proposal to exhume the body.

'It's a strange thing, sir. I know we don't have evidence that supports digging up the grave, but on the other hand, we seem to be running out of leads and we can't explain what the grave disturbance was all about.'

Smith was measured in his response.

'Riley, I warned you about the risks of your personal relationships in this case. I also told you I didn't want any Lone Ranger heroics.'

'I know, sir, but...'

Smith raised his hand.

'I understand what you are saying and maybe it is an avenue to follow. But it's far too early yet. We don't have any reason to support it at this stage. Let me think on it overnight and we'll talk about it tomorrow. I'm not making any promises, just that I'll think about it and if I can see any merit in it, we might just get your pair of amateur detectives to explain their theory in more detail.'

'Ok, sir, thanks for considering it.'

'Riley, you will only hear me say this once, so take note and don't repeat it. Sometimes, good cops do follow out of the box thinking, but they also don't let it dominate sound investigative processes. So don't get carried away, but let the thought develop if and only if you can support it with some real evidence.'

'Noted, sir.'

Riley left Smith and walked back outside the station. He called Sally.

'Sal, I've just spoken with Paul. He won't back the exhuming, not yet at least.'

'Oh, no. Why not?'

'Well, as I said, the evidence doesn't support it. But, don't get too disheartened. He hasn't eliminated it totally. He has said he will think on it, so he might still come around. In the meantime, can I just ask you and Carl to leave the investigation to us?'

'Ok, what if we uncover something?'

'Like what?' Riley asked tentatively.

'I don't know. We may find something else at the library, for example.'

'That's fine, just don't do anything. And don't say anything about what I've just told you. It's unofficial.'

'Ok, and thanks, Riley. You're the best.'

Chapter 35
Friday July 22 2016

It's shortly after 8.00 when I get a call from Sally.

We had spoken late last night after I had been to the Richards' place and I figured she wanted to see how I felt about it this morning.

Instead, she said, 'Hiya, I've just been talking with Riley. We had a bit of a dust-up this morning because I persisted with him to ask Paul Smith about exhuming the body. We're ok now, though, thank goodness. Anyway, he's had the chat with Smith.'

My hopes start to lift.

'Oh, how did that go? I wasn't sure Riley would actually do it.'

'Well, he did. In fact, I think he is starting to see that your theory might have something to it. So, Paul Smith won't apply for the exhuming. He doesn't think there's enough evidence to justify it.'

'Did Riley go through the whole story about the necklace and Joseph Tripp's trial?'

'Yes and while Smith hasn't agreed yet, he hasn't said he won't. He wants to think it through. I guess that's fair enough.'

'I guess so, but I just wish we could get on with it. I feel like I'm in no-man's land. I'm not being accused, but I'm also not cleared yet. As well, I really want to know what the connection is between me and Alexander.'

Sally laughs, 'Patience, my love. Anyway, how are you feeling this morning?'

She is, of course, following up on my call to her last night after I had gone out to Amy's parents' house.

As I had driven there, it was clear that another cold change was coming through and the prospect of rain on Friday was looking highly likely. I wondered what that would mean for digging up the grave, assuming Riley is able to get approval.

When I knocked on the front door of the Richards' house, I was surprised to be met by Brock, Amy's brother.

'Oh, hello,' I had said, my surprise obvious. 'You must be Brock. I'm …'

'Yeah, I know, Amy's coach. What do you want?' he said through the half opened door.

'I was wondering if your mum and dad were home.' I was surprised by Brock's curtness and wondered if he might have been under the influence of something.

'No, they're not, but I don't expect that they will want to see you.'

'Why?' I asked.

'Use your brains. Now that Kyle fuckhead Hooper is dead, you're the last living person that saw my sister alive. What do you think that means? I always thought you were some kind of freak, hanging out with a young girl like that.'

'I didn't harm her.'

'So you say. Frankly, I don't give a shit. All I know is that the cops should be dragging you in, instead of me and dad.'

'What did they call you in for?'

'Fingerprints. And because I had a go at that moron Travis.'

'Travis? Amy's friend?'

'No, not Amy's friend, you idiot. He was Kyle's friend. It wouldn't surprise me if he killed them. He's weird. Anyway, my parents aren't here, so fuck off.' Brock had moved to close the door. As he did, I saw the half empty bottle of Sailor Jerry in his hand.

'Wait. When do you think they will be back?'

'Dunno.' The door slammed behind him.

I am brought back to the present by Sally's voice.

'Carl?'

'Yes, sorry. Yeah, I'm ok. I'm just not sure what to do today. I don't really want to go back to Michael and Karen's. I could do without running into that little shit Brock again.'

'Listen, why don't you come to the library again? I can't help you today but why don't you try to find more about Alexander? Oh remember, I'm going to mum and dad's for dinner tonight... for mum's birthday. You can come if you like.'

'Thanks Sal, I would love to but I have to meet a guy from Adelaide on the island. He's after a quote for some work on his new holiday home. I will try to catch you in the library a bit later but in the meantime, I suppose I'd better catch up on a few of the jobs I've put off this week.'

Chapter 36
Sunday December 24th 1854

Joseph Tripp sat on the bench in his jail cell. This had been his home since being transferred to the Goolwa six weeks before. The cell was not too bad. At least he had a bed, a pan for his toilet and three meals a day. Best of all was the roof over his head, which protected him from bad weather. Not that there had been much since he had been arrested. The transition from spring to summer had heralded early heat and no rain had fallen in nearly five weeks.

After his flight from the Goolwa and his capture at Mannanarie, he was grateful for the relative comforts of the jail cell. But incarceration had not given him the one thing he had sought – shelter from the millions of eyes in the sky that had so haunted him every night. His cell had one small window only, but it was enough. They still watched him, invading his mind every night, conducting their own trial, condemning him, sentencing him. Every night he protested his innocence. *He hadn't meant to kill Alexander or Rubina.*

He screamed his objections, raising his head to the window, confronting his tormentors, before eventually realising they would not listen. Resignedly, he would go back to his cot, lying awake for the rest of the night, trying as he could to stop them from watching him by pulling a blanket tightly around his head.

What more did they expect?

He had confessed to killing Alexander and Rubina, although he had steadfastly maintained his innocence of murder. At his trial, the magistrate had patiently listened to him and had spoken kindly to him while he explained his story.

He had related his recollection of the night in the Goolwa Hotel where he and Alexander had plotted the search for Albert's Folly.

'And tell me, Mister Tripp, what happened once you found this Albert's Folly?' the magistrate had asked.

Tripp was relieved that someone, at last, was prepared to listen to his story. He told the courtroom at great length about how Alexander had taken custody of the necklace but had then for some reason become secretive about it. He said how eventually he had realised that Alexander clearly planned to cheat him of the proceeds.

'And so, sir, I decided I int going to put up with that. So I arranged to meet with Alexander on the Lady Augusta. He dint want to meet me but I made him. Anyway, when I get there and asks him, he tries to fob me off. I says I int going to be cheated and he gets up to leave.'

'And then, Mister Tripp?'

'Well I follows him out onto the deck and grabs him. He knocks my rum to the floor, trying to get away he was. Anyway, we has a scuffle and Alexander pulls away from me. I don't think he knew how close he was to the edge of the ship and he topples over. It were just an accident, see.'

The prosecutor then questioned Tripp on the detail of the fight.

'So, Mister Tripp, is it correct to say that you had consumed a lot of rum on that night?'

'Well, not a lot, sir. I only had the one bottle and it were still quarter full.' There was a titter from the observers in the courtroom.

'But it would be fair to say, would it not, that you were affected by the liquor?'

'Perhaps, sir.'

'Perhaps, sir. So, is it then possible that your memory of the events of that night is mistaken? Or perhaps you do not remember them clearly. Isn't it conceivable that you may have pushed Mister Johnston over the side? After all, he was an experienced seaman who had spent much of his life on a ship. I suggest such an experienced seaman would not have fallen in the way you have described. I also say to you, Mister Tripp, that you likely helped him overboard.'

'I don't remember, Sir.'

The magistrate then asked him to explain in his own words his visit to Rubina the following night. Again, the magistrate's tone was gentle, better than the silent accusations of the night skies and the aggressive tone of the prosecutor.

'Sir, I went to Alexander's house just to get the necklace. I asked Rubina politely, sir, where it were hidden. I meant her no harm, sir, but she came at me with a knife, like a mad woman, sir.

'She were so ferocious, she cut me arm. Then she came at me again and I had no choice, sir. I grabs her hand to protect mesself and somehow the knife went into her. I dint mean her to die.'

The prosecutor went over all his statements in detail, challenging every sentence. *How much force did he use? Was it excessive? Couldn't he have simply taken the knife from Rubina? Did Rubina have the knife or did Tripp pick it up in the kitchen before Rubina even appeared? Why did he go to the house in the middle of the night if he did not have evil intent?*

By the time the cross-examination was over, Tripp was shaking.

Police Trooper Brackenridge took the stand and described Rubina as a short but stout woman. There was no doubt she was strong for her size, but surely she was no match for Tripp who was over a foot taller and double her mass. Common sense, he said, suggested that Tripp could have fended her off, had he wished.

As he listened to the trooper, Tripp grew more sullen. They did not understand the woman's fury. She could not be resisted, despite her smaller stature. Since his visit to the Johnston house, he had fallen into a whirlpool of guilt and confusion. His mind was muddled with what was fact and what he may have imagined. Now, he couldn't tell the difference.

Initially, it had not been too bad when he had left his boat in the Finniss River. He had made his way north by foot, slowly but steadily for two days until he reached the town of Strathalbyn. He knew that suspicion would fall on him for the killings so he had bypassed the farms and the road when he could, travelling by night, sleeping under a bush or a rock overhang during the day.

When he arrived in Strathalbyn, he thought he could look for work in the Breadalbyn copper and silver mine. He had walked the road to the mine taking care to watch for any signs of a search party. He was nearly at the mine when he overheard the conversation of two men walking a couple of paces ahead. They were travellers that had come from the goldfields where they had lucked out. Their journey had brought them across the overland route from Melbourne passing by the Coorong until they reached the Goolwa. Finding no work available for miners there, they had secured a ride to Strathalbyn the previous day.

'I heard in the hotel two poor souls were murdered in the Goolwa. The trooper told the inn keeper that they already have parties searching for the killer.'

Tripp was not surprised

'So they know where he's gone?'

'Well, no they don't. They have sent one search party east, along the Coorong and up to Wellington town. Then they have another group coming this way, north toward the hills circling Adelaide. The trooper said they sent word to all the local towns they are looking for a burly man named Tripp.'

Tripp had allowed himself to drop back from the men and as soon as he could, he had broken off and headed down to the bank of the river Angas.

Giving up on the idea of seeking work in the town, he had decided to flee further away. As night fell he climbed back onto the roadway, walking a brisk pace through the night then resting the following day. He continued that pattern, avoiding any contact, until he reached Mount Barker.

As he arrived at the town, he saw the flour mill that had just opened in the township and asked discreetly whether it was hiring men. By this time, Tripp had not washed for several days and his clothes looked ragged. The mill works supervisor looked him up and down and sent him on his way.

He arrived in Adelaide a week later, intending to look for work on a boat to Melbourne. He thought that from there he could go to the goldfields, where he was sure he would be invisible. Perhaps better, he may find a ship on which he could crew his way back to England. On his second day at the port of Adelaide seeking work, he heard that Messrs Johnston and Murphy were due from the Goolwa to arrange purchase of their own river boat. While Adelaide's population was growing rapidly, he could not risk being seen by George Johnston, so he again took to the road.

There was no point going south so he took the opposite direction out of Adelaide. Before he left, he had heard about men travelling to work in the mines at Burra Burra, far north of Adelaide. He decided that he could easily sit out a few months there until they gave up the search.

Tripp skirted the towns, stealing whatever food he could from neighbouring farms. He had no money for lodgings, so he was forced to sleep where he could in the open.

In the weeks that followed, his nights became more tortured. When he tried to sleep, he had nightmares, re-living the nights he had taken the lives of two others. Soon he started to have recurrences of his first night of the terror he experienced sleeping in his boat off Hindmarsh Island. The stars had started spying on him again, watching and waiting.

By the time he approached Burra, he was filthy, dejected and confused. He had simply kept moving, aiming to steer clear of the searchers but he was unable to elude the watching skies. Some nights were better than others. If there was cloud cover, he felt protected and started the next day with vigour, confident he could escape. As the season changed and the clouds abandoned him, he would be forced to face the witnesses above. The further north he travelled, the clearer the nights became.

When he reached Mannanarie Run, he was starving, desolate and quite mad. He had been relieved when he was captured by the farmer and his men, regardless of the consequences. Nothing could be worse than the hunger, thirst and torment that he had suffered.

He still could not understand why they had not believed him in court when he insisted that he and Alexander had found the valuable necklace. But then, they had searched the house even more thoroughly than he had. Brackenridge was adamant that it was not hidden in the house. Alexander had told him that he did not have it on his person and Tripp believed him. There was no reason for him to say otherwise.

Had he imagined the whole thing? The deal he had struck with Alexander, the night on the Coorong, the camp with the aboriginal man, Lenny, the finding of the necklace. No, of course not. But then why can't it be found?

Had he killed Alexander and Rubina for no reason?

Joe tentatively looked out the window into the night sky. He sensed the stars starting their nightly vigil. To his horror, the moon hung like a silver scythe ready to part his head from his shoulders. He recoiled in shock, stumbling over his toilet pan onto his cot.

Tomorrow was Christmas Day. The following day, Tuesday, the magistrate would pronounce his verdict and sentence. He knew they would hang him. *It mattered not – he would at least be free of the nightly torment.* He was not a religious man, but knew if there was a heaven or hell he need not be concerned about going closer to the stars. *No, he would rot in the ground, in a cold comfort.*

Christmas Day dawned as the day before had and the one before that. The court would not sit on this Monday, being a holy day. Even for a man in jail, there would be some privileges - hearty meals, perhaps even a mug of ale and a more genial mood amongst his guards.

However, the guards were in no hurry that morning.   Their prisoner was not going anywhere, so he wouldn't complain if his breakfast was a bit late. In any event, the entire town said that tomorrow he was to be sentenced to hang, so if he had protestations, it mattered little.

The guard whistled happily as he took the prisoner his breakfast. In a few short hours, his shift would be over and he could be with his family, enjoying roast lamb and a few ales. He placed the tray of fried eggs, fresh bacon and beans on the floor as he fumbled for the right key to unlock the cell door.

In the solid wooden door was a small grated window that provided a view into the cell. There was a similar window on the opposite wall, one that faced out to the open sky, the one through which the stars continued to spy on Joe Tripp each night. Still whistling a Christmas tune, the guard absently looked through the window in the door as he slipped the key into the lock. His whistling stopped abruptly as he saw Joe Tripp suspended from the opposite window. He was tied to the grate by a strip of the blanket he had used to hide from the stars, but which now freed him from their view forever.

With Tripp's death, the whereabouts of Albert's Folly would not be questioned for over one hundred and fifty years. The next time would also have deadly consequences.

Chapter 37
Friday July 22 2016

The gravedigger now knew he must take a risk if he was to finish the job. With the attention around the cemetery and the discovery of Kyle's body the town had been abuzz with rumours and speculation.

At least, he believed, there was nothing that could tie him to the crimes that have been committed there. He had decided he would wait until the activity and interest around the cemetery had faded before he would make another effort at the grave. He had been determined that he would remain strong against the temptation to finish the job.

As long as he kept clean, eventually the investigation would die off and he would be clear for a second attempt. To attempt prematurely could only potentially attract attention to him.

He continued to toss up whether he should wait a few more days. Now Kyle's body had been found, there was increased risk that the reason for the grave's disturbance could be exposed.

Impetuously, he thought he should be able to do what he needed to do and restore the grave to its current condition without anyone knowing.

He remembered how hard the ground was and went to the shed to get a pick and spade. He had been concerned all week that he had discarded the spade he used last time on the side of the path leading down to the creek. *Surely they have discovered it by now.*

He packed his car in readiness and waited for darkness to fall. By the time he left, the wind had come up and light rain was falling. For him that was good news and bad. The rain would soften the ground but it would also increase the chance he would leave foot prints around the grave. He dwelt on that conundrum as he drove through the town.

The Friday evening crowd was starting to congregate at the town's two main street hotels. For the patrons, it was another night of casual dinner, drinking and good company.

After leaving the town limits, he continued to the parking area near the creek. He decided that, like last time, it made sense to park well away from the cemetery to minimise the chance of his car being seen and identified.

With spade and pick, he made his way along the path and up the hill to the cemetery. Unlike last time, he thought, he would be ready for unwelcome interruptions, but he hoped beyond hope he was alone. Looking up at the sky, he hoped the foreboding clouds and the rain already falling would be a deterrent to any other would be visitors to the cemetery.

He walked purposefully through the cemetery toward his target, taking care not to make too much noise. He knew the police were active in the area during the day.

He crept past several areas where tape was drawn across to restrict access but there was no sign of anyone guarding the site now.

Still, can't be too careful. He was past half way across the cemetery, when he first sensed a movement. Moving forward quietly in the darkness, he looked to the sky. The moon was up but hidden behind clouds that formed a full cover across the sky. At least for the moment he felt there was minimal risk he would be seen.

With carefully placed steps, he stole through the headstones, choosing the cover of larger monuments where he could, pausing frequently to listen and look, assessing his solitude.

Then he saw it. There was a dim light at the top of the hill. It looked like the interior light of a car. After a moment the light went out and simultaneously, he heard the soft thud of a door closing.

'Damn,' he muttered to himself. He contemplated whether to call off his venture for the night, but quickly reminded himself that this may be his final chance. The only question was whether he had the courage to wilfully attack someone to get what he wanted.

Last time it was different, he had no choice and he certainly didn't plan to kill them. This time, he needed to plan an attack rather than respond to an instant of surprise.

He laid the pick on the ground. He glided slowly forward, spade gripped between both hands like a woodsman with an axe.

He saw the figure switch on a flashlight as it entered the gate, waving it around from left to right before settling on a course straight ahead down the centre path of the cemetery.

The gravedigger crouched behind a large gravestone, only twenty metres ahead and to the left of the stranger. He waited for him to pass before making a move.

Chapter 38
Friday July 22 2016

After I'd finished the jobs I had scheduled for the day, I dropped into the library to see Sally and to see if I could learn anything new about Alexander Johnston, Joe Tripp, Albert's Folly, anything that would help me prove my innocence. Unfortunately, the pool of history had dried up and I felt no wiser than I had at the start of the day. I need that exhumation of Alexander's body.

Sally and I leave just after dark stepping out to face a cold, stiff breeze. She is off to have dinner with her parents and leaves me at the corner wishing me good luck with the quotation for the landscape job. I decide not to go home before heading over to Hindmarsh Island in an hour or so.

Since arriving in the town I have avoided the local pubs as much as I can, but tonight I am going to eat at the Goolwa Hotel. I walk into the dining room where members of the football club committee are congregating at a table toward the back. It is a tradition for the committee to eat there the evening before a home game to finalise the rosters for all the match day duties. A few seats are empty and I see that Riley hasn't arrived yet.

I wander over to the bar passing the old table and chairs displayed in the corner. While I wait my turn, I read the laminated card on top of the table. The card details how they had been salvaged from the old barge, the Mozambique, which sank somewhere off the coast near here in the 1850's They were apparently given to the hotel publican by the barque's captain in gratitude for providing food and lodgings for the passengers that were rescued from the boat. Out of curiosity, and with a new-found interest in the Mozambique, I look at the chairs. In the research I did this morning into the shipwreck, I had read that the chairs still bore the teeth marks of the sailors who had run races on the ship carrying the chairs in their mouths. The chairs actually show the marks. I'm impressed.

I wait at the bar and a few moments later I am served by Cheryl Higgins, Peter's wife, who I had met for the first time only the day before.

'Oh, hello Cheryl, I didn't know you worked here.'

'I wouldn't be, except we've just bought a place in Sage Street. We can't really afford it but it has a large shed that Peter uses for his joinery work. This job just gives us a bit of extra money.'

Seeing her reminds me that I want to check with Peter about the timing of the construction of Alexander's house. After all, if there was no house built at the time, my theory that the necklace was with Alexander may not be worth anything. *One more piece of the puzzle.*

'Fair enough. I'll have a pint of pale ale thanks. Is Peter coming in for the committee dinner tonight?'

'Apparently he's got too much work on at the moment. He hasn't missed one of these dinners for years. Maybe he's got himself a girlfriend.' She laughs as she turns away to pour my beer.

I take my beer to the food counter and order the roast lamb special. As I walk to an empty table, I look up at the figurehead mounted on the wall above the salad bar. Sally had told me earlier today that the figurehead had also been given to the hotel after the shipwreck. One hundred and fifty years later it was the feature of the dining room, aptly named the Mozambique Restaurant.

I sit at my table intrigued by it. I try to visualise how there can be a link between this inanimate object and the mystery I am embroiled in. The figurehead is a half-body carving of a fair skinned woman with black curly hair and a somewhat noble countenance. She is wearing a scarlet red dress with a blue sash that sits under her ample bosom. Her pale neck is adorned with a necklace made of large pearls. Matching earrings drape elegantly from her ears.

She strikes me as a lady of nobility or at least wealth. I wonder what conversations she has heard over the years and what secrets she carries. *What would she know about the mystery necklace and whether it was ever recovered?* I remind myself to check to see if I can find out whether Catharine Delaney ever claimed insurance for her loss. *Maybe that could provide a clue as to whether the jewels were ever recovered. Perhaps they were recovered and my theory is all wrong. That would take me back to square one – but then why has Alexander Johnston's grave been tampered with?*

The waitress is approaching with my meal as a sudden thought strikes me. I have a nagging feeling about a comment made when I was at Alexander Johnston's house with Riley and Sally yesterday. I'm also puzzled by the comment Sue made about all the sudden interest in George Johnston. My mind is racing and I leap up from the table. I see the bewildered look on the waitress's face but I don't have the time or inclination to worry about that now. I walk through the front door of the hotel and straight to my car parked on the other side of the road. Since I walked into the hotel only thirty minutes earlier, it has started raining. I am at my car before I notice the change.

It is a very short drive to Newacott Place and less than a minute later I sit in my car outside Alexander's Johnston's house. I had hoped Peter would have still been working there but see that his car is not parked out the front and no lights are on inside the house.

I am disappointed as the question that I know Peter can answer is nagging at me. I figure that Peter may be working on some cupboards or other furnishings in his new shed rather than at the cottage, so I start the car and wind my way back to the road that will take me to Goolwa Beach.

As I turn into Sage Street, I am acutely aware that I don't know the street number but I expect that, like most people in Goolwa, Peter parks his car in the driveway or on the roadside. In this town, garages are reserved for far more important chattels such as boats, windsurfing and surfing equipment or, as in Peter's case, a home business. I drive up and down Sage Street and see no sign of his Toyota Hilux. The rain is now falling in a steady curtain. My wipers drag across the windscreen continuously, providing clear vision for only brief intervals. I see no sign of lights on in any of the side buildings in the street. *Damn.*

I sit in my car frustrated, pondering the questions running through my mind. Working through the scenarios, I have another idea – *no this could be a brainwave.* Filled with inspiration and a burning desire to put this thing to bed, I grab my mobile phone and pick a number from my 'Favourites'.

The phone rings four times and I frown with annoyance that my call might go to voicemail. However, the frown dissolves when I hear the voice.

'Hiya. Can't be without me, huh?'

'Yes, I mean no. Hey, is Riley there?'

'No, it's Friday night. He'd be at the Goolwa with his beloved footy club committee. You know that. Why do you want him?'

'Ok, doesn't matter. Listen I need to meet you at the library.'

'When?' Sally asks.

'Now?'

'Carl, I have just finished eating. I'm just starting to help mum clean up. What's going on?'

'I think I might be onto something. I know it's a big ask, but this is really important. Please come.'

My exasperation must have hit a chord.

'Alright! I don't have my work keys so I'll have to swing by and pick them up. You owe my mum big time. See you soon.'

'Great, thanks. Tell your folks I'll make it up to them. Hey, love you. Hurry.'

I drive back into town and park in the side street next to the library. It seems forever since I spoke to Sally and she hasn't turned up yet. The rain is still coming down and the roads will be slippery. *God, I hope she is driving carefully.*

I have my phone ready to call her again when I see her Honda Civic round the corner from Cadell Street and pull up behind me. I jump out of my car and together we run across the road to the side door of the library. I hold my jacket over Sally's head as she fumbles her key into the lock and opens the door.

'Wait here,' she says and walks through to a control pad to disarm the security system. I hear a couple of beeps and she waves me in.

'What is this all about, Carl? Surely it could have waited 'til tomorrow?'

I look at her face, dripping with rain, a strand of hair plastered to her forehead. In spite of my haste, I don't think she has ever looked more beautiful.

'I don't think so. If I'm right, our man will be making a move very soon. I think he has stumbled onto the whereabouts of the necklace that went missing from the Mozambique, the one that Joe Tripp went on about at his trial.'

'But they didn't find anything to support his claims.'

'I know, because they didn't know where to look. They assumed that Alexander had it hidden in his house. I don't think it was.'

'Ok, I know you think it could have been buried with him and that's why the grave has been disturbed. So what?'

I look into her sky blue eyes and hold them while I answer, slowly and purposeful.

'I came to that conclusion because we did the research and concluded that was the most likely way that Joe's story could be true. It would also explain why the jewels were never found. What if the killer reached the same conclusion the same way?'

'Explain.' Sally is gradually aligning her thinking with mine.

'He or she or someone they know went to the same resources we did. Remember Sue mentioned the sudden interest in George Bain Johnston lately? Because the killer did exactly what we did.'

'So,' Sally said, now becoming more animated, 'we need to know who has looked at the books we did.'

'Can we do that?'

'If he or she borrowed one of the books we looked at, we might be in luck. If not, it's a dead end unless one of the staff, maybe Sue, remembers someone asking for those specific books.'

'All right, let's start with the easy option. How do we find out who borrowed them last?'

Sally almost sprinted to the other side of the counter.

'You go get the books while I fire up the computer.' It takes me less than a minute to grab one of the books. I'm relieved no-one else has borrowed it since we looked at it yesterday. The computer is still going through its initiation when I return. Sally and I look at each other in anticipation until we see the home screen come up.

'Ok, let me just get to the screen that we need. There can you just place the books on the RFID reader?'

'The what?'

She points to a rectangular metal plate on the counter.

'Radio Frequency Identification. It uses electro-magnetic fields embedded in the book. They allow us to access all the information about it.'

I place "The Early History of Goolwa" on the reader and Sally turns to the computer screen.

'Ok, here's the last person that borrowed the book. The last activity date shown here, that's the day it was returned, or close enough, was only three weeks ago.'

'So who was it?' I ask a touch impatiently.

Sally lifts her eyes to look at me scornfully.

'Just a minute, one more step. I need to copy the UserID and then go to this screen... here... and paste in the UserID. Let's see who we've got.'

The name comes up and she looks at me quizzically.

'Is that what you expected?'

'Mmmm, could be. I couldn't find the other book, "SA Murder Trials 1851 -1899". How can we be sure?'

Sally thinks for a minute and then says, 'Oh, that's right, we got that in the History Room, so that's not available for loan.'

'So that's a dead end?'

'Not necessarily. When people use the History Room, Sue gets them to write their name in a visitor's book. It's mainly for follow up if the historians find something in the field that the person is looking for.'

'But, surely he wouldn't have put his name in, knowing it could lead to him.'

'Well, Sue's pretty persistent and, remember, he wouldn't be expecting anyone to be following up. And because he's a local, he's not going to put in a false name or make a big issue about leaving his name. That would only draw attention.'

She leads me into the History Room and the visitor book lies on the table, opened to the current page. The ledger shows the date of the entry, the name and contact details of the person accessing the records, who and what they were researching and any comments.

'I didn't fill this in when we were looking,' Sally says, 'but I'm pretty confident that Sue would have made sure anyone else would have.'

We scan the current page, but there is no sign of the name we are looking for. Sally, turns the book back to the previous page and there it is.

Sally stares at me again.

'You knew it was him, didn't you? How?'

I draw in a sharp breath.

'Can I tell you later? I want to get going,' I exclaim.

'Where to?'

'The cemetery. I think he's gone to finish the job because he has figured we will get Alexander's body exhumed.'

'I'm coming too.'

'No, Sally, it could be dangerous.'

'All the more reason why I'm coming. You're not going alone,' she screams as we run to the door.

It's late and still raining as we drive through Goolwa, heading north. We pass the police station and I suggest to Sally that she call them for assistance. We leave the 50 km per hour zone and accelerate out of Goolwa.

'There's no answer at the station. It's diverting to another number. I'm going to call Riley.'

She redials and waits.

'Hey, Sal, listen I can't talk right now. We're cleaning up a car accident at Middleton.'

'No listen, Riley. We know who the killer is. We're going out to the cemetery now.'

'You're what? No, stop right now. This is a police matter. We'll come as soon as we can. Anyway, I've got Phil Reid out there on watch.'

'Ok, we'll wait. See you soon but please come quick.'

She hangs up. 'He wants us to wait.'

I ponder the consequences and turn to Sally, without slowing the car.

'I can't wait. He could be gone before Riley gets there. I'll let you out back at the station and you can wait for Riley if you want.'

'Carl, we are in this together and you'll lose too much time turning back now. Keep going. Riley says he's got Phil Reid out there and hopefully it's all under control anyway.'

Chapter 39
Friday July 22 2016

We drive across the cattle ramp onto the dirt road and toward the cemetery. The road is wet and slippery and I have to slow to 30 kilometres per hour. The rain has eased slightly but our vision is still limited and it feels ghostly, surrounded by the shadows of trees on either side of the narrow road.

In my haste, I let the car drift up to 50 kilometres per hour and as I take the right hand bend before the shooting range, I feel the back end of the car slide out. I turn the steering wheel sharply back to the left and resist the urge to brake. The car spins and it's only a split second before the rear of the car is taking the lead. I feel Sally's eyes on me as the car starts to slow, but it is still spinning, seemingly in slow motion.

We feel a jolt as the car comes to a sudden stop, the rear wheels embedded in a mound of dirt on the side of the road. Shaken, we undo our seat belts and get out of the car. I run to the back of the car and look at the rear wheel - the tyre has been knocked off its rim.

We are still a few hundred metres from the cemetery, but at least the rain has stopped now.

'Sally, stay with the car and ring Riley again. I'm going on.'

'I'm coming too,' she says.

'I'd rather you stay locked in the car. I can get there quicker on my own, but if you insist on coming, have a good look before you enter the cemetery. And stay quiet ... just in case.'

'Carl...' she screams, but I have already started running down the road.

I slow to a walk as I reach the car park. A police car is parked near the gate but there is no sign of Phil Reid. I figure he is probably doing a round of the cemetery. I am surprised that there's no sign of the car I expected to be there.

I start to doubt my theory. *Perhaps he didn't see the need to come back and finish. Perhaps he's not even connected to this whole mess.*

I enter the cemetery and hear the wind in the trees. In the moonlight, I see a shape on the ground near the small shelter across the path from Alexander Johnston's grave.

I walk over to find Phil Reid, his head bloodied. He has a nasty gash stretching across his forehead. He is lying on his side facing me. His hands have been tied behind his back using his own shoelaces and his feet are bound with his belt. He has a cloth, looks like a handkerchief, stuffed into his mouth.

I bend over him and reach to remove the cloth from his mouth, when his eyes open as wide as golf balls. He is looking over my right shoulder. Sensing the danger, I throw myself to my left but not quickly enough and I feel a searing pain as something smashes into my upper right arm, leaving it with no feeling. I am certain that it's smashed.

I manage to scramble just a couple of metres away, enough to force my attacker to come after me. I'm still on the ground and my arm is useless, but I manage to lash out with my foot as he is raising a spade for his next big hit. Luckily, I connect with his knee and it buckles beneath him. Although he recoils in pain, he recovers quickly, enough for another onslaught by the time I am on my feet.

His next blow connects with my stomach and I double over winded, gasping for breath. I have been able to grab the spade handle before he pulls back. I am gripped by the fear that his next hit will be a killer blow if I can't stop it. The next voice I hear is Sally's.

'Carl', she screams.

He looks at her. Instead of trying to wrench the spade from me, he lets it go and runs deeper into the cemetery.

Sally rushes to me as I fall to the ground, still gasping like a fish out of water.

'Carl, are you alright?'

'I'm ok,' I mutter as I get to my knees. 'Take care of Phil. I don't think he's too good.'

'Oh my god,' she says when she sees his face. 'Riley's on his way.'

'I hope he's brought back up. Tell him where we've gone,' I say as I stumble after my attacker.

He is far enough ahead of me that I can't see him now but I figure he has gone down toward the creek, just as he must have done a few days before.

Even though it's almost a full moon the cloud cover blocks its beams from pushing through. The wind is howling through the trees now and I feel like I am in some 'B' class horror movie, except I know that this is real.

I am trying to run at full pace, but the going is hard. The ground is uneven and I continually trip over stones and tree roots. So far I have been able to hold my feet and I have made it about half way through the cemetery grounds. I have only been here once before but I remember there is a stile at the north western corner. I hope that he has gone that way; otherwise I'm convinced I will lose him.

As I run further down, the tree roots have gone so I pick up my pace. What I don't know and don't see, is that over the years rainfall has created tiny rivers in the ground. When it is dry, they are uneven, but hard. Right now, with the rain they have become slushy and slippery. I am running full speed when I need to swerve left to dodge a gravestone that I hadn't noticed. As I do, I step in one of the rivulets and my foot slips out from under me. I fall heavily and slide straight into the gravestone I was trying to avoid. A pain in my ankle shoots up my leg and for the second time in just a few minutes I feel like I may have broken a bone.

I lift myself so I can lean on my elbow and as I turn, I see the silhouette of a figure standing over me. All I can see is a large bulk blocking the moon and I am shot with a fear that he has come back to finish me off. He stands, towering above me, while I feel powerless to defend myself. *I'm scared shitless.*

'Here', he says, offering me his hand. As I rise gingerly, I realise two things. Firstly this is the kid from the supermarket, Amy's friend, Travis. The good news is he's not my attacker.

'What are you doing here?' I ask.

'I sometimes come over from my house just there,' he says pointing to the hills. 'I like walking here. He nearly pushed me down, that bloke.'

'Which way did he go, Travis?'

'He went over there.' He points to the corner that I was heading to.

The second thing I realise is that I haven't seriously hurt my ankle and I am able to comfortably put weight on it.

'Thanks,' I call back, running in the direction he had pointed. 'Can you go and help the others at the gate?'

As I run, I am rapidly losing confidence that I can make up enough ground. It might be up to Riley and his men to find him.

I finally reach the stile and almost fall over it in my haste. The pathway down the hill is narrow and there are thorny shrubs that grow on the side, branches occasionally hanging over and catching on my clothes and skin. I wince with each stab.

There are logs set into the path to make steps so that the downward slope is easier to traverse, but I am running so fast, there is every chance I will miss one and end up rolling head over heels to the bottom. I only hope that bastard is having as tough a time of it as I am.

I'm not familiar with this area. I know that to the right is the road from Goolwa to the townships of Currency Creek and Strathalbyn, while left goes to a waterfall and I suspect a dead end. I figure that if I was trying to escape someone chasing me, I'd head for the road, so I turn right.

The path is narrow. On my left, the creek side, the bamboo reeds stretch nearly two metres in the air, hiding the creek itself. I know it's there, because I can hear the water flowing. On the right is the side of the hill I have just scrambled down. Growing on the side are eucalypts and various types of bushes. One type in particular has more thorns and because of the narrowness of the path I am forced to slow frequently to disentangle myself. The floor of the path is even rougher than the cemetery and the path down the hill. Rocks jut out from the ground and getting a reliable foothold is hard. My ankle is sending needling jolts up my leg every time I ask it to support my foot on an angled rock.

I feel wretched, but I tell myself that I need to keep going to bring Amy's killer to justice and to make sure my name is not again tainted.

I reach the railway bridge that towers over my head. I see a pool of water between the pylons and now that the moon has come out from behind the clouds, the reflection of the night sky provides a sense of serenity that I can't quite connect with at the moment.

I keep running despite feeling a stitch in my side. I can see the reception centre on the left on the other side of the creek so I know that it can't be much further to the road.

The rain has started again and the moon has timidly shrunk back behind the clouds as though it is also trying to shield from the rain. I see blue and red lights flashing ahead and a split second later the headlights of the police car come over the hump into the driveway. The police car pulls into the car park and even though the ground is wet I hear the crunch of sudden braking on the gravel. To the right of the police car, a four wheel drive is parked hidden between a bush and the toilet block.

Riley stands in the headlights of the car as a second patrol enters the car park. I am bent over, panting, grateful for the reinforcements.

'Carl,' Riley calls, 'you've figured it out. How did you know?'

'I didn't know, but I just thought it was a bit odd that he said yesterday that he didn't have any work other than at Alexander's house and then tonight his wife tells me that he is too busy working so he breaks a habit he's had for years. On top of that, he seemed to know a lot about people living in huts rather than houses in the 1850's. That's almost word for word what Sue told Sally and me at the library yesterday. The sealer was that I'm sure he overhead me ask you about exhuming Alexander Johnston's body. That's why he's come tonight'

'He wasn't at the footy committee dinner? How did you know he wasn't working?'

'Well, he wasn't at the Johnston house, and or at his house either. I've already been there. Cheryl jokingly said he could have a girlfriend but she said it with a lot of confidence that it wouldn't be a real possibility.'

'So where is he now?' Riley asks.

'I've lost him. If he hasn't come out here, he must be back there somewhere,' I say, pointing back over my shoulder.

Riley deploys some of his men to go back to the road and search possible escape routes, especially away from the direction they have come.

'How did you know to come down here?' I ask Riley.

'I saw Sally and Phil. Where's Travis? He apparently came after you'

'I haven't seen him since the cemetery.'

'Come on, let's go back along the path,' says Riley, already running as he passes me.

Soaked to the skin, I turn and start running after him. The rain is now coming down in sheets and the wind has lifted, growling as it powers into the narrow pass ahead.

We have gone only thirty or forty metres, when a massive fork of lightning lights up the sky ahead of us. For the briefest of moments, I think I have seen a movement ahead. Not on the path ahead but on top of the railway bridge.

In the darkness after the lightning strike, it is only a couple of seconds before the thunderclap booms above us.

'Did you see that?' I yell to Riley about ten metres ahead of me. He stops.

'Yeah, I think so. He must have scrambled up the side of the hill.'

I catch up to him and we stand shoulder to shoulder, straining in the darkness to catch a further glimpse.

As if knowing it has a role to play, the moon seems to summon courage and pokes out from behind the cloud. It is almost directly above the bridge from where we stand and its silvery glow is just enough to highlight any movement.

Momentarily we glimpse the silhouetted figure of Peter Higgins. He is almost half way across the bridge.

'Peter,' Riley yells. 'Wait.'

'What for?' He answers, the strain in his voice dissolving the strength it had always previously shown.

'We need to talk. There's no point in running now. Why don't you come back down?'

'No point in that now either, is there? I've fucked everything up.'

'It's not too late to salvage something, Pete. Let's just talk it through.'

Higgins stops and seems to be considering what to do next.

'I didn't mean to hurt them, Amy and that boy. If they had just let me be, none of this needed to happen.'

'What were you doing at the grave, Higgins?' I ask.

Riley glares at me. 'Let me handle this,' he mutters. 'I don't want him to jump.'

Higgins looks up at the black sky and then back to us. The cold wind is ripping through my wet clothes and I suddenly realise that I am shivering uncontrollably.

'Bloody treasure. I should have known it was only going to bring trouble. Don't even know if it's there for certain.'

As he talks, we see another dark figure walking across the bridge. Higgins hasn't noticed.

Riley looks at me puzzled and it comes to us both at the same time.

'Travis Schultz' I whisper, barely audible in the howling wind even though Riley and I are standing right next to each other.

'Travis, stop!' Riley yells.

Higgins turns to face him. For a terrifying moment it appears that he will rush at Travis.

Travis continues to walk toward him. They are of similar build and their silhouettes as they face each other create an image of some sort of weird puppet show.

'You killed Amy and Kyle. They were my friends.'

'I'm sorry. It was all a horrible mistake.'

They are yelling at each other yet we can barely discern their words. Riley tries desperately to regain control. 'Come on Peter and Travis. Come down here so we can talk this through. It's not safe up there.'

Travis stops momentarily and looks down at us, not sure whether to do what Riley asks.

Higgins breaks the impasse. 'No, Riley, it's too late for talk. It's got to be made right. Tell Michael and Karen I'm sorry. Kyle's mother too. And tell Cheryl I love her.'

'No, don't.' Riley calls.

In Peter Higgins' moment of hesitation, Travis rushes him. With head down, he buries his shoulder into Higgins mid-drift. They fall onto the sleepers of the train track, inches from the edge. We can see the shadows of them wrestling, but can't distinguish them apart.

'Oh, Christ.' Riley runs to the base of the bridge, set to scramble up the hill to the top.

The moon is now shining brightly as I stand back, watching. One of the shapes on the bridge rises to his feet and moves slowly away from the other. As he does, a hand stretches out, enough to cause the standing figure to stumble. He regains his balance but in his haste to escape the outreached hand, he steps back, the heel of his foot catching on the rail track. His momentum causes his upper body to keep moving backwards, over the edge of the bridge.

The body almost floats through the air until it splashes into the pool of water beneath. It lies still.

Riley races into the water, sinking to his upper chest by the time he reaches the body. It's face down. When I get to the side of the pool, Riley has turned it over and I see the lifeless eyes of Peter Higgins staring into the moonlit sky above.

I call up to the bridge. 'Are you alright, Travis?'

'Yeah, I'm alright. He killed my friends.'

'I know. Come on down. It's all over now.'

Chapter 40
Two months later

It's now September and for the last two weeks, warmth has begun to find its way into our days. The bitter chills off the Antarctic have been replaced by sweet breezes carrying the scents of fresh pollen and freshly cut grass.

Sally and I are walking along the beach and for the first time in months, this morning we have bare feet. The sand between my toes is warm and sensual and the sun on my face is a welcome change from the dull winter days. There is a light breeze coming from the north, gently teasing the grasses in the sand hills as they wave at the sun in some kind of welcome to the change of season.

As we look to the west toward Middleton and Port Elliot, the surf and the breeze join to create a fine mist over the sea, a surfer occasionally riding the top of a wave, breaking through the curtain.

The brilliance and goodwill of this beautiful spring day is a stark contrast to the bleak winter night when Peter Higgins fell to his death from the railway bridge.

Paul Smith and Riley wrapped up the investigation within a couple of weeks of that night. If Smith was disappointed that he wasn't there when the case unravelled or the way that it came together, he didn't show it. In fact, he was very gracious and passed the plaudits onto the team, particularly to Riley going so far as to endorse his entry into a specialised investigative course in Adelaide. According to Smith, it's quite likely that Riley will be promoted to the rank of Senior Sergeant on his return to Goolwa.

After Higgins' death, police went to work to understand why he had an interest in Alexander Johnston's grave and why he killed Amy and Kyle. Of course, his revelation on top of the bridge that the treasure may not have been in the grave supported my theory that he had at some time discovered information that led him to believe that it was the most likely place it was hidden. Poor Amy and Kyle must have stumbled on him while he was digging at the grave, but we all remain bewildered how that led him to commit such brutal, heinous and unnecessary murders.

Forensic scientists were able to match the fibres found in Amy's ears and nose with fibres in the tray of Peter's Hilux, most likely from the hessian used by him in his building activities.

The real shock to us all was the discovery in the glove compartment of Peter's car of a jewellery bag, marked Geo. Fotheringham & Son, London, 1840. It turns out that George Fotheringham was the jeweller reputed to have made Albert's Folly, the valuable emerald necklace referred to in Joseph Tripp's file and lost from the Mozambique over one hundred and fifty years ago. Peter's discovery of the bag was no doubt the catalyst for his research that led him to be aware of the existence of the necklace.

Cheryl, Peter's wife, knew nothing of the discovery, but we assume that somehow Peter uncovered the bag while renovating the little cottage in Newacott Place. On the night Peter secretly made his first attempt on the gravesite on the night of the murders, Cheryl was babysitting her grandchildren and had slept overnight.

She was overwrought by Peter's death and the shame of the subsequent enquires. The few people she spoke to after suggested that, as well as the shame of the crimes Peter had committed, she truly did not know whether Peter's plan for the future even included her. She wondered if he intended to start a new life without her. She left Goolwa to make a new start in Adelaide as soon as Peter's funeral service was over.

His funeral was a quiet affair with only a handful of people outside his family attending, an ignominy for a man who was once highly respected in our community.

Amy and Kyle on the other hand had several hundred turn out for their joint service.

Of course, Travis was there and gave a simple but touching eulogy for his friends. He still works at the supermarket, but spends time with Vicky Hooper and has been a great comfort to her in dealing with the loss of her son. At Vicky's insistence, Travis often stays at her house during the times his father is working away.

Brock Richards attended the services for Amy and Kyle. Somewhat subdued nowadays, the feeling around town is that Michael may have clipped his wings to some extent.

I am still gardening, but I do admit that I am thirsting for the opportunity to get back into the teaching ranks. I was flattered when the Goolwa Surf Lifesaving Club asked me to train a team of young lifesavers. Kayak turns out to be great winter training for surf ski paddlers. They even contributed to the cost of the kayaks so that I can expand the program further.

Sally moved in with me two weeks ago which was timely given Riley's temporary relocation to Adelaide but it has also given us the opportunity to deepen our relationship. In many ways, I am a different man now. I have moved my old demons on and I haven't noticed the dark shadows following me for a long time. I've got a much more positive outlook and am certainly the most self-assured I have been for two years. Sally is coping with the new me very well.

Maybe the biggest obvious change for me has been that I now live by the name I was born with, Callum Johnston, although to Sally, it's usually Cal. The change was not as great as I expected. I first had to convince myself to let go of Carl. Even though that identity had served me well, I also learned with Sally's help that it was just an escape.

Finally, the necklace.

It seems that Albert's Folly did exist. The details of its loss, then discovery at the Coorong (I still can't call my ancestor a thief), followed by its disappearance, remains a mystery. Paul Smith did ask me, as apparently the only known living relative of Alexander Johnston, whether I wanted to pursue the application for exhumation.

He didn't say whether an application would be successful, but in the end I decided that the necklace should remain where it is, assuming it is actually there.

I can't honestly lay any claim to its ownership and somehow it seems like it would be opening up the past again. I would prefer for Alexander's grave to be as it had been for one hundred and fifty years – left alone.

'What are you thinking about, Callum Johnston?'

I turn to Sally. 'I'm thinking it's time to turn back so you can buy me a coffee.'

Author's note

This story is (almost) entirely fictional. It is fact that the Mozambique was washed aground near the Goolwa. The prologue of this book is a re-print of the article that covered this event as reported in The Register courtesy of the National Library of Australia

It is also true and that the occupants of the ship were offered hospitality by the publican of the Goolwa Hotel which, by the way, is still in its original location in Cadell Street and does feature the figurehead prominently in its dining room. Other artefacts, including the table and chairs (with bite marks) are also there.

Some other historical elements are based on actual events, for example the race between Frances Cadell and William Randell to sail the length of the Murray River, but most is fiction of my own imagination.

Many of the historical characters did exist and I have tried to do justice to their personalities, but in the end it is of my creating. Those people include George Bain Johnston, who indeed seemed a remarkable man, his wife Elizabeth, Francis Cadell, John and Mary Varcoe, Thomas Goode, all of the Goolwa, and William Marchant, of Mannanarie.

All other characters are fictional and are intended to resemble no person living or dead. In some cases, surnames have been used that were common in the area in the 1850's but there is no intended connection arising from this.

Acknowledgements:

Sue Geisler, a volunteer in the History Room at the Alexandrina Library, Goolwa. Sue provided a great source of information in the files held in the History Room, much of which was collated over many years by Goolwa icon, Walter Pretty. Sue was also kind enough to lend her (slightly amended) name for the character Sue Geisen in the book.

Barbara and Andrew Stannaford, owners of Cockenzie House, George Bain Johnston's residence in Goolwa. Andrew is George's great, great grandson

Cicely Findlay who owns Thomas Dowland's house (built in approximately 1860) in Newacott Place Goolwa and who provided me with a rich history and understanding of the style and construction of homes in Little Scotland in that era.

The surname Johnston was entirely coincidental, given the relationship of Alexander to George Bain Johnston. However, in developing the characters for the book, I was always attracted to calling Alexander's wife Rubina and I would like to acknowledge our dear friend, Ruby (Rubina) Johnston for allowing me to use her name. Likewise for Alex Johnston, son of Neal and Marie-Claire, I hope you enjoy Alexander's character.

Most importantly, I owe huge thanks to Wendy & Judy, who spent countless hours poring over the iterations of the book, offering healthy debate over the plot and the characters. Our late night trips to the Currency Creek Cemetery and the Beacon 19 Ramp allowed us to experience the beauty of the places but also the sense of vulnerability and aloneness that I hope I have been able to convey in the book. In particular, I would also like to thank them for the uplifted masculinity of Carl Johnson/Callum Johnston in the final version.

There were a number of people who read this book at various stages and provided valuable feedback. Thanks to you all and my apologies if I have left you off the list – Sarah (my daughter, always honest in her feedback), her husband Ryan, Roy and Ruby Johnston (who helped with the Scottish perspective), Marie-Claire Johnston, Peter Young, Bruce and Florence Levia (who as Canadians sense checked that the story made sense outside Australia), Cait Halsey, Michaela Moss and Melanie Reid.

Thanks also to author Felicity Fair Thompson for her early guidance on how to build an effective plot and maintain intrigue.

June Taylor has provided wonderful support in the launch and promotion of the book in the Fleurieu region and corporate supporters Bendigo Bank Goolwa and Artworx have been generous in selling the book in their outlets.

Finally, I want to thank my friends in Goolwa Sandwriters, who have provided continued guidance and encouragement for my writing. It is an extraordinarily talented group of people who enjoy writing for writing's sake as well as hungrily consuming the work of others in the group.

This book was seeded following my attendance at Adelaide Writers' Week in February 2016. I had the great pleasure to listen to, and to meet, the fabulous Peter May, whose story telling in the crime thriller genre I have enjoyed for a number of years.

I walked away from Adelaide Writers' Week truly feeling like I could write a book and as I have heard so many times since, the best way to become a writer is to start writing.

Shortly after I put the threads of the plot together, I announced to my family that I was writing a book but that I had no idea if I could write well enough(and I still question) to have it published. My grandson, then aged seven, overheard my comment, looked up and said,

'You know, Grandpa, everyone's got it in them. You just have to want to do it.'

Thank you for these sage and profound words, which have inspired me to maintain a belief that this has been a worthwhile project.

The moral – listen to the unencumbered, unfearing wisdom that kids so freely share.